# THE DUKE'S SHIELD

## The Duke's Guard Series, Book Three

# C.H. Admirand

## ARE YOU SIGNED UP FOR DRAGONBLADE'S BLOG?

You'll get the latest news and information on exclusive giveaways, exclusive excerpts, coming releases, sales, free books, cover reveals and more.

Check out our complete list of authors, too!

No spam, no junk. That's a promise!

### Sign Up Here

www.dragonbladepublishing.com

*Dearest Reader;*

*Thank you for your support of a small press. At Dragonblade Publishing, we strive to bring you the highest quality Historical Romance from some of the best authors in the business. Without your support, there is no 'us', so we sincerely hope you adore these stories and find some new favorite authors along the way.*

*Happy Reading!*

*CEO, Dragonblade Publishing*

# Additional Dragonblade books by Author C.H. Admirand

**The Duke's Guard Series**
The Duke's Sword
The Duke's Protector
The Duke's Shield

**The Lords of Vice Series**
Mending the Duke's Pride
Avoiding the Earl's Lust
Tempering the Viscount's Envy
Redirecting the Baron's Greed
His Vow to Keep (Novella)

**The Lyon's Den Series**
Rescued by the Lyon

# Dedication

For Arran McNicol, my new editor, who helped me find the perfect balance between trimming away unnecessary verbiage while keeping my voice. Thank you!

# Special Thanks

To author extraordinaire Tara Nina, for reading…and bugging me for more pages when I wasn't writing fast enough!

# Author's Note

I love strong women and the hardheaded men who meet their match in these heroines. What can I say? I married a hardheaded man and loved him in this life until he breathed his last...I will love him through eternity.

*Settle into your comfy reading spot with a cup of tea while I tell you a story...*

# PROLOGUE

"All I'm saying—"

Pain, sharp and swift, sliced through Michael O'Malley's head, dropping him to his knees.

"Bloody hell!" James Garahan knelt by his cousin's side. "If this is yer way of winning the argument, 'tisn't funny and won't work. Ye're wrong!"

O'Malley couldn't speak, couldn't catch his breath. He tried to block it, but knew it was no use…the unwanted glimpse of death would come with or without his permission.

Garahan placed a hand on his shoulder. "What's wrong? Where are ye hurt? Was it something ye ate?"

*The scene unfolding before his eyes was washed in blood. Two faceless men stood in an open field. Dueling pistols pointed at one another's hearts.*

He felt the pressure of his cousin's hand as it squeezed harder to get his attention, but the echo of pistols firing speared through his already aching head.

*Both men fell to the ground. Though he could not make out their faces, he saw crimson spreading on one man's chest and the other man's abdomen. There were no seconds, no physicians. No one came forward to tend the wounded men.*

*Their garbled gasps ended abruptly. Every ounce of color faded from their faces, leaving a waxen yellow behind as their souls left their earthly bodies behind, seeking the afterlife. As he watched in horror, their bodies decomposed before his eyes until they were dust. A gust blew across the field, scattering their ashes to the four winds.*

O'Malley came to with a jolt as his cousin tossed him over his shoulder. Garahan ran as if the fires of hell were licking his boots. The pain in his head receded, as it always did once the vision ended, and his wits returned.

His gut ached from the pounding it was taking as his cousin ran toward the stables. Garahan had never witnessed O'Malley in the throes of one of his "spells," as Da liked to call them. Would James wonder if he'd lost his mind, or mayhap that he'd been bitten by a demon? His staid cousin did not believe their cousin Emmett had the gift of healing that had been passed down in the O'Malley family for longer than anyone could remember. His seeing visions of what could happen today, or five years from now, would drive Garahan back to Tipperary and his da's jug of *Poitín!*

He could use a swig of the illegal brew himself. O'Malley snorted with laughter.

Garahan jolted to a stop. "Ye bloody *eedjit!* How can ye laugh when I didn't know if the devil was prying the brain from yer head?"

O'Malley's eyes watered, he was laughing so hard.

"Faith, I thought the *banshee* had a hold of yer soul!"

That comment hit too close to the bone. O'Malley stopped laughing. He'd wondered, was he somehow connected to the O'Malleys' harbinger of doom? Ma never seemed bothered by his visions. Mayhap 'twas because of the O'Gradys—Ma's side of the family, one of the five ancient Irish families without Norman blood in them. It had long been rumored that prominent families had their own *banshee* who would appear keening outside their home before a family member was taken from them.

When he didn't respond, Garahan grumbled, "I've heard ye do this sort of thing."

O'Malley didn't know what to say; he was too busy sorting through his family members, trying to figure out who would be involved in a dual. No one that he could think of. Had the visions changed to encompass those somehow connected to his family? If that were the case, how would he be able to figure out who the victims were going to be?

Bloody hell, he couldn't think upside down, when the blood was throbbing in his head!

"Bugger it, Michael, 'tis the last time I try to help ye!" Garahan heaved his cousin off his shoulder and onto the hard-packed dirt path.

O'Malley gasped, trying to draw in the breath that had just been knocked out of him. When he finally managed it, he glared up at his cousin. "What did ye do that for?"

Garahan grinned at him. "Got yer attention."

Pushing himself up off the ground, O'Malley brushed the dirt from the seat of his trousers. "Ye have no idea what it feels like when it happens!"

Garahan frowned. "Ye're right. I don't. From what ye were blathering, I'm not sure I'd believe ye if ye swore on our family Bible." Pulling his cousin by the arm, Garahan opened the door to the stables and tugged O'Malley inside. "Stay here for a bit. The scent of horse and hay will clear yer head."

"How did you know?" O'Malley asked.

Garahan shrugged. "Whenever I'm troubled, I come to the stables, talk to the lads." With a nod at the pair of geldings stabled on one side of the building, he lowered his voice and whispered, "They tell me they'd like to cover a mare, but can't remember what to do once they're standing behind one."

O'Malley snickered, and Garahan grinned. "Sure and a little barnyard humor makes ye laugh every time."

"Yer ma would box yer ears if she heard such talk," O'Malley predicted.

Garahan smirked, reminding him, "Me ma's not here."

O'Malley needed to feel grounded again—with an emotion they could both share. Knowing his cousin's sense of humor like it was his own, he chuckled when one of the geldings nudged him in the back. He turned to run a hand along the horse's neck. "Did ye really forget what to do with a mare in heat, then, lad?"

Garahan snorted with laughter, and O'Malley joined him, purging the vision from his heart and his mind until he felt like himself once more. Someday he'd have to ask Ma why she never worried about his spells, and if she knew of an ancestor rumored to be connected to the *O'Grady banshee*. No point in asking Da. He'd leave the cottage whenever O'Malley suffered his visions.

"Emmett has the gift of healing," Garahan said once he stopped laughing.

"That he does," O'Malley agreed. "Like his mother and grandmother before him."

"Goes farther back than that, Ma always said."

"Did she now?"

"Aye. We Garahans never had a healer in our family." Garahan locked gazes with O'Malley, adding, "Or one who dreamed while he was wide awake." O'Malley was about to tell him they weren't dreams when Garahan sighed. "I'm not meaning to make light of the pain when whatever's happening happens."

"I know ye weren't." O'Malley opened the side door to the stables and stepped outside.

"Well then." Garahan's eyes gleamed as he followed, closing the door behind him. "Say I was to toss a punch at ye." He clipped O'Malley on the shoulder, emphasizing his statement. "Would ye be interested in sharpening yer bare-knuckle skills, or would it add to yer aching head?"

O'Malley's jab was his reply.

Fists raised, the cousins faced off, taunting one another as they traded swift and painful blows.

O'Malley's face ached where his cousin's fist connected with his jaw. "Is that all ye've got?"

Garahan's dark eyes narrowed, and O'Malley taunted his cousin, "Ye'll be eating yer words and apologizing when what I've seen comes to pass."

His cousin shook his head. "I still don't believe—" Garahan's eyes rolled back in his head as he slumped to the ground.

O'Malley slowly smiled. "Me right cross shuts yer *gob* every time."

Satisfaction filled O'Malley as he bent down to haul his cousin's inert form over his shoulder. "God, I love a good dust-up."

"Dust-up, is it?" Viscount Chattsworth asked from where he stood a few feet away.

O'Malley groaned. "I didn't see ye, yer lordship."

Chattsworth narrowed his eyes, staring at O'Malley until he felt the need to squirm. "No doubt, as you and Garahan were going at one another again."

"'Tis practice, yer lordship. Ye know we have to keep our fighting skills as sharp as our skills with a pistol, rifle, and blade."

"So you've mentioned time and again."

"Because 'tis the truth. Ye can ask His Grace, if ye don't believe me."

Chattsworth sighed. "I'd prefer if you would have a set schedule for practicing your bare-knuckle skills. I do not like surprises, especially while my wife and I are waiting on tenterhooks for the arrival of our firstborn."

The lingering aftereffects of the visions cleared, and O'Malley was mortified that he'd forgotten the viscount's request to keep their fighting skills behind closed doors—preferably their quarters—until after the countess safely delivered the viscount's heir. "I beg yer pardon, yer lordship."

Chattsworth inclined his head, accepting the apology.

Garahan groaned and started to come to. O'Malley set him back on his feet, steadying him with one hand.

"Faith ye've *bollocks* for brains, Michael!"

"*Bollocks*, is it?" the viscount asked.

"Yer lordship," Garahan mumbled. "I didn't see ye there."

"How could you, when O'Malley knocked you out cold?"

Without missing a beat, Garahan said, "He didn't."

Chattsworth chuckled. "I may not have the same fighting

abilities as you men, but I know when someone is bloody unconscious."

"Beg pardon, yer lordship," Garahan murmured.

"I'll leave you two to resume your patrol. I need to check on my wife."

"Aye, yer lordship," Garahan responded.

"Thank ye, yer lordship," O'Malley replied.

As the viscount walked away, Garahan shoved O'Malley. "Keep yer bloody right cross to yerself, or I've a feeling heads will roll—*ours!*"

# CHAPTER ONE

"NEARLY FINISHED, MUM!"

Harriet Mayfield—Harry to her closest friends— smiled at her son. He was as dark as his father had been. She silently wondered how long it would take to get used to the fact that her husband was gone. It was their son and his father's namesake, Bartholomew, who worked alongside her on their tenant farm. At four and ten, Bart shouldn't have to work so hard. He should have more time to read...spend time with friends his age.

"I'm right behind you." Brushing the back of her hand across her forehead, she sent up a silent prayer of thanks that their son was able to step into the role and had been working tirelessly for the last few years. Never complaining. Cheerful at dawn when their day began. Still smiling at dusk when it was nearly over.

Removing the heavy work gloves from her hands, she straightened to her full height, stretching the kinks from her back. Her gaze swept across their land as pride swelled within her. "We'll have a fine harvest this year, thanks to you, Bart."

"You could have done it without me," he chided, coming to stand next to her.

Side by side—as she and her husband had been for too many years to count. Her heart lodged in her throat. For a moment, she couldn't breathe. Grief threatened to overwhelm her, but she fought against giving in to it. To do so would have devastating aftereffects—for herself and her son. "I don't think so," she managed, wishing she had more to offer her son. Her son should have been able to make the choice: continuing his studies or working on the farm. But her husband's death had taken so many choices away from them.

She drew in a deep breath, exhaled slowly, and put her arm around her son's shoulders. "We make a good team, but I still wish you had continued with your studies. Mayhap we could convince the viscount to let you work with Mr. Rowland. You'd be a fine steward's apprentice."

Bart chuckled. "Mum, I don't want to be a steward. I'm content working the land, planting in the spring, and harvesting in the autumn."

"You should have more time to yourself. You could—"

"Get into trouble with Matthew and Robbie?" he quipped.

Harry laughed despite the soul-deep ache that filled her whenever she remembered the day her son stepped into his father's shoes. He had lost a part of his childhood that he would never get back. They worked from sunup to sundown. Every. Day.

At thirty—She shook her head. No, that wasn't right; she'd been thirty the year her husband died…three years past. Lord, she was tired. No matter what time she laid her head down, she hadn't been able to sleep more than a few hours a night. She would drag herself out of bed in the morning and force herself to finish the same number of tasks she and her husband had accomplished when he was alive.

Her nose twitched, a prelude to tears she refused to give in to. Rubbing her nose, she willed them away and concentrated on the next task—checking the stew that had been simmering all day. "Would you—"

"Bring in a bucket of water," he finished for her.

Harry shook her head at Bart's cheerful mood. "Is there something you aren't telling me?"

He looked out over their fields before turning to face her. "I'm an open book, Mum."

They both jolted at the unmistakable sound of a rifle being fired nearby. "Who do you suppose—"

"It's coming from the Clarkes' farm!" With a steely determination, he ordered her, "Stay here, Mum!" Bart dashed to the corral, opened the gate, grabbed hold of their plow horse's mane, and leapt onto his back. "Close the gate."

"Bart, wait!"

"Stay here, Mum!"

*"Bartholomew Tristin Mayfield!"*

He never looked back as he galloped toward his friend's farm. It took her a few moments to find her husband's blunderbuss and follow him on foot.

Flames licked the south side of the Clarkes' barn when she arrived. Their neighbors on the other side of the Clarkes had already formed a bucket brigade. Bart burst through the barn doors, leading the family's heavily pregnant mare to safety.

"Bartholomew!"

Her son turned toward the sound of her voice. "Mr. Clarke's been shot! Mrs. Clarke needs you."

Harry dashed away from the barn toward the thatched cottage. Afraid of what she would find, she knocked before opening the front door. "Mary, what can I do?"

Her friend's eyes were red-rimmed from crying as she pressed a cloth to her husband's shoulder. "He's lost so much blood, Harry."

A glance around the cottage revealed blood-soaked linens on the floor, a pitcher of water, and a bowl that needed to be emptied and refilled. "I'll wash my hands and bring more water."

Her friend did not bother to speak, instead concentrating on stanching the flow of blood from her husband's wound.

Harry worked quickly, willing her hands to stop shaking. She wouldn't do her friend any good if she let her fear show. Calm was needed now.

"I have the boiled threads. Where are your needles, Mary?"

"On the table. You'll have to sterilize them in the fire."

They worked together, Mary sewing the wound closed as Harry held Mr. Clarke's arm still. Afterward, Harry added more soiled linens to the bucket outside to be laundered later.

She straightened the cottage while Mary bathed her husband's face with cool water. "Can you tell me what happened and why anyone would shoot your husband?"

"I was inside getting ready to put supper on the table when I heard the shot. I ran outside in time to see four men on horseback riding away…" Her voice broke as she continued, "My Ethan was lying in the road…bleeding."

Harry's belly clenched in fear. "Did you recognize any of the men? Have you seen them before?"

"No, not one of them."

"Where was Matthew?"

"Over by the barn, trying to put out the fire."

"We've never had anything like this happen before," Harry remarked. "What reason could strangers have for shooting Ethan and setting fire to your barn?" Her heart lodged in her throat at the worrisome thought spearing through her. "Are they strangers to Ethan?"

"Aye," Ethan rumbled, "and too late to question them."

"You're awake!"

Mary's husband held out his hand to her. Drawing his wife to his side, he held her close. She laid her head on his chest and sobbed. "I'd thought I'd lost you."

Ethan held his wife to his heart and let her cry.

Watching the couple, Harry's heart hurt. She had lost *her* husband, but that was not important right now—Ethan and who was behind the attack was. "I'll go check on Matthew."

She was out of the door before either Mary or Ethan could respond. Relieved to be away from the couple, who had been close friends of Harry's family for years, and thoughts of what might have been if her husband were still alive…Harry walked over to stand beside her son. "Is the fire out?"

Matthew answered, "Aye. For now. Only the one wall is damaged. You have our thanks, Mr. Johnson, for organizing the bucket brigade."

Their neighbor placed his hand on Matthew's shoulder. A dark look shadowed the man's face before he replied, "You and your family would do the same for us."

"Let's hope it doesn't come to that," Harry remarked.

"How's Ethan?" Johnson asked.

"I helped Mary patch him up," Harry replied. "He's awake, but weak. She'll have to watch him closely… Fever may set in."

Johnson's gaze met hers. "Why don't you and Bart go home? Cynthia or I can sit with Mary tonight."

Harry shuddered, remembering the virulent fever that took her husband's life. It had come on him suddenly. Before she'd been able to get it to break…he was gone.

"Bart and I will be by first thing, to help with the morning chores and breakfast," she said.

Mary stepped outside and walked over to Harry, throwing her arms around her friend. "Thank you for coming."

Harry hugged her back. "Send for me if you need me to-night."

"I will."

"Promise?"

"Of course," Mary replied. "See you in the morning."

Bart helped her mount. She didn't mind the lack of saddle and was adept at riding bareback. Her husband had insisted both she and Bart learn to ride without a saddle, stressing one never knew when they'd be called upon to help a neighbor. Saddling the horse would take precious time in the event of an emergency.

"Aren't you going to ride with me?"

Bart shook his head. "I need to walk."

Harry knew then that Bart had something difficult to work out in his head. He'd tell her when he was ready—when he'd come up with an answer.

They were nearly to the first of their fields when he said, "Matthew was in the hayloft when the men attacked." His shoulders tensed with every step. "He saw the face of the man who set the fire, Mum."

Harry tamped down the crippling fear sweeping up from the soles of her feet. Was Matthew in danger? Their neighbor said one of them would stay with Mary and her family tonight—and Robert Johnson would have already come to the same conclusion. He would be able to handle the situation.

Her mind and heart calm once more, she said, "I'm certain we will know more in the morning."

They both fell silent covering the last of the distance between their farm and the Clarkes'. Harry's mind could not let go of the puzzle of the mysterious attackers and why they chose the Clarke's farm.

She slid off the horse's back and smiled at her son. "If you'll put the horse away, I'll get our supper on the table."

"Aye, Mum."

"Do not worry, Bart."

The grief on her son's face cut her to the quick. "I can't help but remember...Father died from a fever."

"Of a different sort," she reminded him. He was so tall, and the muscles filling out his frame hinted he would be as broad through the chest and shoulders as his father had been. She was proud, while at the same time worried. He still had the heart of a young man, one who had lost his father too soon.

"A fever can rage out of control no matter the reason."

She held his gaze. "Where did you hear that?"

"From Robbie. His grandfather died of a lingering fever—he'd been caught in a heavy rain in late autumn. Never recovered."

Harry drew in a deep breath and frowned at her son. "Enough morbidity. Life is for living. None of us know how long the Good Lord has planned for us to be here. We'd best make the most of every day."

"One last question, Mum. Do you think Father would have planted another field, adding to our yield of crops, if he'd known that he wouldn't be here to help you harvest it? I wasn't as strong as I am now at the time, and I wasn't much help."

Harry wrapped her arms around her son and assured him, "You were a great help to me. Every day, you climbed out of bed ready to work until your arms were too sore to lift them."

He slowly smiled. "I wanted to prove to you that I wasn't too little to help tilling the fields, planting, weeding, and harvesting."

"The first year your father and I came to work the land for the earl, we shared the workload. It wasn't divided into my chores and his. It was simply work that needed to be done."

"You're so strong," he rasped. "I hate that you have to do back-breaking work to put food on our table. I want to be the one to handle the heavier load."

She brushed a lock of dark brown hair from his eyes and smiled. Her sweet son wasn't a boy any longer—he had the mind and heart of a man. She'd do well to remember that and treat him as such. It was the least she could do while he chipped in and shared more and more tasks around the farm.

"You are handling most of the heavier tasks already, and I'm grateful. I've been able to spend a bit more time baking midday knowing you're outside plowing the fields or tending the animals."

His quick grin had her wondering what he was thinking. She wasn't left to wonder long.

"If you spend a little extra time baking, do you think you could bake some of your scones?"

Her laughter eased the worst of the tension of the last few hours. "Aye," she replied, "I'll bake some scones." She nodded toward the barn. "Off with you. See to the horse and let me get supper on the table."

"Aye, Mum!"

HEAVY POUNDING ON their door woke them in the middle of the night. "Mrs. Mayfield! Bart! Wake up! It's Robbie Johnson! We need help!"

Bart had already pulled on his trousers and beaten her to the door, wrenching it open. His friend's face was bruised along the jaw and one eye was swollen shut. "Who hit you?" Harry asked.

Robbie ignored the question. "It's Matthew. I had to leave him in the field—" His voice broke, and his eyes filled. "He's hurt bad. I'm afraid to move him."

"Did Mary ask you to come for me?"

The young man shook his head. "She didn't answer the door, and I didn't know what to do."

Pulling Robbie inside, she put her arm around him. "Is he bleeding?"

"Not that I could see—they beat him up. When I tried to stop them, they started on me."

"Where is your father?"

Robbie stared at his feet before meeting her direct gaze. "Home. He knows I was to stay with Matthew tonight in case there was more trouble. I was to fetch him right away, but there wasn't any time. The attackers set fire to the barn again. Father would be more likely to chase after the attackers than seeing to Matthew's injuries. Please hurry!"

She glanced through the open doorway. "Can your horse hold two people?"

"Aye."

"Bart, go with Robbie. Keep Matthew as still as possible until I get there. Robbie, fetch your father. You'll need his help moving Matthew or fashioning a litter to carry him to his house."

The look of desperation on his face touched her deeply.

"Don't worry, I'll dress quickly and gather the herbs and salve we may need. I won't be far behind you."

⟫⟫⟫✤⟪⟪⟪

MARY WAS HALF-ASLEEP when she finally answered the door. "Harry? What is it? Why are you here?"

Harry glanced over her shoulder. "Matthew's been hurt. Those men must have come back to finish the job. They set fire to your barn again. I've just sent Bart to the manor house to get help. Robbie and his father are bringing Matthew. They are right behind me."

Mary's face lost every ounce of color as the Johnsons carried her son inside and gently placed him on the kitchen table. Harry laid a hand on her friend's arm and told her, "There's a nasty bump above his left ear, which could be why he still hasn't come to."

"We were waiting near your barn, Mrs. Clarke," Robbie explained. "Matthew was certain the men would be back."

"Why?" Mary rasped. "Why would he think that?"

Robbie glanced at Harry before answering. She nodded, encouraging him.

"He saw the face of the man who set the first fire. Matthew didn't want to worry you and tell you the man glared up at him."

"The attacker came back to hurt my son?" Mary's tears dried in a heartbeat. "They will live to regret shooting my husband, beating our son, and setting fire to our barn—twice! The constable shall hear of this!"

"After the viscount," Johnson reminded her. "If his lordship is not awake, you can be certain one of the duke's guard will be on patrol and come at once."

Harry needed to cut through the anger and vows of vengeance to bring everyone's attention back to the more crucial matter—Matthew's injuries. "Robbie, would you and your father please draw some water for us? I'll put a pan on to boil. Mary, you wash up first and check that lump."

Mary's gaze met hers. "I'm so glad you're here, Harry."

"Friends help friends through the good and the bad." Harry reached for her friend's hand and squeezed it briefly, promising, "We'll get through this."

# CHAPTER TWO

"I BEG YOUR pardon," Lord Chellenham grumbled. "Did I hear correctly? There was a witness and you left him alive?"

The four men facing Chellenham visibly flinched.

The spokesman for the group drew in a breath before speaking but was cut off before he could utter a word.

"There are no excuses!" Chellenham barked. "See that you finish the job. Leave no witnesses! No one must be able to uncover my name in connection with the attack."

"Aye, your lordship."

The men bowed and took their leave, aware that they would have to return to Sussex and finish the job.

"One moment!"

The group turned around and waited to hear what the peer had to say.

"You will continue with the rest of the plan, destroying one tenant farm at a time, until Viscount Chattsworth is left with no revenue coming in from his farmers. I want the man financially ruined. Do you understand? Broken!"

"Aye, your lordship." As one the men retreated, uncertainty clouding the very air surrounding them.

HALF AN HOUR and a dozen miles away from the angry lord's home, the men pooled their coin and shared a bottle of whiskey.

"I never signed on to kill anyone," their leader Stiles mumbled.

"Break a few bones, is all," the strongman of the group added.

"Trampling crops," the one with the crooked nose groused.

"He was just a lad," the tallest one in the group rasped. "Same age as my oldest nephew. Isn't right, I tells ya."

When the bottle was empty, they'd come to a decision.

"We're gonna have to kidnap the lad."

"It's fer his own good."

"At least he'll live to see another day."

"We're agreed, then," Stiles said.

The men filed out one at a time, meeting in the alley behind the waterside pub. Under the cover of darkness, they stood firm in their decision.

"We tell his lordship that we killed the lad." Stiles slipped a wicked-looking blade from his sleeve. "And make a blood oath never to tell him the truth." He sliced the palm of his left hand and handed the knife to the man beside him, who did the same. One by one, they clasped hands with their leader, sealing their oath in blood.

# CHAPTER THREE

O'MALLEY'S GUT ICED over. "The Clarkes' farm, is it?" He watched the boy's face and the myriad emotions displayed for all to see. *Worry. Regret. Fear.* He remembered meeting the lad and his widowed mother the last time he'd been at Chattsworth Manor. He'd been impressed by how hard Bart worked alongside his mother...Harriet Mayfield of the sunset hair and eyes the color of morning mist.

"Aye," Bart answered. "Mr. Clarke was shot earlier—but the attackers came back."

O'Malley felt his cousin stiffen at his side. Before Garahan could say something to frighten the lad, he asked, "Why didn't ye come for help then?"

"Mum was helping take care of Mr. Clarke."

"And afterward?" O'Malley asked.

Bart shrugged. "We were tired and hungry." He shuffled his feet as if uneasy asking for help. "She's always worrying I don't eat enough."

O'Malley motioned to one of the stable lads and sent him to fetch Hargrave, the viscount's butler.

Garahan grumbled, "What about you, Bart? Did ye not think his lordship had a right to know what was happening on his land?"

Bart met his gaze and blurted out, "Aye. Mum's always worrying about his lordship and our farm—" He clamped his jaw shut and placed his hand on the big plow horse's back. "I've got to get back...my friends are hurt."

O'Malley laid a hand on the young man's shoulder. "Ye may be needing more than our brawn to help ye, lad."

Garahan asked, "Which friends, and what happened to them?"

Bart shifted his gaze to Garahan and answered, "Matthew Clarke is unconscious—Mum noticed a lump by his temple. That's what has Mrs. Clarke worried. Robbie Johnson's got some bruises on his face and has one eye swollen shut. He tried to fight them off."

Hargrave arrived with two of the viscount's brawnier footmen. "Master Mayfield. Are you all right?"

Bart nodded. "Aye, Mr. Hargrave. But Mr. Clarke and my friends..." He drew in a deep breath and continued, "My friends were injured, too. Mum sent me to get help."

"And help you shall have," Hargrave said with a determined glint in his eye.

The men quickly apprised the butler of the situation. Hargrave nodded, then asked, "O'Malley? Garahan? What do you need me to do?"

"Tell his lordship what's happened." Eyeing the two footmen, O'Malley added, "Hartman and Sweeney, mount up and follow us."

The trio took off at a gallop with Bart in the lead—the footmen not far behind them.

O'Malley and Garahan shared a look as they noted the burned wreckage of the barn and the trampled crops in the field behind it. Johnson and his son were standing guard outside the Clarkes' cottage. Father and son were armed, expecting trouble.

Johnson appeared relieved, acknowledging the men with a nod. "Good to see you've brought reinforcements, though there has been no further sign of the attackers." With a steely glance at his son, he added, "I'm still not sure why they returned in the first place."

Bart dismounted and walked over to stand beside his friend. "It wasn't Robbie's fault, Mr. Johnson. Matthew swore him to secrecy."

Sensing there was a bit more to what occurred earlier, O'Malley asked, "How many men did you see the first time?"

Robbie shrugged, and his father nudged him in the shoulder. "You'd best tell the men all you know. We owe his lordship an accounting of what happened."

Bart placed his hand on his friend's arm. "Matthew was right. They came back. Tell him, Robbie, so the duke's men can go after them!"

Robbie nodded. "Four of them. Matthew was in the hayloft and saw the man who set fire to the barn. Said the man looked up and glared at him."

Garahan frowned. "Where were ye when they came back?"

The young man glanced at his father and then back, answering, "Hiding behind those trees." He pointed toward a stand of oak trees not far from the smoldering ruins.

"The attackers found you," O'Malley said.

Robbie nodded.

"Why didn't you tell me Matthew had seen one of the men?" Johnson demanded of his son.

"We didn't want you to chase after them," Robbie answered. "We needed you to stay here and protect Matthew and his father."

The door to the cottage opened, and Bart called out, "Mum! I've brought help."

O'Malley's heart lurched as he stared at the tall woman standing in the doorway. Soft lantern light added to the illusion that her hair was on fire.

It had been some time since he'd met the widow. Though it took more effort than he'd care to admit, he had consigned her to a tidy little box in his heart that he firmly closed.

But aye, he had not forgotten her. He was annoyed to discover the same pull in his gut and pounding of his heart at the mere sight of her, just as it had the first time he laid eyes on her.

She was tall, with generous curves. The widow was built like a goddess. A queen! He knew she was strong. She had to be to keep the farm going alongside her son. Watching her now—her strength, resolve, and beauty—threatened to take him out at the knees.

"Mr. O'Malley, Mr. Garahan." Her husky voice beckoned him closer. He widened his stance, not giving in to the urge to close the gap between them as she continued, "Thank you for coming."

Her words called him back to the present and the dire situation they faced. "Why didn't ye send for us earlier?"

She frowned at him. "Mary needed my help while she sewed closed the damage a lead ball did to her husband's shoulder."

O'Malley inclined his head, acknowledging her words.

Garahan grunted. "After ye both tended to him, why did ye not send for help? The least ye could have done was to let his lordship know what happened."

Her shoulders sagged as if under a huge weight. "All I could think of was getting home and feeding Bart." She glanced at her son, then back. "He shoulders so much of the heavier work and is still growing."

"I already told them that," Bart scoffed.

Harriet stepped over the threshold, placed her hands on her generous hips, and glared at O'Malley and Garahan. "Then why did you ask if my son already answered your question? You're wasting time when you could be following those men!"

"We could have followed them earlier and ensured they did not return, if ye'd come to us for help in the first place," O'Malley countered. "Then neither Matthew nor Robbie would have been injured."

Her hands fell to her sides as she seemed to crumble in on herself, worry evident in her troubled gaze. "You're here now. Do you think his lordship will be angry with me that I did not send my son sooner?"

O'Malley noted the play of emotion in her gaze and shrugged. "I haven't spoken with his lordship yet and couldn't say." He wanted to ease the worry plain as day on her lovely face. "His lordship is a fair man—don't waste yer energy on what might happen. Ye need to concern yerself with the Clarkes' son."

Bart urged his mother inside, but she paused in the doorway. "Thank you for coming."

The men gruffly nodded, watching as she closed the cottage door.

O'Malley turned to the lad, asking, "Robbie, can ye show us what direction ye think the men came from?"

The young man pointed toward the dense line of trees separating the Clarkes' farm from the Johnsons'.

O'Malley and Garahan shared a look. Time was of the essence if they were to pick up their trail. Neither wanted the lads following them.

"Hartman, ye'll come with us," O'Malley told the footman.

"Aye, O'Malley."

"Sweeney, stay behind and guard the others."

The other footman moved to stand beside Mr. Johnson.

"Robbie," Garahan said, "ye should have the ladies tend to yer injuries, so ye can tend to yer duties."

"Duties?" Robbie asked.

"Aye, lad, it'll be up to yerself and Bart to be the last line of defense should anyone breech the door."

"What about Sweeney?" Robbie asked.

The older footman snorted. "Don't worry about me. No will get past me this night."

"Good man, Sweeney," Garahan remarked. Turning to Robbie, he asked, "Can ye handle that pistol using only one eye?"

Johnson answered for his son, "He's a better shot than me, and nine times out of ten, I don't miss what I aim at."

Garahan grinned. "Well then, the Clarkes and Mayfields are in good hands."

O'Malley frowned. "Johnson, is there anyone else at home

with yer wife?"

"No one," Johnson replied.

"Ye should go home," Garahan said. "Protect yer wife. The attackers may still be in the area."

"She will be worried by now," Johnson admitted.

"Best go to yer wife," O'Malley added. "And be ready to apologize."

Johnson chuckled. "Have you met my wife?"

"Nay." O'Malley grinned. "Me ma would have me head on a platter if I didn't make certain all concerned were protected—and no one was left alone to fend for themselves at such a time."

"So would my Cynthia." Johnson hauled himself up onto the seat and took hold of the reins.

As he released the brake, Garahan said, "Send our thanks to yer wife."

"I will." Johnson waited a beat before asking, "You'll let us know what happens?"

"Aye."

"Robbie can stay the night if you need him."

O'Malley considered the offer and replied, "Thank ye. If things change, me cousin and I will escort him home."

Johnson nodded, snapped the reins, and drove off.

O'Malley stared after the man and his wagon, his mind racing over his mental list of those who may be responsible for the attack and whose whereabouts would be questioned.

Who were the attackers? Why here? Why now?

O'Malley wondered if the viscount had more than one enemy. He'd be speaking with his lordship after they uncovered as much information as possible in the early hours before dawn.

The cousins and Hartman set off in the direction of the attackers, keeping their eyes and ears open, praying the wan moonlight would be enough to find their tracks.

It was going to be a long night.

# CHAPTER FOUR

A FEW HOURS later, the group arrived at the stables, dismounted, and turned their horses over to the stable master.

"Thank ye for taking care of the lads for us," O'Malley said.

The older man chuckled. "I know you two would rather be brushing your mounts and spoiling them with an extra cupful of oats, but his lordship is waiting to speak with you." With a glance at the footmen, he added, "Hargrave asked me to send you to him when you returned."

The footmen set off to report to the viscount's butler.

Garahan nodded. "We'd best not keep his lordship waiting."

"Ye'll spoil them with the oats for us?" O'Malley asked.

"I will," the stable master replied.

"Thank ye."

Side by side, as they had been for years growing up, O'Malley and Garahan strode to the door to the kitchen.

Garahan had his hand on the knob when it pushed open. He caught the edge of the door before it smacked him in the nose. Cursing, he took a step back and stifled a groan as the viscount stepped through the doorway. "Yer lordship! I didn't see ye there."

The viscount stared at the men. A muscle beneath his left eye twitched—the only indication he was angry. "I'll try not to take issue with you because I know you did not want to disturb

Calliope. However, in the future, you will keep me apprised of any, and all, issues that arise here at Chattsworth Manor—regardless of the time, the weather, my wife's health...or my mood."

Garahan leaned toward O'Malley and grumbled, "Faith, reminds me of that time we stayed too long at the public house after ye won that bout against O'Doyle from Kerry."

O'Malley grinned. "Aye, Ma was waiting to ring a peal over me head."

"Mine too," Garahan said.

"Wasn't it yer fault that I'd agreed to fight O'Doyle in the first place?"

Garahan slowly smiled. "'Twas a bout to remember."

"If the two of you are quite finished," the viscount declared, "I'd like to speak to you in the library."

"Aye, yer lordship." O'Malley was desperate for a cup of tea and something to fill the hole in his gut, but would starve before ignoring a request from the viscount. Though he and his cousin were members of the duke's guard, they reported directly to Viscount Chattsworth, the duke's distant cousin, until they were reassigned during the rotation of the guard. Although now that his brother, Sean, and their cousin, Patrick, had recently been married and were no longer a part of the rotation, who knew how often they would move to guard another location—either the duke, the duke's brother, or their distant cousins.

"Whoever the men were," O'Malley began as soon as he closed the door behind him, "no one recognized them. There was just enough moonlight to follow their trail until it disappeared into the wooded area to the north of the Clarkes' farm."

"Bloody devils shot Ethan Clarke and set fire to the barn!" Garahan spat out.

"The *first* time they attacked," O'Malley finished for his cousin.

The viscount's gaze intensified. "First time?"

"Aye," Garahan said. "Apparently, Mrs. Mayfield and her son

heard the shot a few hours earlier and rushed over to their neighbors' farm."

The need to shield the widow from censure, for not reporting the first incident, filled him. Before the viscount jumped to the wrong conclusion, O'Malley explained, "Mrs. Mayfield was exhausted when we arrived. She helped repair the damage a lead ball did to Ethan's shoulder. Bart got the animals out of the barn in time, then joined the bucket brigade."

"Did you ask her why she neglected to inform me of the attack?"

"Aye," Garahan answered for his cousin. "Though we asked her son first."

O'Malley met the viscount's steady gaze and responded, "Questioned separately, they both gave the same answer. She was concerned with feeding her son. He's built like a man, though he's just a lad of four and ten. Bart has been holding down the farm with his ma since his da passed on."

The viscount scrubbed a hand over his face, then shoved to his feet to pace in front of the fireplace. "I know the family and their situation. No need to plead their case." He fell silent, staring past them. O'Malley was about to speak, but the viscount continued, "I am unaware of anyone who may be harboring ill will toward me—other than Lord Chellenham."

"Ye foiled his plan to shoot Lord Coddington when he turned his back on the blackguard," Garahan said.

"And took the pistol ball yerself," O'Malley added.

The viscount shrugged then asked, "Have either of you heard of his whereabouts in the last month?"

"Sean reported that he'd been in the Lake District a few months ago but seemed to have disappeared," O'Malley replied.

Garahan looked up at the knock on the door.

The viscount frowned. "Enter."

His butler and valet walked into the room and stood at attention.

Chattsworth addressed his butler, "Hargrave?"

"Mary Kate is attending Lady Calliope," Hargrave replied. "She promised to come down as soon as she convinces her ladyship to remain in bed and rest."

The viscount sighed. "I never expected one tiny woman to be so difficult about staying where she's put."

O'Malley swallowed his laughter. Garahan didn't bother—he laughed out loud.

"Do you think this is funny? I am trying my damndest to protect my wife. I will not see her harmed."

O'Malley elbowed his cousin in his gut to get him to stop. Garahan swallowed his laughter to answer the viscount's question. "'Tisn't what ye think, yer lordship. 'Tis just that her ladyship is acting like our mas would."

"Aye," O'Malley agreed. "Their tempers flare when anyone tries to tell them what to do."

"I still cannot believe how far out of her shell my wife has come. She was so shy, reticent…and now—"

"She's happily married, expecting your heir, and willing to go to any lengths to protect the both of ye," O'Malley finished.

The viscount's eyes widened. "Yes. That's it exactly. But she's not a warrior."

"Ah," Garahan murmured. "But she has the heart of one. 'Tis dangerous in a woman of her petite stature."

The deadly glare in the viscount's eyes softened. "As soon as she delivers our babe, I mean to speak to her about her ideas."

"Good luck with that," Garahan mumbled.

"What was that?" the viscount asked.

"Nothing, yer lordship," Garahan answered.

Viscount Chattsworth shook his head, then focused his attention on his valet. "MacReady, what have you to report?"

"On your advice, I sent two footmen to the village to see what they could find out. They should be returning soon."

O'Malley opened his mouth to speak, but the viscount forestalled him, saying, "Excellent, MacReady. I need as much information as possible."

The two servants bowed and quit the room.

"I'll wager 'tis Chellenham," Garahan said, watching them leave.

"Aye. The man has connections in high places and has never had to make restitution for shooting ye," O'Malley reminded the viscount.

"It was my own fault for interfering in an illegal activity," Chattsworth reminded the men.

"Ye saved Lord Coddington's life by interfering," Garahan said.

The viscount held the man's gaze for long moments before saying, "Ah, but the authorities do not see it that way. By the by, I've asked Mrs. Romney to have a meal ready, anticipating your return. Take some time now to eat. When the others return, we can question them together." With that, the viscount turned and walked away.

"He's worried about her ladyship," Garahan murmured as he and his cousin walked to the kitchen.

O'Malley clenched his jaw. "If Chellenham has resurfaced, his lordship has every right to be."

"Ye know that's not what I was referring to."

"'Tisn't proper to speak of her ladyship's condition," O'Malley reminded Garahan. "This isn't Ireland, and we are not among family. His lordship has enough to concern him right now. We'd best eat quickly. No telling what news the footmen will return with."

The cook greeted them as they strolled into the kitchen and waved her hand to two empty seats at the huge, scarred, ancient oak table.

"Faith, O'Malley, we won't starve this day," Garahan declared with a grin.

O'Malley thanked Mrs. Romney as the two sat down to steaming plates of eggs, ham, potatoes, and scones with fresh berry jam and a pot of tea.

The cook smiled watching the men devour the food she'd

prepared for them.

Wiping his mouth, Garahan told the cook, "That was a fine meal, Mrs. Romney."

O'Malley added his thanks: "Filled the hole in me gut."

She smiled and said, "I'll be baking an extra batch of scones and mayhap a butter cake for this afternoon's tea."

The cousins grinned at one another, but it was Garahan who repeated the question he asked every time he finished one of Mrs. Romney's meals: "Have ye decided to run away with me? Ye'd spend yer life cooking for one man—me!"

Her normally staid expression softened as she shook her head at Garahan. "Not today, James."

"Mayhap if ye could burn one of the meals ye serve us," O'Malley suggested. "Then me cousin would stop asking ye to run away with him."

The cook smiled at the men and shook her head. "I've baking to do. Best let me get to work, or there won't be anything sweet for you to eat when you swing back through the kitchen between your rounds."

Those words had Garahan striding to the back door and yanking it open. "Hurry up, O'Malley! I'm not about to miss out on butter cake and scones because of yer lazy *arse*."

"'Tisn't lazy," O'Malley griped, and pushed his cousin through the door.

⇶❯❮⇷

MARY KATE WALKED into the kitchen and sighed as the men closed the outside door behind them. "I missed him again?"

Mrs. Romney glanced at the young maid. "You'll have to move faster to keep up with that one."

The older woman's smile had Mary Kate asking, "Did he ask you to run away again?"

The cook lifted her chin and loftily replied, "Never you

mind."

Mary Kate glanced out the window in time to see Garahan staring at her. She felt her face heat but ignored it and managed a small smile. He nodded, turned, and walked away. Why did he never seem to have time to speak with her these days? He always rushed out of a room just as she entered it.

Going over the list of duties she had to see to before bringing a breakfast tray to Lady Calliope, she knew now was not the time to ponder that great mystery.

In her heart there was a kernel of hope that James Garahan cared for her—even the tiniest bit would give her hope. No good would come of falling for a man who had absolutely no interest in her. Though, at times, she would feel his gaze upon her and wonder if mayhap he did feel something.

One day, she'd gather her courage and go in search of the difficult man and simply ask him!

*Not today…but someday soon.*

# CHAPTER FIVE

ARRY LEANED AGAINST the washtub and wiped her forearm across her forehead. Her arms ached from working the land, but she knew it was pointless to complain while there were clothes to launder. After drawing in a deep breath…and then another, she resumed her chore.

Scrubbing, rinsing, and wringing, she finished washing the shirts and trousers her son had nearly outgrown. She knew she would be spending more than one night sewing larger clothes for him. If only she could manage to squeeze in time to make the trip to the village and purchase fabric, Bart would have something new to wear.

Mentally calculating how much more material would be needed to account for the new width of her son's shoulders called up the unwanted image of one Michael O'Malley. Why had she let that tall, broad, irritatingly handsome, green-eyed Irishman get under her skin? He was like a sliver of wood that refused to be dislodged.

Though it was well past midnight when he'd arrived last night, she remembered the visual impact of his strong physique. It reminded her of her husband's frame. O'Malley's grass-green eyes and sunlit hair were a sharp contrast to her husband's dark brown hair and warm brown eyes.

Shaking her head to clear it of ridiculous thoughts of a man she had no business pondering, she returned her focus to the task at hand and lifted the next worn item from the washtub. Staring at the trousers—her late husband's—she remembered taking them in because there was no extra coin to purchase a pair closer to her own size. Putting her back into it, she scrubbed at stains that had been too stubborn to remove when her husband had worn them.

A tear slipped past her guard as she carefully washed his cambric shirts. His scent was long gone…only her own remained mingled with the dirt from working their land. Her eyes welled with more tears, but she blinked them away, saving them for a time when Bart wouldn't see her crying. Resolved to finish the laundry and move on to the next chore, she dug deep to ignore the emotions she had no time to deal with.

Lifting the last piece of clothing, she was dismayed to discover the fabric of one of her husband's shirts had frayed, leaving a hole the size of her fist in it. Biting her lip, she knew she'd be sacrificing the last of her gowns—the pretty blue one she wore the day she'd pledged her love and life would be sacrificed in order to sew shirts for her son and herself.

No matter—she couldn't recall the last time she'd worn a gown, let alone had a need for one.

"Serves you right for letting your mind go down a path it has no business traveling," she told herself.

"And what path might that be, Mrs. Mayfield? If I may be so bold as to ask."

Harry snorted with laughter before she could think to hold it back. The man who'd been front and center of her thoughts, disturbing her sleep and interrupting her chores all day, sat atop a beautiful roan gelding.

His beautifully sculpted lips curved into a smile that simply stole her breath. Michael O'Malley's face and form would make a weaker woman swoon.

But Harry was not weak. She lifted her chin and frowned. "What brings you back this afternoon?"

"His lordship."

The bottom dropped out of her stomach. The viscount must have finally realized that the revenue from their farm had decreased to the point where he would have no choice but to demand she and Bart leave so he could install someone far more capable of earning their keep. After all, it was his right.

Her mind whirled as the familiar ache tore through her heart. Where would they go? What would they do?

She swayed, clutching the worn, damp shirt to her breast.

O'Malley dismounted and swept her into his arms, holding her against his pounding heart. "Are ye ill, lass?"

Harry's eyes burned as tears threatened yet again. She had not given in to weakness since the night she'd sobbed her heart out on the fresh dirt covering her husband's final resting place. Mortified she'd let her fear overwhelm her, she struggled in his arms.

"Until ye answer me, I won't be setting ye down."

Their gazes clashed. Wide gray eyes met steady green.

She refused to believe he wouldn't set her on her feet. "Unhand me!"

His grip tightened. "How do I know ye won't keel over and crack yer head against the washtub?"

He was far stronger than she realized. He lifted her easily— and she knew her sturdy bones alone were heavy. It was futile to continue. Struggling to move past her embarrassment, she managed to reply, "I am fine, just a bit more weary than I thought." When he did not budge, she added, "I did not stop at midday to eat."

He held her gaze for long moments before repeating his unanswered question: "Are ye ill, lass?"

She clenched her jaw as indignation swept up from her toes. "I am not ill, and I am a widow—not a *lass*."

He chuckled and gently set her on her feet, holding her arm to steady her. "Well now, as ye're a woman younger than meself, ye're a lass. If ye prefer, the Gaelic for it is a wee *cailín*."

Though her shoulders and upper back ached, Harry stiffened her spine and straightened to her full height, surprised she was nearly a foot shorter than the giant of a man currently smirking at her. "I am not a small woman."

O'Malley's eyes slid from the top of her head to the tips of her toes. "Aye, that ye're not, though a *cailín* is a young girl."

She squinted up at him. "As a matter of fact, I am probably older than you."

"I doubt it, lass."

"My son is four and ten…I was just shy of my twentieth year when he was born."

"Well now, Mrs. Mayfield, ye are a wee bit older than me, though ye don't look a day over five and twenty."

She felt the flush heat her cheeks, but for the life of her did not know how to respond. It had been years since a man looked at her the way her husband had—as if she were pleasing to the eye. Unbidden, her emotions tangled into a tight knot. Praying she would not disgrace herself and dissolve into a puddle of useless tears, she tucked a stray strand of hair behind her ear and cleared her throat. "Why did his lordship send you?"

His eyes narrowed for a moment before he responded, "He wanted to come himself, but Lady Calliope was not feeling well, so he asked me to deliver a message."

Worry filled her heart. She knew from experience that as a woman's time drew near, exhaustion and labor pains were to be expected. She herself had thought she was about to deliver a sennight before Bart was born. The midwife had assured her it was normal for some women to go through laboring pains for days—even a week or two before delivering.

Concerned for her ladyship, she asked, "Has Old Miriam been to the manor house to see Lady Calliope?"

"Aye, which is the only reason she's resting and not pulling up behind me at yer door. She wanted to see for herself how the Clarkes, the Johnsons, yourself, and Bart fared after last night."

She smiled. "Lady Calliope is caring and kindness itself. We are beholden to her and his lordship for so many things. After they married, our homes and plows were repaired. There was enough seed to plant to ensure a harvest worth celebrating. We owe his lordship and her ladyship far more than we can ever repay."

Understanding, and an emotion she could not quite place, filled O'Malley's gaze. "I'll be happy to pass on yer words."

Throat tight with emotion, she nodded in reply.

"Where would I find yer son? I need to speak with him before I ride over to speak with the others."

"In the far field between our farm and the Clarkes'."

"I'll take me leave of ye, then, lass."

Indignation at his insistence on calling her lass surged up from her toes, but his crooked smile had her chuckling instead. "You are a stubborn man, O'Malley."

"To hear Ma tell it, I'm hardheaded too." He mounted his horse. Holding her gaze, he inclined his head. "I'll bid ye good day, then, Mrs. Mayfield."

"Good day, Mr. O'Malley."

Harry watched as he rode off toward their neighbors, belatedly wondering if he would deliver the same message to her son, or if he had something else entirely to say to Bart. She should have asked him about the message.

Pinning the rest of the clothing to the rope stretched between two posts, she shook her head, admitting to herself, "He probably wouldn't tell me."

She bailed out the washtub, watering her household gardens. *Best check on the stew. Bart will be here soon, and hungry enough for three men.*

And just like that, her thoughts returned to O'Malley. Staring at her handiwork drying in the midday sun, she marveled that he seemed to have the strength of two men. How else would he sweep a woman her height and weight off her feet as if she weighed but three stone?

Exasperated with the unexpected direction of her thoughts,

she firmly put the handsome man from her mind. After setting the washtub against the back of their cottage, she stepped inside, ready to take on the next task.

Hands washed, she checked the pot on the back of the cookstove, stirred it, and replaced the lid. The mindless task had her mind repeating the viscount's message. Gratitude filled her.

"We won't be evicted from our farm today, my love," she whispered to her heavenly husband. She felt a sense of peace surround her, as if he agreed.

Stronger for having felt it, she moved about the cottage with a spring in her step, ready to face whatever the night would bring.

IT WAS QUIET for the next few nights. Harry felt confident the attacks were an aberration and not something to worry over. She had enough to do with the daily visits to the Clarke farm to help with whatever chores were left to do. Mary did not have the time to add their daily chores to her duties. She had her hands full caring for her husband and their son.

Bart and Harry worked between the two farms for a sennight before he spoke up. "Mum, you cannot do it all. I'm more than capable of working both farms. You don't need to."

She frowned at him, not willing to admit she had no idea how much longer she *would* be able to continue. The idea that he was younger and as strong as a bull—just as his father had been—wasn't the issue. The fact that he felt the need to point it out to her was. It irked her—though, in truth, even her fingernails ached from the hours of hard labor she'd put in between their place and the Clarkes'.

"Are you saying I'm not capable?"

Bart frowned and released a deep, gravelly rumble.

"Bartholomew Tristan Mayfield! You did not just growl at your mother, did you?"

Her son had the sense to beg her pardon and apologize. "I cannot help it, Mum. You're not Father. You're working too hard, and you're not strong enough."

Anger tore through her belly as the need to shout at her son took hold. Shouting at Bart wouldn't get through to him when his mind was made up—only her husband's calm voice had been able to.

She swallowed the words poised on her tongue. "Is that what you truly think, young man?"

"I'm nearly five and ten! I am not young!"

Borrowing her own father's oft-used phrase, she barked, "As long as you live under this roof—"

To her utter shock, Bart got to his feet, spun on his heel, and walked out the front door, slamming it behind him.

Dear God, what was she supposed to do now? Chase after him? Demand he listen? Apologize for telling him he was a young man when he was half her age? Bloody hell, he *was* a young man compared to her!

Common sense returned as she walked over and placed her hand on the door. If she opened it, would he be standing there, about to turn around and stalk back in? Or would he be halfway to the barn, to let their plow horse out of his stall?

Hands shaking, heart breaking, she added water to the tea kettle and set it on the cookstove. Busy hands had helped when she'd lost her husband, and they would help now.

Dear God in Heaven, had she lost her temper *and* her son?

Her throat tightened and her breath hitched in her breast, but she fought against giving in to the emotions clawing at her insides, demanding to be set free. Biting the inside of her cheek until she tasted blood distracted her as it had before.

She was a woman, but God help her, she was not weak, and she bloody well would not give in and weep!

The tea helped settle her worry to the point where exhaustion forced her to give up her vigil praying Bart would return.

⇶❮❮❮

SHE HEARD THE door quietly open just before midnight, and her son pause next to her sleeping pallet by the fireplace. Harry had preferred sleeping there after injuring her back a year ago.

She struggled but managed to maintain her slow breathing pattern until she heard Bart slowly walk to the other side of the cottage, where he slept on the bed his father had built to accommodate his height. It wouldn't be long before Bart matched his father's height. He may even surpass it.

Heart heavy, mind racing, she wondered if she should speak to her son. Mayhap she should let it go until the morning, when calmer heads would prevail. Unable to decide, she finally fell into a fitful sleep.

⇶❮❮❮

THE SOUND OF hoofbeats and wood breaking woke her as Bart called out, "Stay inside, Mum!"

She was on her feet and out the door when she heard the first guttural shout. *Bloody hell!* The attackers were back!

Harry grabbed her husband's blunderbuss, then remembered the task she'd forgotten the moment Bart walked out—she was supposed to mold more lead balls. What could she use instead? They needed the nails she hoarded to make repairs around their farm.

She made the split-second decision to leave the gun. Sprinting around the cottage, she grabbed the shovel she'd left there earlier in the day, too tired to put it away in the barn where it belonged.

"Grab him!" a deep voice shouted.

"We need to leave now," another barked.

"Hit him over the head and be done with it," a third grumbled.

"I've got him. Quit fighting, boy!" another voice commanded.

"Bloody hell, I'm not a boy," Bart growled. "Let go!" His deep voice carried to her on the still night air.

Without thought to the consequences, she lifted the shovel above her head and screamed as she ran toward the man struggling to hold her son.

The larger man jolted in surprise, and she had the advantage. She swung with all her might. The blow reverberated from her hands to her shoulders as the shovel connected with his knees. With a grunt, she swept his legs out from under him. He landed hard on his back.

The others leapt into action when the big man fell, grabbing for Bart while the third man reached for a pistol tucked into his waistband.

"Mum, go get help!"

Rage filled her at the sight of three men trying to hold her son down. He was fighting as if he outweighed the men, his fists flying, his feet kicking. Raising her shovel, she swung again, and this time the blow landed across one of the attackers' shoulders. He grunted and let go of Bart.

*Two on one.* Much better odds… Her confidence soared. She'd keep the men at bay.

Bart pushed free and roared, "No!"

The breath whooshed from her lungs as twenty stone of muscle tackled her to the ground. Dear Lord, she couldn't draw a breath. Her eyes watered until her vision blurred. The weight of the man was crushing!

She heard her son calling to her, but she couldn't answer.

An eerie battle cry in the distance rent the night air. The cry must have startled her attacker, as the weight shifted off her.

The sickening sound of flesh battering flesh seemed to surround her as she gasped to fill her burning lungs. Turning her head to the side, she watched her son deliver an uppercut that knocked his attacker to his knees. Pride filled her. Bartholomew had taught their son how to defend himself.

Another took the fallen man's place, while she struggled to catch her breath to warn her son. White-hot pain sliced through her. She braced a hand to her side and felt a bump that hadn't been there before. She'd dealt with her husband's cracked ribs more than once and knew what she would have to do—and what she would not be able to do until she healed.

But her son's life was in danger. She fought the pain and moved past it, bellowing, "Bart, behind you!"

Her warning had him spinning around and laying out another of the men with a wicked right cross.

"Ye bloody bastards!" a familiar deep voice roared. "I'll skin ye alive!"

"O'Malley," Harry rasped, watching the duke's man leap from his horse and enter the fray. Between her son and O'Malley, they quickly turned the tide, overpowering the attackers. Gaining control of her breathing while her son and their rescuer bound the attackers' hands behind their backs, she was finally able to roll onto her hands and knees and push to her feet.

"Mum! Where are you hurt?"

She lifted a hand to her son's cheek and cupped it. "Just a scratch," she lied.

"What were you thinking going after the largest one of the bunch with a shovel?"

She narrowed her eyes. "That he was about to beat you to within an inch of your life." Speaking cost her—her vision wavered. The light of the moon faded as the ground shifted beneath her feet and darkness claimed her.

# CHAPTER SIX

EAR HAD O'MALLEY'S heart pounding as he stared at the woman cradled against his chest.

"You can't leave us here!" a deep voice bellowed from behind him.

He ignored the curses of the attackers and the demands to set them free. He had to take care of Mrs. Mayfield. The door was still open, and he followed Bart inside. "What happened?"

Bart's pained expression washed over O'Malley. Instead of trying to reassure the lad, he needed facts. The men were going to pay for the destruction of yet another of the viscount's tenant farms.

Glancing down at the bruised face of the woman who'd fought like a warrior to free her son, he vowed the price the men paid would be dear.

Bart raced to the other side of the room and smoothed the linens on a large bed. "Put her here."

O'Malley noted the unusual size of the bed. It would more than accommodate his height. Pushing thoughts of Widow Mayfield's bed from his mind, he gently laid her down. "Did anyone strike her head before that bleeding bastard tackled her?"

Bart shook his head and swallowed. His Adam's apple bobbed up and down as he struggled to regain control. The lad's fighting skills, and the way he fought to keep his head while his ma lay unconscious, impressed O'Malley.

"Are ye certain the bastard didn't hit her with his head as she was falling?"

"I was too busy trying to break free."

O'Malley knew he needed to bring the widow around quickly to ascertain the extent of her injuries. "Can ye stir the fire and see if ye can coax a bit of flame out of it? We'll need the warmth, and I'll be needing more light to see where yer ma is injured."

Bart did as he was asked, returning with a lighted candle.

There were bruises on one side of her face, but what worried O'Malley was the possibility of an injury hidden beneath her braided sunset hair.

"Can ye fetch a bowl of clean water and a cloth? I need to bathe yer ma's face and see if there's a lump or cut at the back of her head."

The young man rushed to do as O'Malley asked and returned with the water and cloth.

O'Malley dipped the cloth in the water and smoothed the cloth across her forehead. Carefully, as if she were made of fragile china, he repeated the motion along the line of her jaw before bathing the other side of her face. She moaned, and her dark lashes fluttered, but she did not open her eyes.

"Why won't she wake up?"

O'Malley asked himself the same question but wouldn't be telling that to the worried lad leaning over his shoulder. "I need to check the back of her head." Bart steadied her while O'Malley carefully palpated her head.

No lumps. No warm, sticky substance coating his fingers.

Relief swept up from his toes, easing the worst of the knots in his gut. "No sign of an injury to her head. Just the bruising on the side of her face."

Mrs. Mayfield moaned louder this time as her lashes slowly lifted. Their eyes met, and she blinked. "Mr. O'Malley?" Confusion swirled in the misty gray of her eyes.

"Ye've nothing to fear, lass. Bart and I have everything well in hand." Without looking away from the battered woman, he asked, "Can ye fetch a cup of water for yer ma to drink?"

"Aye."

O'Malley leaned close and pitched his voice low so as not to be overheard. "I need to bring the men to the manor house, where I'll have help carting them off to the constable. I don't have time to send for a woman to preserve your dignity."

"What does my dignity have to do with taking the men away?"

Relieved with the irritation in her voice, he struggled not to chuckle. "I'll be needing to check yer limbs for injuries. Will that be a problem?"

She lowered her lashes, and for a heartbeat, O'Malley wondered if she'd fainted on him again. But then her eyes opened, and she licked her swollen lip. Had the bleeding bugger struck her in the face?

Before he could ask, she replied, "No need waiting. I'm not a maid whose virtue needs to be protected."

Bart heard his mother's words and glared at O'Malley. "What does she mean by that? Do you plan to take advantage of my mum?"

Exasperated, O'Malley shook his head. "I asked yer ma if I had permission to check her limbs to see if anything's sprained or broken. I don't have time to wait for ye to fetch Mrs. Clarke. I have to deliver the men to the manor house, tell his lordship what's happened, and send someone to fetch the constable."

Bart held his gaze for long moments before turning back to fetch the cup of water.

"I felt my ribs shift when I hit the ground. There's a bump on my left rib cage." She paused to catch her breath, before adding, "Might be broken."

O'Malley drew in a breath and stared down at the woman. "I shouldn't be here with ye dressed in yer nightrail. Mayhap yer son can help ye change into something else? I don't want any rumors flying around questioning yer virtue, lass."

"Hang my virtue! Those bastards tried to kidnap my son! Take them to Chattsworth Manor so they can be tossed behind bars!" When he opened his mouth to reply, she cut him off. "I'm fine," she assured him. "My husband suffered broken ribs a few years back. I know what to do."

Admiration for the woman trebled as he stared into the depths of her gaze. There was pain, plain as day, but more, there was worry…worry for her son.

A shout from outside galvanized him into action. Turning to Bart, he asked, "How quickly can ye ride to the Clarkes' farm?"

"If I take your gelding, I'll be able to ride like the wind."

O'Malley nodded. "That's a lad. Has yer friend recovered enough to help?"

Bart nodded. "Aye. Right as rain. Mr. Clarke is moving slowly, but I know he'll want to come too. Do you need him to help you take the men to the manor house?"

"Nay. Ask Mrs. Clarke if she can come and tend to yer ma's ribs. I'll need yer friend and his da to stand guard, in case the four bastards brought company."

Bart looked at his mother. "Mum, will you be all right while I'm gone?"

She grabbed hold of his hand. "O'Malley needs to guard the men until you get back. I'll be fine right where I am."

O'Malley breathed a sigh of relief as Bart rushed from the cottage. The sound of hoofbeats pounding past the front windows had him turning toward Mrs. Mayfield. "Now then, lass, why don't ye tell me where else ye're injured."

Her mouth opened, but she snapped it closed and glared at him.

Pleased she'd gotten a bit of her grit back, he nodded. "Seeing as ye're too embarrassed to tell me, I have to guess that ye landed on yer *arse* and bruised it."

The shock on her face quickly faded. Her snort of laughter was followed immediately by a groan of agony.

Too late, he realized that, in his bid to ease her worry, he'd forgotten laughter would only add to her pain. "Lass. Forgive me for making ye laugh!" Without asking permission, he placed a hand to her left side and held it there, supporting her rib cage.

"I'm fine," she said, clearly lying. "You can remove your hand."

Their eyes met, and the long-buried emotions broke free, hitting him in the gut. With a will of iron, he forced the feeling aside. "I didn't mean to cause ye more pain."

She winced. "You didn't."

"Ye haven't told the truth once since ye opened yer mist-laden eyes."

She frowned at him, and he wondered if she'd have as sharp a tongue as his ma. Instead, her frown disappeared, and her eyes filled with uncertainty. "Mist?"

"Aye, yer eyes are the gray of a morning mist. Entrancing. Mysterious."

"You don't have to flatter me to get me to cooperate, O'Malley."

He was about to protest when she laid a hand on his forearm. "Check on the men. I don't want them escaping before they're brought to justice!"

"Have no fear of that—me da taught me well. The knots I tie stay put."

"Please? I promise not to move until Mary gets here." When he did not answer right away, she grumbled, "Fine, then—I'll just get up and see for myself that the blackguards are still bound and waiting for you."

He shot to his feet and leaned over her. "Ye'll do nothing of the kind. I'll tie ye up meself if you move a muscle."

Her eyes widened.

"I'll have yer word on it, Mrs. Mayfield. Ye'll not move from this bed until Mary or I give ye permission!"

The soft gray of her eyes changed in a heartbeat to the color of winter sleet. "Go to blazes! I do not need your permission to do anything!"

Shouting at him obviously cost her dearly. Her face turned white as flour and her eyes welled with tears. She clenched her jaw tight and blinked them away.

"Ah, lass. Ye're back to breathing fire like when ye were protecting yer son. Don't waste any more of yer precious breath. Don't move and have one of yer ribs poke through yer lung. I won't see ye hurt more than ye already are." O'Malley watched the anger leave her by degrees. "Please stay here—I'm meaning what I said about the possibility of a rib poking through yer lung."

Eyes wide, she quickly agreed.

"Now then, if ye hear any grunts or blows being exchanged, ye won't be worrying."

"Blows? What are you up to, O'Malley?"

"Extracting a bit of information."

She seemed pleased with his response. "In that case, do your worst."

He cocked his head to one side. "Are ye sure ye won't try to get up and spy on me through the window?"

"Get the names of those bloody bastards!"

O'Malley grinned. "Aye, lass." He turned and walked to the door. Pausing with his hand on the edge of the door, he reminded her, "Stay put."

Irritated, she huffed, clearly with more force than she'd intended, and grimaced.

Shaking his head, he closed the door behind him. He stepped outside and forced himself to put his worry for her aside to deal with the men.

He strode toward the group and kicked the foot of the closest man to him. "Who are ye working for?"

No reply.

He did the same to the next two men, receiving the same response. Silence.

The last man in line locked gazes with him. He was the biggest of the bunch, the bleeding bugger who'd broken Mrs. Mayfield's ribs. O'Malley grabbed the man by the throat and lifted him until his feet were dangling in the air. "If ye want to see another sunrise, ye'll tell him his name."

The man's surprised expression pleased O'Malley. He may not carry the same bulk as the man he had by the throat, but O'Malley was very strong, and very, very angry.

The man's face was mottled red before O'Malley realized he'd been squeezing the bastard's neck. He grunted and eased up on his hold, but didn't set the man on his feet. Frustration gave way to anger at the man's insolent glare. It tore through O'Malley, raking his guts to shreds. "Ye yellow-bellied piece of *shite*! Picking on women and children! Ye'll give me the name, or I'll crush yer windpipe."

"Tell him!" the man next to them said.

"It's not worth dying over," another told him.

O'Malley increased the pressure, waiting for the man to give a sign he was ready to talk. When the man's body went lax, he tossed him face-first on the ground. "Eat dirt, ye bloody cur!"

Cracking his knuckles, he stood in front of the next man in line. "Now then, ye know what I want. Ye know the consequences."

Before O'Malley could grab hold of the man's throat and lift him in the air, he shouted, "His lordship'll kill us if we tell!"

O'Malley paused. The viscount was right to be concerned about Chellenham. Though the men hadn't given him the name, he could still play on their fear and get them to confirm his suspicions.

His look of boredom seemed to ease the man's worry. O'Malley grabbed him and squeezed the man's neck just enough until he too lay unconscious, face down in the dirt.

O'Malley did not even bother to ask the next man—he grabbed hold of him, rendered him unconscious, and tossed him on the ground.

Coming to stand before the fourth attacker, he sighed. "Now then, I'm tired, and I could use a glass of the Irish."

The man nodded, fear lurking in the depths of his eyes.

"Let's try a different tack—I'll mention a name, and ye can nod yer head for aye or shake it for nay. Yer friends can't hear ye, if that's yer worry. Ye won't have to utter a word." Flexing his fingers as he leaned over the man, he asked one last question: "Chellenham?"

The man's eyes bulged, and he nodded vigorously.

O'Malley patted the man on the shoulder. "That's grand now. Wasn't that painless? Too bad yer friends weren't as smart as yerself." He smiled. "One last question. Remember, all ye need to do is nod."

Jaw clamped tight, the man waited.

"Is Chellenham in Sussex?" The slight nod was all the answer O'Malley required. "Since ye've been so helpful, I'm thinking of offering ye a boon. What do say? Would ye like to spy on Chellenham for me?"

"He'll kill me if he finds out."

"How will he find out?" O'Malley asked.

The man nodded toward his fallen comrades. "They'll know as soon as they wake up and see me just sitting here."

"Well now, if I can guarantee they won't suspect a thing, will ye agree?"

The man nodded, and O'Malley slowly smiled.

The sound of hoofbeats and wagon wheels approaching had him acting quickly. "Ye won't regret yer decision," he told the man before he reached out and squeezed the man's neck until he was limp in his grasp.

After tossing the unconscious man beside the others, he wiped his hands on his trousers and turned, ready to greet Bart and the Clarke family.

Mr. Clarke had his arm in a sling, but otherwise looked no worse for having been shot recently. His wife glanced at the men sprawled facedown and started swaying. Clarke was quick to grab hold of her with his free hand to keep her from falling off the seat. "They're not dead," he assured her.

O'Malley grinned. "Faith, far too many people would be put

out with me if I'd done more than rough them up a bit."

Bart dismounted and led O'Malley's horse to him. "How's my mum?"

"She demanded I extract information from these four"—he glanced at the still-pale Mrs. Clarke and amended what he was going to say—"men. Assuring me she wouldn't move until ye returned with the Clarkes."

Bart rushed to the door and flung it open. "Mum!"

O'Malley held out his hand and helped Mrs. Clarke down from the wagon. "Thank ye for coming."

Mrs. Clarke found her voice. "Of course, Mr. O'Malley. She has done the same for us. I couldn't refuse to help if it was within my ability to do so."

He turned to her husband. "Do ye need a hand?"

Mr. Clarke set the brake and tied off the reins. "I can manage." Proving it, he jumped down and landed next to his wife. "Carry the basket for your mother," he told his son. "I need to speak to O'Malley for a moment."

Matthew hopped off the wagon, reached for the large basket, and held out his arm to his mother. She smiled at him and slipped her arm through his.

Mr. Clarke waited until they were inside before asking, "Who hired them? Did you get a name?"

"No one had to utter a word." With a glance at the largest of the bunch, O'Malley added, "I've all the information I need."

Clarke didn't ask for details, just nodded. "What do you need Matthew and me to do?"

O'Malley eyed the wagon. "I need to borrow yer wagon while ye guard the Mayfields."

"Done." Clarke reached under the seat of the wagon and pulled out a rifle.

O'Malley eyed it with interest. "Mind if I have a look at yer long rifle?"

Clarke handed it over.

"Kentucky .50 caliber?"

"Aye. You've seen one before?"

"Two of me cousins have them."

"It was a gift from my brother-in-law."

"'Tis a fine, accurate weapon." O'Malley handed it back. "I'll not be worrying about Mrs. Mayfield or Bart with yerself standing guard. What'll Matthew be using?"

"He's the true hunter in the family," Clarke said with pride. "He prefers a bow and arrow."

O'Malley grinned. "Does he now? That's fine, then. I'll load up the men and be on me way." With a glance at the cottage, he added, "Ye'll send Bart to the manor house if there's trouble?"

"I will."

The door opened, and Matthew and Bart walked toward them. "Mrs. Clarke kicked us out," Bart said.

"As well she should have. Yer poor ma doesn't need you two fine lads hovering when she's getting her ribs wrapped." Staring at Bart, O'Malley asked, "Did you manage to overhear what other injury she has?"

The boy shrugged. "Something about her knee."

"Mum was pushing us toward the door when Mrs. Mayfield told her about it," Matthew explained.

"Well then. I'll leave the women in yer care. Thank ye."

Clarke watched as O'Malley hauled the first man over his shoulder. "Need any help?"

O'Malley tossed the man headfirst into the wagon bed. "Nay." He loaded the other three, hauled himself onto the seat, untied the reins, and released the brake. "Remember, send word to his lordship if ye need me."

"We will," Clarke assured him.

THE SKY WAS growing light as O'Malley drove his prisoners toward Chattsworth Manor. As he pulled to a halt beside the stables, he glanced over his shoulder at the men who were watching him warily. "I cannot say 'tis been a pleasure, but faith, I enjoyed our...*encounter.*"

Garahan strode toward him. "Old Miriam's here. The viscount is beside himself pacing the hallway outside their bedchamber. He could use a distraction."

O'Malley grinned. "I'll leave the delivering of the men to the constable in yer capable hands, cousin. I'd best bring a full flask with me to soothe his lordship's worry."

Garahan chuckled. "Save a drop or two for yerself." He eyed the men, but they had no bruises that he could see. "Ye used that trick, didn't ye? Blocking off their air until they are unconscious."

O'Malley shrugged. "Seemed expedient, as time was against me." The stable master walked over to see to the horse while O'Malley quietly confided, "His lordship was right—'tis Chellenham."

# CHAPTER SEVEN

HARRY WINCED, AND Mary immediately paused. "I'm sorry, there is no way to avoid causing you pain."

She drew in a careful breath as she met her friend's worried gaze. "I knew bruised ribs were painful, but my husband never let on how much worse it was when they were broken."

Mary sighed. "Men do not like to admit to any weakness. At least, Ethan hates to. There is a point when stoic falls by the wayside as stubborn takes the reins."

Harry closed her eyes for a moment to gather her reserves.

When she opened them again, her friend said, "Let me know when you are ready for me to continue."

"I'm ready." Harry silently prayed for the strength to keep quiet while her friend finished wrapping her ribs.

Mary completed the task and added another pillow behind Harry's back. "If I thought you could have managed to get into and out of a tub, I would have suggested it. That miscreant that tackled you ground dirt into your hands, your knees"—her voice dropped to a raspy whisper—"your face. It would not have been as painful if we could have soaked your injuries before cleaning them."

"We both know we don't have time for that, not with the worry the blackguards are in the area."

Mary agreed.

"It feels better to have my ribs supported. Thank you, Mary. It's the bending over to reach my knees that is going to be difficult, but I can wash my face and hands myself."

"We'll work together, then. The sooner we clean you up, the sooner we can finish patching you up."

Mary got up and brought a bowl of warm water, a tiny round of soap, and a worn cloth to Harry. After setting it on the chair seat next to the bed, she dipped the cloth in the soapy water and handed it to her friend.

When Harry was finished, Mary glanced over her shoulder at the door. "To avoid embarrassing you, I think we should uncover one of your legs at a time, using the linens to protect your modesty."

"I'm not worried about that," Harry said, watching her friend gently bathe a long gash caked with dirt. She did her best not to flinch as Mary removed a few pebbles before smoothing on healing salve and wrapping a bandage around it. But she could not hold back a moan of pain when Mary touched her right knee.

Worry filled her friend's gaze. "It's warm to the touch. I need to see how badly you're injured beneath the dirt. I'll be as gentle as possible."

"Go ahead."

Mary examined the leg. "Your knee is badly bruised and starting to swell. You'll have to stay off it until the swelling goes down."

Harry pressed her lips together to keep from crying out. When the pain subsided, she argued, "Not with all of the work Bart and I have waiting for us."

Mary folded an extra blanket and placed it beneath Harry's knee, and another beneath her foot. "There, that should help."

"For however long I can afford to stay off it," Harry whispered.

"I heard that!" Mary barked. "I'm not quite certain which injury will take longer to heal—the gash on your shin, your mangled knee, or your ribs."

"The gash did not require a needle and thread. The swelling in my knee will go down. I'm more worried about how long it will take my ribs to heal. Bart and I have to try to save what we can harvest. We will turn the rest back into our fields."

Eyes narrowed, Mary huffed. "If I could hazard a guess, I'd say your injuries will take twice as long to heal if you ignore my advice and get out of that bed before the fortnight is up!"

"I will do whatever I feel is necessary," Harry told her. At Mary's frown, she confided, "I'm worried the viscount will have no choice but to lease our farm to someone who is capable of bringing in more revenue."

"Harriet Mayfield!" Mary gasped. "You should have more faith in his lordship. He and her ladyship have done more for us in the short time they've been here than his father did in the last few years he was running the estate. Do you not remember the times we had to share what little we could grow because there was no coin for seed?"

Harry stared at her hands, fighting not to cry. "I remember."

"What about the time Earl Lippincott and his wife accompanied her ladyship on her rounds when she delivered those baskets? I cannot remember a time when we'd received such thoughtful gifts. The calves' foot jelly, the sachet of lavender, the round of soap."

Harry met her friend's gaze. "It is not that I disagree." She paused, searching for the words to help her friend understand why she had no other choice. "I cannot help but worry. So much of the burden of running our farm used to be shared." She swallowed to ease the growing lump in her throat. "Now it is all on my shoulders."

"You could let Bart assume part of your worry," Mary suggested. "We've given over a part of ours to Matthew. He's become more responsible because of our trust in him."

"Bart has already shouldered so much of the heavier workload. I have trusted him with more, but I do not want to take away what little time he has left for his studies. He's intelligent enough to handle the job of steward. I asked if he wanted me to speak to his lordship about letting Bart apprentice with Mr. Rowland."

Mary's eyes widened. "What did he say?"

Harry's shoulders slumped. She gasped and immediately straightened until she was sitting with her back upright again, alleviating the strain on her battered ribs. "He insists he likes working the farm alongside of me."

"He's a good son," Mary told her. "Why not let him shoulder more of the responsibility? Need I remind you, to heal properly, you should not be bending, lifting, or twisting for at least a fortnight, mayhap longer."

Harry closed her eyes, battling the urge to let her guard down and weep. "We do not have the time to waste."

"Time spent allowing your body to heal is not time wasted, *Harriet.*"

"What of your crops? What will you do while Ethan heals?"

Mary glanced at the door. "He's already been back in the fields."

"With a pistol ball wound? He needs to fully heal after losing all that blood, or he'll risk infection!"

Her friend's eyes welled with tears. "I've said those very same words to him."

"And he still refused to listen?"

"Aye. 'Tis the same situation you are facing here with your load and your yield of crops. We need to decide what portion of the crop can be saved and what will be plowed under to enrich the soil."

"Mayhap we can ask the Johnsons to lend Robbie out to help us. He will no doubt lend a hand—as we will for one another, Mary. You can certainly ask for help. Although Bart would never let me hear the end of it if I were even to suggest such a thing as needing help with our harvest."

Mary chuckled softly. "He does take after his father in that regard."

"In temperament as well as looks."

"It was providential that Mr. O'Malley arrived when he did."

Harry's heart stuttered in her breast as the feeling of being held against the pounding of his heart took over her thoughts, addling her wits. The breadth of O'Malley's chest and width of his shoulders were equal, if not more imposing than her husband's had been.

"Aye," she finally managed. Her thoughts were in turmoil as she wrestled with the fact that the man had *ordered* her to rest. Not even her husband had dared to order her around!

Mary adjusted her friend's nightrail to cover her legs, then smoothed the covers, tucking them around her. "Is there anything you need before we leave?"

"Not a thing, Mary. We are indebted to you for your help."

Mary scoffed. "We're even. You helped us; we helped you. That is what neighbors and friends do for one another."

"Thank you."

She reached for Harry's hand, squeezed it, and let it go. "Thank *you*, Harry."

The heavy knock on the cottage door was accompanied by a deep voice calling, "Mum! Can I come in?"

"Aye, Bart."

He shoved open the door. "Mr. Clarke is ready to go."

"Thank you, Bart."

He nodded and slowly walked over to the bed. Reaching for his mother's hand, he rasped, "Your cheek is bruised, Mum."

"I have one to match it on my knee."

Mary cleared her throat—loudly.

"And your ribs, Mum?"

"Broken," Mary replied. "Her knee is still swelling, possibly from twisting and the impact when she landed on it. Your mother must remain in that bed for a fortnight. See that she follows my recommendations to the letter, or I cannot guarantee that her ribs or her knee will heal properly—if at all. The chance of infection is too great."

Bart's face paled, and his Adam's apple bobbed up and down twice before he was able to respond. "I promise to see that she rests."

Mrs. Clarke walked over to Bart and gave him a quick hug. "I know you will. If your mother becomes feverish, please let me know. I shall come at once. We may need to send for a physician."

"No physician!" Harry grumbled. "We do not have the coin to cover the cost."

"I'm sure we can barter if it comes to that," her son assured her.

"I still make the decisions around here," Harry reminded him.

Her son straightened to his full height and frowned down at her. "For now." With that, he walked over to where Mary had finished packing her basket. "I'll walk you outside, Mrs. Clarke."

"Thank you, Bart."

With a harsh glance, he commanded, "Stay put, Mum!"

Harry drew in a deep breath to snap at her son but ended up moaning in pain. It was going to take a bit to get used to taking shallow breaths. More so to remember not to laugh or shout her displeasure at her son.

It was going to be a long two weeks.

# CHAPTER EIGHT

"CONGRATULATIONS, YOUR LORDSHIP!" the physician announced. "You and your countess have a healthy baby boy."

William stood rooted in the doorway to their bedchamber, staring at the sight before him.

Calliope beamed at him. "Come and meet our son."

He blinked, then slowly made his way to her side. "Calliope, my love. I am so sorry."

She ignored her husband in favor of the bundle in her arms. "Just look at him. Isn't he perfect? Two eyes, two hands, two feet—and all his fingers and toes. I counted."

"You asked me to do that for you," he reminded her.

"I intended to but was afraid it would embarrass you if you heard me complaining about the slight bit of pain I endured."

"If it was a *slight* bit of pain, how is it that I clearly heard you cursing my name before you started cursing the duke for arranging our marriage?"

She had the grace to blush at his question. "The laboring may have been a bit stronger and harder to deal with than I'd imagined. I distinctly remember Persephone telling me it was a walk in the park."

Their housekeeper, Mrs. Meadowsweet, chuckled. "I have heard more than one mother cry out in pain while she labored to birth her babe, then, after delivering a healthy babe, brush it all aside, replying it was nothing."

"As have I, Mrs. Meadowsweet," the physician remarked, approaching the couple. "I expect you to remain in bed for at least a sennight, Lady Calliope. Even if you feel completely fine, do not overdo it by attempting to return to your normal duties too soon. You could end up on full bedrest for a fortnight."

Calliope readily agreed, for which the viscount was extremely grateful.

Addressing the viscount, the physician continued, "I've given Mrs. Meadowsweet suggestions for her ladyship's diet and cannot stress enough if she tries to do too much too soon, she could hemorrhage." The viscount swayed on his feet, but the physician was quick to steady him. "Mayhap you should sit down, your lordship."

William sat down hard, nearly falling off the chair, but managed to keep his seat. "Hemorrhage, you say?"

"Aye. Even though your wife appears as if she is ready to take on the world, you must coddle her and not let her do too much. I have seen disastrous results from ignoring my instructions."

The viscount locked gazes with the physician. "I shall follow them to the letter."

"Excellent." Turning to the countess, the physician bowed and smiled. "My congratulations again, your ladyship, your lordship."

Calliope didn't bother to look away from the miracle in her arms when she replied, "Thank you."

"Mrs. Meadowsweet, please see the physician out."

"Aye, your lordship."

"Please pass on the good news that her ladyship safely delivered a son. Have one of the footmen deliver the news to our tenant farmers and their families. Let them know we shall have a celebration three weeks hence to welcome..." The viscount glanced at his wife. "What name did you have in mind for our son?"

She beckoned her husband closer and pressed her lips to his. "William, after his father, the love of my life."

# CHAPTER NINE

O'MALLEY AND GARAHAN were the first to hear the news.

"A son, is it?" Garahan said. "Wonderful news!"

"Congratulations, your lordship. How is her ladyship?"

The viscount glanced at the closed door behind him and leaned toward the men. "She insists she is fine, but the physician wants her to stay in bed for a sennight. Does that sound normal?"

O'Malley and his cousin shared a look before O'Malley replied, "I wouldn't be knowing, though Ma was usually chomping at the bit to get back to doing things her way—without help not long after me younger brothers arrived."

"Me ma was the same," Garahan added. "Though I remember Da worrying after me youngest brother was born."

"What happened?" the viscount asked.

"Ma refused to listen and got up too soon. She was pale as flour. Da put me in charge of me younger brothers and Ma while he went to fetch the midwife."

The viscount fell silent. "And your mother is well?"

Garahan snickered. "Well enough to box me ears the last time I was able to visit."

"Mayhap I should insist Calliope stay in bed for a fortnight."

"Begging yer pardon, yer lordship," O'Malley began, "but Ma was always more agreeable when Da *suggested* she rest—stubborn as a goat when he *insisted*."

"Aye. Ma could raise the roof whenever Da started telling her what to do, when, and how," Garahan agreed.

Before the viscount could form a response, O'Malley slipped his hand into his waistcoat pocket and offered his flask. "A wee drop of the Irish'll set ye to rights."

"Ye'll be thinking clearly after another wee sip or two," Garahan remarked, watching the viscount take a drink.

"I did not think I would react this way," the viscount said, handing O'Malley's flask back. "But all of the horrific stories I remember hearing from my friends when we were young are stuck in my head."

"Best not to dwell on what might have happened," O'Malley said.

"Aye. Her ladyship safely delivered yer son," Garahan added as he held out his own flask to the viscount. "Concentrate on that, yer lordship, and have another sip or two."

The viscount smiled as he drank. "Aye. Thank you, men." He handed Garahan's flask back and grinned. "I do believe a few sips of your fine Irish whiskey have settled my stomach and cleared my head."

Garahan elbowed his cousin. "Aye, but remember, more than a few sips may muddle yer head."

"And turn yer stomach," O'Malley said with a grin.

"Wise words. I'll heed your advice, gentlemen." With a nod, the viscount knocked on the door and opened it slowly when his wife bade him enter.

"'Tis a relief to see them so happy," O'Malley said as he and his cousin made their way back to their posts.

"Aye, amid the troubling attacks on his lordship's tenant farmers," Garahan replied.

"I'm not one for overstepping me bounds," O'Malley said, "but I'm thinking we should take it upon ourselves to increase the guard."

"His lordship hasn't asked it of us yet."

"I'm thinking he's been worried about her ladyship and the

prospect of becoming a father." He glanced at his cousin and inclined his head. "I'll speak to Hargrave and ask who he'd recommend from the staff. Why don't you ask MacReady who he'd suggest from the village?"

The two separated and set off to lay the foundation for additions to those guarding the duke's cousin, his wife, and the newborn babe.

⎯⎯➤➤➤◄◄◄⎯⎯

A FEW HOURS later, O'Malley and Hargrave had met and agreed upon two more footmen—the two were younger than Hartman and Sweeney, who'd already been drafted to help. It had been a shock to O'Malley that young men in service to the viscount would *not* know how to wield a knife or blade, let alone fire a pistol or rifle. The newest additions to the viscount's staff had been hired when he was in London. Mayhap it was because those that worked in the city had no need to protect their families and their farms. Either that or his first thought was the truth—the English were an odd lot to figure out.

Garahan agreed to meet with the four young men from the village that MacReady suggested. They were younger than the viscount's footmen, who ranged in age from eight and ten to six and twenty. The village lads were half a decade, and more, younger. MacReady assured Garahan their age would not be a deterrent, as they were from God-fearing families and all of them were hard workers. MacReady sent word with one of the stable hands to have the young men arrive late in the afternoon.

"'Tis best if ye are the one to speak to his lordship," Garahan told O'Malley. "Ye're far more patient than meself and apt to suggest hiring on more men in a way that he'll end up thinking 'twas his idea in the first place."

O'Malley chuckled. "High praise coming from yerself, though ye may be right."

"I'm always right," Garahan boasted.

O'Malley shoved him out of the way with his shoulder. "Unless ye're wrong."

"I'm never wrong," his cousin growled.

O'Malley laughed in his face.

Fists raised, jaws clenched, the two men eyed one another through narrowed eyes.

"I do not have time for this!" the viscount barked from behind them. He raked a hand through his hair and sighed. "I heard an unsettling rumor—something about increasing the guard?"

Garahan nudged his cousin.

O'Malley frowned before turning to face the viscount. "Aye, yer lordship. Given the current circumstances with what's been happening to a number of yer tenant farmers…"

"And…" Garahan prompted.

"And," O'Malley repeated, "with the birth of yer heir, ye'll be needing additional men to guard yerself, her ladyship, and the babe."

Viscount Chattsworth's frown smoothed out as his eyes lit with purpose. "What about Hartman and Sweeney? Hargrave informed me that they rode with you the other night."

"They were a welcome addition to our patrol, but I'm thinking two more men guarding from the inside are needed."

The viscount inclined his head. "Aye. If I hadn't been so preoccupied with Calliope giving birth, I'd have thought of it myself!"

Garahan snorted to cover his laughter. "Naturally, ye'd want to add one someone ye trust. Mayhap one of yer footmen."

"Excellent notion."

O'Malley cleared his throat. "Garahan and I took the liberty of speaking with Hargrave, and he recommended two of yer footmen."

"I spoke to MacReady, and he suggested four young men from the village," Garahan added.

"I take it you've already met with the men and want me to

meet the prospects to round out your guard?"

O'Malley jammed his elbow in Garahan's gut. "Aye, yer lordship."

Garahan stepped on O'Malley's foot. "Hargrave and MacReady came through for ye, yer lordship, as they always do."

The viscount locked gazes with them, but did not reprimand them for dereliction of duty, or acting like a bloody pair of *eedjits* about to pound on one another.

O'Malley wondered if he was waiting for one of them to apologize.

As he opened his mouth to do so, the viscount held up a hand. "I'm anxious to meet with the men. I want the both of you guarding the perimeter of the manor house—On second thought...inside, now that little William has arrived. Assign the patrols to the others."

"The men are waiting outside our quarters."

The viscount glanced over his shoulder. "Bring them to the library. I'll meet with them there."

"Aye, yer lordship."

⇥⟫⟪⇤

O'MALLEY AND GARAHAN left to do their employer's bidding. A short while later, they approached the library, accompanied by the footmen, who followed readily. The four lads from the village were a bit more hesitant meeting the lord of the manor, and hung back.

O'Malley knocked and waited for permission to enter.

"Ah, come in, gentlemen."

When they'd all filed in and stood side by side, the viscount took their measure. Uneasy with the silence, the villagers shuffled from foot to foot.

At the continued silence, O'Malley spoke up. "Deacon and Hornsby were selected from yer staff at Hargrave's suggestion."

The viscount's brows lifted. "Why do you think that is, Deacon?"

The young man squared his shoulders and replied, "I'm a crack shot with a rifle."

The viscount smiled. "I see." He turned to the other footman. "And you, Hornsby? Can you shoot?"

Hornsby grinned. "Better than Deacon, and I'm a fair hand with a knife."

"I have no doubt O'Malley already put you through your paces, or neither one of you would have gotten this far even on Hargrave's recommendation."

"Aye, your lordship," they both agreed.

Turning to the four young men from the village, the viscount seemed impressed by the way they held themselves, standing tall.

Garahan knew he would be, were he the one inspecting the group. "MacReady suggested these fine young lads as additions to yer guard. Every one of them is used to putting in a hard day's work and can handle a pistol, rifle, or knife."

"Have you demonstrated your skill to Garahan?" the viscount asked.

The group readily agreed.

The viscount glanced at Garahan. "Why don't you introduce the men to me?"

"Aye, yer lordship. The tallest of the bunch is Ryerson, who is also the youngest at six and ten. Next to him is Anderson, who is seven and ten, Flanders is the same age, and Kent here is the oldest of the group and eight and ten."

"I've been practicing with my father's blade," Ryerson remarked.

The viscount nodded. "Military?"

The young man grinned. His pride was evident as he replied, "Aye, your lordship. One of the King's Dragoons."

"Can you handle a pistol too?" the viscount asked.

The youth shook his head, "But I can outshoot these three at a distance of four hundred yards!"

The broadest of the bunch, Anderson, elbowed him. "He has an unfair advantage."

"What is that?" the viscount asked.

"He's been practicing with his father's Kentucky long rifle."

Garahan grinned. "A fine weapon, if I do say so meself."

"Not standard issue in the King's Dragoons," the viscount murmured.

"It was a gift from my uncle—he's been living in America," Ryerson said.

"Ah," the viscount replied. Nodding to the youth who'd voiced his opinion of fairness, he asked, "What weapon are you most comfortable with, Anderson?"

"A pistol, your lordship."

"Flanders, what about you?"

The young man replied, "Same as Anderson, a pistol, your lordship."

"Kent? What is your preferred weapon?"

"A blunderbuss, your lordship, unless I'm close enough to use my fists."

O'Malley and Garahan shared a smile.

"Bare-knuckle, is it?" O'Malley asked.

"Aye."

"That's fine, then, lad," Garahan said.

"I won't tell you there is no danger involved, men," the viscount said. The younger ones from the village lifted their chins proudly at being called men, as the viscount had no doubt intended. "You will be counted on to have your weapon primed and ready at all times, and you should not be afraid to use it." When no one contradicted his words, he told them, "I'm proud to have you as a temporary part of the duke's guard here at Chattsworth Manor."

"Will we have to meet the duke, too?" Ryerson asked.

"Not at this time. His Grace trusts my judgment and that of his men implicitly," Viscount Chattsworth told them. The worry in the young man's gaze cleared, and the viscount continued,

"Now then. I'll leave O'Malley and Garahan to advise you as to where they patrol and at what hours of the day. If any of you believe it will interfere with your duties at home, please let them know immediately."

"Begging your pardon, your lordship."

"Aye, Kent? What is it?"

"Before we could come to meet with O'Malley and Garahan, our parents had to agree that we would be working for your lordship and reporting for duty at dawn tomorrow."

The viscount slowly smiled. "I take it your parents agreed." There was a resounding chorus of *ayes* that had the viscount's smile broadening. "Well then, men, welcome. Your service is greatly appreciated."

"We haven't done anything yet," Anderson reminded him.

"I disagree," the viscount said. "You're skilled with weapons, hard workers, and are willing to work under what could be hazardous conditions, and somehow you managed to convince your parents to let you work for me. I would say that is quite a feat."

The first chuckle was soft, gradually increasing in volume as, one by one, those from the village joined in.

"Until tomorrow, men," the viscount said. "Garahan, kindly show the men where their quarters are."

"Aye, yer lordship. 'Tis in the outbuilding his lordship converted into quarters for those of us in the duke's guard." With a wave of his hand, Garahan said, "Follow me, lads."

"Deacon, Hornsby, a word."

The footmen straightened to attention at the viscount's command. "Aye, your lordship," Deacon said.

"O'Malley, I want Deacon and Hornsby stationed inside, along with Hartman and Sweeney."

"Aye, your lordship," O'Malley replied. "Hargrave and I already discussed that may be what you would prefer."

"Men, I know you did not anticipate moving into a position of protection rather than service, but Lady Calliope and I are most grateful that you are skilled using a variety of arms and are willing to join O'Malley and Garahan, knowing that we are currently besieged with unprovoked attacks against our tenant farmers."

Deacon was the first to speak. "We heard the rumors, your lordship."

"Aye," Hornsby agreed. "We stand ready to defend you and your family."

"You'll start immediately," the viscount said. "I'll let O'Malley fill you in on the hours, patrol stations, and such."

"It is an honor," Deacon replied.

"Definitely an honor," Hornsby chimed in.

"Thank you, men."

O'Malley turned to the men. "Let's start with the hours and rotation of your posts."

$$ \Longleftrightarrow \diamond \Longleftrightarrow $$

# CHAPTER TEN

H ARRY STRUGGLED TO keep her balance while not putting pressure on her injured knee. Every time she leaned forward to drag the hoe through the dirt, a sharp ache slashed through her bound ribs.

Mayhap they were not wrapped tight enough.

Though the sun was still low in the sky, it was quiet. Too quiet. She missed the companionable chats she and her son normally had while working their land. A glance from the side of her eyes revealed the dark and forbidding cloud that had wrapped around her son from the moment she announced she intended to get out of bed and work in the fields.

Bart protested, using every reason Mary had stated the day before, to no avail. He stopped short of bodily putting her back in bed. They'd argued over every little thing from that moment until she walked to the end of the row and began to loosen the weeds from their grip on the soil—the job she'd assigned herself. It did not require the bending Bart was doing as he sorted through their damaged crops to see what could be harvested.

Her son ignored her presence and had been silent since then. Each tugging motion of the hoe added another layer of pain—to her body and her soul.

In her heart she knew there was no way her son would be able to accomplish what needed to be done alone. It had taken her working alongside her husband for years to tend to their crops and bring in the harvest. Bart needed her. She would not lie abed when there was work to be done.

Sweat beaded on her upper lip and gathered between her breasts, trickling beneath the linen bandage. Exhaustion pulled at her, but she ignored it. She'd worked through her grief when she lost her husband, and she would work through the pain of her paltry broken ribs while ignoring her knee.

The sound of hoofbeats approaching had her shielding her eyes with one hand while she leaned against the handle of the hoe to keep from falling on her face. As the rider drew closer, irritation began to simmer in the pit of her belly.

"O'Malley!" her son called out, striding toward the man who had been front and center in her mind since he held her to his heart the night before.

*Because you were injured and not able to stand,* her head reminded her.

*Because he admired your strength and your courage while protecting your son,* her heart insisted.

"Bloody hell!" He leapt from his horse and strode to where she stood. "What in the name of God do ye think ye're doing?"

She frowned. "Weeding."

His grass-green eyes darkened as an all-too-familiar emotion surfaced. O'Malley was angry with her? Why?

"Are ye daft?"

She dropped the hoe, put her hands to her hips, and drew in a breath to lambast the man for suggesting she was crazy. But the words got caught in her throat as spots danced before her eyes. Her head felt as if it floated above her body when darkness pulled her under.

"Mum!" Bart shouted, rushing to where O'Malley stood, once again cradling the daft woman in his arms.

"What in the bloody hell is wrong with yer ma, lad?"

Bart's hands were shaking, but O'Malley wasn't sure if it was from fear, or the need to restrain himself from shaking his mother until she saw sense.

Eyes of the deepest brown met O'Malley's gaze. "She's bull-headed and argued against everything I said." Bart lowered his voice to add, "Mum does not like to be told what to do."

"We don't either, now do we?" Without waiting for Bart to answer, O'Malley continued, "But 'tis me opinion she knows she's wrong—and is just too stubborn to admit it."

Bart snorted. "Aye, but I'd not have her any other way." Worry creased the young man's brow. "Do you think she's injured her ribs further?"

"Three of her ribs are already broken. Cannot get more injured than that."

Bart opened the door to the cottage and waited for O'Malley to carry his mother inside. "I overheard you mention something about a rib poking a lung. Do you think that's what happened just now?"

O'Malley dug deep to set that particular worry from his own mind while he laid the stubborn woman on the bed she'd abandoned to work in the fields. "We'll know once she rouses."

"Can you tell me? I need to know, because as sure as the sun rises, she'll be fighting to get out of bed to work in our fields."

O'Malley scrubbed a hand over his face. "Is there a reason she insists on working until she drops, or is it something more…something tangled up with what happened to yer da?"

Bart shrugged. "She's had to be strong after my father died. He wouldn't have given up—Mum won't either." He poured water from the pitcher into a cup and set it on the table by the bed. Without O'Malley asking, he then poured water into the bowl on the table, dipped a worn cloth into it, and wrung it out.

"May I?" O'Malley asked, when Bart was about to bathe his mother's face.

"Aye, since you saved her from a serious injury to her hard

head last night and just now."

O'Malley's lips twitched as he fought not to laugh. "She's protective."

"Aye," Bart agreed.

"Stubborn to a fault."

"My father said that a lot."

"What else did he say?"

Bart slowly smiled. "Said he was smart to marry a strong, courageous woman instead of a fragile flower."

"Oh? And what was yer ma's reaction to that?"

Bart chuckled. "She'd whack him with whatever was handy."

O'Malley slid the cool cloth along the curve of her cheek. "Did she now?"

"Aye. Then my father would smile and tell her he couldn't imagine his life without her in it."

"Yer da was a lucky man." With a gentle touch, he blotted her forehead before laying the folded cloth across it, partially covering her eyes.

"Aye."

Turning his full attention to the lad, he told him, "Ye are, too."

"She's always protected me. I know when I've pushed her too far and can get her to laugh when she'd rather take a whack at me."

"A smart man knows when to push and when to retreat."

"My father knew that. They worked tirelessly to keep the farm going, especially after he expanded what we planted to include a third field."

"But ye helped."

"Aye." The lad's eyes clouded, and O'Malley sensed what was coming before he spoke. "I wasn't as much of a help back then, but I am now. If only…"

"Yer da was still here," O'Malley finished for him.

The lad struggled to hold his emotion in check, but tears welled in his eyes. Four and ten was young enough to be embarrassed by his emotions, so he ignored the way Bart blinked and recovered his composure. "The men would never have hurt Mum, if he were here."

"Would she have chased outside after him to stop them?"

Bart shrugged in answer for a second time.

"I'm thinking she would."

The boy blew out a breath. "Aye, and would have gotten an earful from my father, but she'd have stood beside him defending what was ours just the same."

"As ye did."

"Aye," the lad rasped. "The three of us would have done serious damage to the attackers."

O'Malley placed his hand on Bart's shoulder. "Ye held yer own against the attackers, when there were three to yer one."

"Well, I—"

"And with your doing so, I was able to take care of the bloody bastard who'd tackled yer ma."

"Have I thanked you for that?"

O'Malley grinned. "Aye, lad. Now, let's see if we can convince yer ma to open her eyes instead of listening in on our private conversation."

"Mum would never—"

"You were speaking about me as if I weren't here!" Harry accused them, snatching the cloth off her forehead.

"That we were, lass," O'Malley said.

"The things you said about me—"

"All true. Weren't they, Bart?"

"Aye, Mum," Bart said. "They were true. Father used to say those very same words I told O'Malley."

Harry frowned at them but remained silent.

O'Malley held her gaze for long moments, relieved to note her cheeks had a hint of rose—not deathly pale or with a grayish cast. "Yer eyes are a clear, soft gray."

Bart leaned over his mother. "They are. That's good, isn't it?"

"Aye. As is the flush on her cheeks, soft enough to be a blush, not bright enough to be a fever."

"Stop talking about me as if I am not present!" Harry demanded, then gasped.

"She hasn't grasped the need to keep her breathing even, not trying to suck in too much air at once to rage at us or argue."

"I wish she would," Bart mumbled. "It's hard to watch her gasping for breath."

The widow's gaze met O'Malley's, and he nearly choked on his laughter. She was mad enough to spit nails. "I think she's recovered enough to give me a large piece of her mind." When she opened her mouth to speak, he held up his hand to stop her. "But yer ma's intelligent enough to know she'd only end up out of air again, unless she chooses to use a gentler tone. One that requires less air and less effort."

Turning to glare at the widow, he said, "I told ye I would be by today to help with yer chores. Why did ye not wait for me?"

Harry closed her eyes, then slowly opened them. "Bart, would you please help me sit up?"

"Are you still lightheaded, Mum?"

"Nay."

Bart looked to O'Malley, waiting for him to agree before obliging her.

"Thank you."

He immediately handed her the cup of water he'd poured earlier. As she was drinking, he asked, "Why did you let us think you were unconscious? It isn't a game, Mum."

"And well she knows it, lad," O'Malley said. "I knew she was conscious."

"How?" Harry and Bart asked at the same time.

O'Malley chuckled. "I think I'll save that bit of information for a more opportune time."

"What do you mean by that?" Bart asked.

"Let it be, Bart," Harry said.

His gaze lingered on her face for long moments before he rasped, "I thought you agreed to stop treating me as if I were still a child."

"It's not that at all, lad," O'Malley assured him. "Yer ma is embarrassed that I knew she was feigning unconsciousness, when the both of us were worried for her. She knew it was wrong and is probably unsure if we would accept her apology for such a cruel trick."

Harry's face lost every ounce of color—not what O'Malley had intended, but at least there was no doubt in his mind that his point had hit home.

"Now then, lass. Drink yer water and apologize to the lad. He was worried sick, though he didn't show it."

Bart's eyes rounded. "How did you know?"

"If it were me own ma, I'd have been. Seeing's how much ye love yer ma, I knew ye'd feel the same as meself."

"I do love you, Mum. I just wish you'd listen to reason and stop being so difficult."

"Difficult?" she asked.

"Aye. You should have listened to Mrs. Clarke and stayed in bed until you were well enough to get out of it."

"I know how I feel."

"Oh, aye, Mrs. Mayfield," O'Malley barked. "Right now ye feel like *shite*, and it serves ye right for going against common sense and scaring the life out of yer son."

Tears welled up and spilled over.

"Don't cry, Mum."

After handing her the handkerchief from his waistcoat pocket, O'Malley patted Bart on the shoulder. "Sometimes a woman needs to cry."

"Mum never cries."

"Then mayhap it's time she let go of her worries and the grief balled up inside of her and had a good cry."

O'Malley remembered the last time his ma dissolved in tears. They'd been waiting outside the gaol for his da and Uncle Patrick to be released. When the doors finally opened, 'twas his da carrying his uncle with tears staining his proud face that had Ma weeping. Da had lost his best friend, his eldest brother, jailed for a crime neither had committed.

Rather than share that memory, he shrugged. "Let's give her a few moments to collect herself, then. Have ye a kettle ye can put on the boil?"

"If you help me up, I can—"

"Stay in that bed," O'Malley barked. "Ye've caused enough trouble between yer stubborn insistence that ye work in the fields, and then making yer son fear ye were at death's door, feigning unconsciousness."

Harry had the grace to accept his harsh words.

'Twas about time the woman listened to reason. "I'll have yer word ye'll stay put while we brew some tea."

She nodded.

"Well then, we may let ye share a cup with us, won't we, lad?"

"Aye, Mum," Bart said. "But you'd best listen this time, or I'll leave you here to fend for yourself. Then you'll see reason and understand why we want you to rest your swollen knee and busted ribs."

"I promise, Bart."

O'Malley was proud of the lad for speaking his mind. His ma needed to know the error of her ways. Bart may be nearly grown, but he had a tender heart that still needed his mother.

Bart reached for the tin of tea leaves and stared at his mother until she inclined her head as if she understood her son's silent entreaty. The lad's shoulders relaxed as he busied himself pouring the hot water over the tea leaves. He put the lid on the pot, and set it to steep.

Turning to meet O'Malley's gaze, she cleared her throat. "I'm sorry, O'Malley. I should have known better than to ignore Mary's and your advice."

O'Malley accepted her apology with a nod. "Do ye have a biscuit or scone to go with the tea?"

Bart chuckled. "Aye. In that tin on the table. If you'd set a few on a plate, I'll pour our tea."

O'Malley did as the young man asked, then proceeded to clear off the table beside Harry. "I thought we'd join ye for tea, if ye don't mind."

"I'd like that."

"Bart, lad, the lady of the house has deigned to have a spot of tea with the likes of us."

The young man grinned. "We are fortunate she's not whacking us with her favorite cast iron pan."

O'Malley's laughter rumbled out and filled the room. "Me ma has wicked aim with her broom, rolling pin, or cast iron pan. Me da, me brothers, and I learned to be quick on our feet."

Harry was smiling as she lifted her cup. "Bart is fast on his feet." As she started to reach for her plate, she paused, grimaced, then asked, "Would someone mind handing me my plate?"

"With pleasure, Mrs. Mayfield." O'Malley held her plate where she could grasp it easily.

"Thank you." After carefully setting it on top of her cup, she bit into the day-old scone and slowly chewed. "Since you've saved my stubborn head from bashing against the ground twice now, I think you can call me Harry."

Bart's gaze bounced from O'Malley to his mother and back, but he did not say anything.

Pleased that the lad hadn't balked at his ma's suggestion, O'Malley inclined his head. "These scones are delicious, Harry. Thank ye for inviting me to tea."

Her smile was radiant, though he could see exhaustion begin to creep into her mist-colored eyes.

When they'd finished off the tea and the scones, he motioned to Bart. "Why don't we see about a few of those chores while yer ma has a bit of a rest?"

"But I'm not—" Harry began, only to wilt under the hard stares of her son and O'Malley. She let go of a sigh. "I'm not going to argue with either of you. Mayhap I will rest my eyes."

"And you'll remember your promise, Mum?" her son asked.

"Aye, Bart."

"Ye'll not be hopping out of yer bed the moment we close the door?" O'Malley added.

"I won't."

"Yer word, lass."

She ground her teeth together. "You have my word, O'Malley."

"That's fine, then, lass."

"We'll be in to check on you after we finish weeding and sorting," her son told her.

"I'll be waiting right here," Harry grumbled.

⇒⇒⇒⇒◄◄◄◄

THREE HOURS LATER, the men found her sleeping soundly.

"Thank you for your help today, O'Malley," Bart said.

"Me pleasure, lad. I'll be back tonight."

"Tonight?"

"Aye, I've a feeling the attacks may start up again."

"But you turned those men over to the constable."

"I've a feeling more will follow," O'Malley said.

"I hadn't thought of that."

"Garahan and I have reason to believe more will be coming."

"I'd best warn our neighbors," Bart said.

"Garahan was to see to that today while I worked with ye here."

"And tonight?"

"I'll help ye stand watch."

Bart looked over to where his mother lay sleeping. "I owe you a debt I doubt I can repay."

"Ye already have, lad, by the way ye care for yer ma, and how hard ye work alongside of her. Between the two of ye, ye keep the farm producing enough revenue to help the viscount get Chattsworth Manor back on its feet."

"He won't send us packing, will he?"

O'Malley shook his head. "That he won't. Viscount Chattsworth is a man who can be trusted to keep his word."

Relief filled the young man's face. "I'll see you tonight."

"Aye. Tonight."

# CHAPTER ELEVEN

Harry's head hurt and her heart ached when she opened her eyes to find her son quietly standing in front of the cookstove stirring a pot. She hadn't had time to prepare anything since yesterday and had no idea what was in the pot.

She braced her hands on either side of her and attempted to sit up. The pain surprised a moan out of her.

"Mum! You're awake." He rushed over to help her sit up. "Easy now. Don't twist," he warned her, taking a step back.

"Thank you."

He nodded and returned to the stove. She wanted to ask what he was cooking, but the growing silence had her remembering her earlier actions and Bart's reaction. Why hadn't she told her son and O'Malley that she was awake?

"I was tired of feeling out of control," she whispered.

"Control?" He snorted, sounding very much like his father.

"Aye. I'm not accustomed to sitting while others do my chores for me."

Bart glanced over his shoulder at her. "But you're hurt."

She drew in a shallow breath and let it go. "I hate feeling useless," she confessed.

Her son set the spoon aside and walked over to crouch by the bed. "Mum, you are not useless. But I wish you'd remember I'm not a child anymore and can handle more of the workload you hesitate to share with me."

Harry cupped his face in her hand. "No matter how old you are, you'll always be my precious little boy." His groan had her smiling. "I will do my best to only say such things when it's just the two of us. Would that be all right?"

He put his hands on his thighs and pushed to his feet. "Aye, Mum. I hope you're hungry. Mrs. Clarke stopped by and dropped off a hearty soup."

Harry blinked, shocked that she hadn't woken up when Mary arrived. "How long was I asleep?"

"Until not that long ago."

She glanced out the window, surprised to see the sky darkening toward twilight. "I must have slept longer than I intended to."

Bart ladled soup into two bowls, sliced the last bit of bread she'd baked the other day, and set it all on the worn oak table. "Do you think you can manage to sit and eat at the table, or do you prefer to remain in bed?"

She frowned at him. "I was ordered to stay in bed." Her son turned away, but not before she saw his smile. "What is so humorous?"

He fetched the teapot and poured hot water over the leaves before answering. "Mrs. Clarke said that if you felt well enough, and let me help you to stand, she thought it might do you good to sit at the table and eat."

"What about staying in bed for a fortnight?"

"Mum. She knows you almost as well as I do. We both know how hard it is for you to sit while others toil. Given the fact that you've already been out of bed and working in the field, she thought being out of bed to eat one meal a day would help you heal faster."

"Well then, I do believe I would enjoy sharing a meal with you at the table."

He inclined his head and returned to her side. "Lean on me."

His strength was a constant surprise to her, but shouldn't be, considering he was built like his father had been.

As he eased her onto her chair at the table, he grinned. "I was going to offer to carry you."

She chuckled and braced a hand to her side.

"I'm so used to making you laugh, Mum, I forget that you shouldn't."

Harry dug deep and conquered the pain in time to reassure him that she was fine.

They ate in companionable silence, until Bart's shoulders slumped. "I have something to tell you, but I'm not certain how you will react."

She set down her spoon and folded her hands in her lap. "Is this about the attack?"

"How did you know?"

"Aside from my injuries, it's been on my mind. Although you are your father's son, there are parts of me that you inherited as well—the part of me that picks apart situations and worries until all has been resolved."

"O'Malley said the attackers were turned over to the constable."

"He told me that as well. What is your worry, then?"

"O'Malley's coming back tonight."

"Why?"

He held her gaze for long moments before confiding, "He believes more men will come to finish the job."

"Our barn?"

"Aye, Mum. He didn't say as much, but he's coming to stand watch with me."

"I can—"

"You promised, Mum. You're to stay inside. I know how hard it is for you not to be standing beside me."

"You may think so, but I cannot imagine that you understand."

"Every time you told me to go back inside when you and Father were facing a problem, I felt as if I was not strong enough, smart enough, good enough to stand with you."

She reached for his hand and held tight. "We never meant for you to feel that way. It's hard for a parent to let go of the protective hold they have on their children—even when in their heart they know it is past time to do so."

Bart's eyes glassed over. He looked away, and when he turned back, they were clear again. "Like the night we lost Father. We leaned on one another, drawing strength from one another."

"I was so proud of you, shouldering the burden of such a loss, and willing to do what had to be done."

"Lean on me now, Mum, like I leaned on you back then. I won't let you down."

Harry did not blink back the tears that spilled over. "You never have, Bart. I love you so much."

He handed her his handkerchief. "I love you too, Mum."

She dried her tears and blew her nose. "Since I'm already up, if you gather the ingredients, I can whip up a batch of scones and loaf of bread."

He frowned at her. "You're not to work."

"It isn't work," she replied. "It's a pleasure to bake. Unlike the laundry—that's a chore."

Her son rose to his feet and gathered their dirty dishes. "If I see that you are tiring, I'll finish the baking," he warned her.

"Lord help us then, Bartholomew," she teased.

He snorted with laughter. Shaking his head, he smiled at her. "I'm glad you're feeling a bit better. I was really worried."

"I know, but you needn't worry. I gave my word. I'll heal faster if I do as Mary and O'Malley have suggested."

"Aye." With his back to her, he asked, "What besides flour and salt do you need for the scones?"

"Should I bake them?"

"If you would, please."

Her smile bloomed. She wasn't *entirely* useless. She would bake for her son—and mayhap he would share a bit with Michael O'Malley. "Butter, eggs, sugar, and cream."

He laughed. "How much of each do you need?"

She told him and watched as he set the ingredients on the table he'd cleared. "I can wash the dishes if you—"

"I can handle the washing up. Baking is a bit daunting."

"It's not hard. Just measuring carefully, and sometimes tasting as you go."

His eyes lit up. "I'm your man. Although I'd rather wait until the sugar and the cream is mixed in before I taste the batter."

HARRY'S ARMS WERE tiring, but she kept a smile on her face. She still had bread to knead and set to rise overnight before she could go back to bed. Remembering how exhausted she'd been after Bart was born and there were so many chores to see to, she slowed her movements as she had done back then. Taking each task at a slower pace had worked then, and it would work now.

"Can I stir that for you?"

She looked up and saw the concern on his brow. While she did not relish giving in, she sensed his need to help hid the worry in his heart. He'd already lost one parent; it might be preying on his mind that he'd lose another.

"Yes, if you wouldn't mind."

Harry sat back and watched her son incorporate the last of the cream into the batter. It was smooth and a lovely shade of pale yellow.

"That looks perfect. Thank you, Bart."

He leaned down to kiss her cheek. "You're welcome, Mum."

She smiled until she realized he'd distracted her and scooped a fingerful of scone batter into his mouth. "You should use a spoon."

"Finger's quicker." He reached for the bowl, but she smacked the back of his hand.

"We are not the only ones who will be eating these scones."

"Are you planning on entertaining?"

She lifted her chin. "If O'Malley is coming back later tonight, he may need a cup of tea and a few scones before he leaves."

Bart fell silent, and she wondered what he was thinking. Before she could ask, he nodded. "O'Malley's a good man. He works hard for the viscount and the rest of us. Keeps his word and isn't afraid of anything." Bart stared down at his hands, then looked up and met her questioning gaze. "He reminds me of Father."

"When you put it that way, I guess he does."

"You like him."

She shook her head. "We need him. There's a difference."

"Mum. I saw the way he looked at you when he scooped you up out of the dirt. He cares about you."

"He would be just as worried if it was Mary Clarke that had been injured."

He snorted. "I've also seen the way *you* look at *him*."

Her belly clenched. Had what she was thinking shown on her face? "Oh, and how is that?"

"You admire him. He's built like my father was, helps those in need, keeps his head in an emergency, and thinks your eyes are a mist-laden gray and your hair the color of sunset."

She felt her face flush but didn't deny her son's words. "We need his help right now. It would be wrong not to be kind to him and share whatever we have to eat with him."

A light of mischief shone in the depths of Bart's eyes. "He's fond of scones."

Harry's lips curved into a smile. "I know."

# CHAPTER TWELVE

O'MALLEY RODE DOWN the lane to the Mayfield cottage. The viscount's happiness lingered in his thoughts, distracting him from what may lie ahead of him tonight.

Pain, sharp and swift, shot through his head. He gripped the reins and leaned forward, hugging his mount's neck. He braced for the vision, refusing to fall off his bloody horse!

The location of the scene had changed. It was not Chalk Farm—the infamous dueling field in London.

*Two men weren't facing one another across a field of honor…they were standing in the fallow field by the Mayfield Farm!*

The position of the participants had changed, and one man's face was immediately recognizable.

*Chellenham was propped on his elbow with his hand holding his bloody abdomen. Though the black-powder cloud from his discharged pistol lingered in the early-morning air, O'Malley could see the evil glint in Chellenham's eyes. Following the direction of the lord's gaze, he noted the opponent lying facedown in the field, his arms outstretched—hands empty, crimson staining his upper back.*

The pain seared from his forehead through to the base of his skull. Chellenham had shot an unarmed man! Dear God in Heaven, O'Malley had to know who the other man was. Was it the viscount? He had to warn him! Chellenham was not to be trusted.

Was it himself?

"O'Malley?"

He strained to see the other man's face. He had to see it! He was running out of time. The third time the vision came, both men would already be dead. Fear tangled with purpose. Michael O'Malley was the Duke's Shield! He would not fail whoever was to face Lord Chellenham over a brace of pistols at dawn...or had it been cold-blooded murder? Bloody coward! The other man was unarmed...shot in the back.

His breath snagged in his lungs as he felt himself falling into the abyss of the dark vision.

"O'Malley!"

His throat was as tight as his chest, but he managed to draw in one breath and then another.

"What happened? Where are you hurt?"

The worry in the youthful voice tugged at him, bringing him all the way back. He blinked, and Bart Mayfield's expression changed from worried to relieved.

"I thought you were having a fit of some kind."

"Close enough," O'Malley groaned. Bloody hell, he *had* fallen off his horse. "Help me up, lad." With Harry's son supporting him, he was able to draw up the will to clear his muddled thoughts. "Have they come yet?"

"Nay. I've been watching for them while I was waiting for you. Mum promised she'd stay inside, but if she slipped out of bed and is watching out the window, she'll come running."

"She gave her word."

"All bets are off when someone she cares about is hurt."

O'Malley patted the younger man's shoulder, the signal that he was fine and could stand on his own. "She'll be able to see that you are fine. Nothing's happened to you."

Bart hesitated, then released his hold on O'Malley. His face showed concern and something more.

"What's wrong?"

"I didn't mean me...she'd be worried about you."

O'Malley's eyes narrowed. "What are ye saying, lad?" Bart's bark of laughter had O'Malley grinning. "Are ye after letting me in on the jest?"

"You don't know?"

"Nay. We'd best get to our hiding place soon. Save us both the time and just tell me what's funny."

"Mum cares about you."

O'Malley's gut tied into a double knot, but he struggled not to let it show. "Ye don't say."

Bart nodded. "We need to tell her you're here and then we can slip into the spot I've picked to hide tonight."

"Lead on, then, lad."

BART GAVE ONE swift knock before opening the door. "Mum! O'Malley's here."

"Mrs. Mayfield—"

"It's Harry. Remember you agreed?"

"Aye. Harry," O'Malley said. "How are ye feeling this fine evening?"

She slowly smiled. He was entranced at the way her features lit up as if her inner light and goodness shone through for all to see. "Better. Thank you."

"I let her eat at the table," Bart told him.

"Well now, whose idea was that?" O'Malley asked.

"Mrs. Clarke's. She knew Mum would be itching to do something and decided eating a meal at the table once a day might satisfy that need for a bit."

"How was dinner, lass?"

"Delicious," Harry replied. "Then I baked—"

"Ye know ye need to rest more before ye're on yer feet slaving over a hot cookstove!" Her gray eyes darkened, but O'Malley did not care a whit. "If ye move wrong one time—just one"—he held a finger in front of her face—"yer rib could puncture a lung, and ye could bloody well bleed to death. Do ye want yer son to be without a father and a mother?"

Tears filled Harry's eyes, but she didn't seem to notice. She stood stock-still, staring up at O'Malley until he shifted from foot to foot.

"Lass. Do ye understand what I'm saying?"

Harry gripped the covers with both hands as if to anchor herself to the bed. "I don't believe you."

"Believe it. Me da described it in detail… 'Tisn't pretty. Bart, be a good lad and bring yer ma a cup of water." O'Malley knelt beside the bed and brushed a lock of hair out of her eyes. "I'm not after scaring ye, but if that's what it takes to get through that hard head of yers, then so be it."

"Who was it?"

O'Malley's gaze slid to the floor. "No one ye know."

"A friend? Family?"

O'Malley's voice broke as he replied, "Me uncle Patrick. He died in Da's arms an hour before the jailer set them free."

The emotion in Harry's eyes humbled O'Malley. Mayhap she truly cared. But it was too soon for deep feelings to be involved—wasn't it?

She laid a hand to his cheek. "I am so sorry, Michael. I shall not trouble you with any more questions. I'll do as you ask, and Mary suggested."

Relief smoothed out the sharp edge of fear. He rose to his feet. "See that ye do, lass…for yer son's sake."

"Aye."

Bart handed her the cup of water and hung back while she sipped from the cup. When she'd finished it, he placed it on the table beside her. "Do you want me to refill the cup in case you're thirsty while we're standing watch?"

"Won't you be right out front?" she asked.

"Nay, lass," O'Malley said. "Yer son's assured me he has the perfect hiding spot for us."

She sighed and asked Bart to pour her half a cup.

"If ye have need of us"—O'Malley turned to Bart to gauge his expression—"we'll be within hearing distance."

"No need to shout, though, Mum." Bart handed her their largest pot and a wooden spoon. "Bang on this. We'll hear you."

"Mayhap when you get back, we can use your father's iron mold and make more pistol balls for his blunderbuss," Harry said. "I did not realize we used them all."

"Have ye the lead?" O'Malley asked.

"We do," Bart replied.

"I'd be happy to help Bart. 'Twouldn't be wise for ye to be handling the mold over a fire, working with hot lead just yet, lass." She started to protest, but his smile stopped her. "When ye're healed, I'm certain ye'll be up to the task."

"Well, I suppose I shall have to wait."

"Thank you, Mum," Bart said.

"I don't know how long we will be gone," O'Malley said.

"Do not give me another thought," Harry said. "I'll just lie in bed and worry."

Bart snickered. "Don't let her gift trick you, O'Malley."

"Gift?" O'Malley asked.

"Aye, Mum's crafty and adept at handing out the guilt whether or not it's deserved."

O'Malley's heart settled down after lodging in his throat at her words. "I'll not be forgetting this, lass."

"Neither will I."

⋙✖⋘

THREE HOURS LATER, they returned, with nothing to report.

"I'm glad you're back." Harry's voice carried through the dim room.

"Mum! I should have left you with more than one candle burning."

"You and O'Malley had more important things on your mind." Her gaze slid from her son's face to O'Malley's. "How did it go? I didn't hear anything."

"Nothing to report. All was quiet," O'Malley replied.

"Is that good or bad?"

"'Tis both, I'm thinking. Good because I should have brought one of the other men with me. Bad because we'll be holding the same vigil tomorrow night."

"How about some tea and fresh-baked scones?"

He turned at the sound of water pouring.

Bart grinned. "Just putting the kettle on. Why don't you tell Mum about the new babe?"

"I thought Garahan brought the news earlier today?" O'Malley said.

"Aye," Bart agreed. "But he was in a hurry and only told us her ladyship safely delivered a son."

"Are ye interested in hearing more, then, lass?"

Harry's eyes were bright with anticipation. "Aye. Tell me."

O'Malley relayed what details he could remember: a boy to be named William after his father, healthy with all of his fingers and toes—her ladyship counted—healthy pair of lungs for such a wee lad, and not one hair on his head.

"Please tell her ladyship and the viscount how thrilled Bart and I are for them. A healthy babe is what every mother hopes and prays for."

"Well now, I'd have to agree, having heard me own ma say the same only once after I was born."

"I thought you had three brothers," Harry said.

"Aye. Sean is the eldest, then meself. Then Thomas and Eamon."

She snorted and covered her mouth with both hands, while her eyes danced with merriment. She lowered her hands. "Even I know that would be twice after you were born."

"Think ye're smart, don't ye?"

Her eyes twinkled in the candlelight, and he was entranced.

"Sean, Michael, Thomas, and Eamon—four sons. Four births."

O'Malley rose to his feet. "Hah! Thomas and Eamon are twins!"

Her eyes rounded. "Twins?"

"Aye. Three births, four sons."

"Your mother must be a saint."

O'Malley laughed. "Sure and that's what me aunt Eileen tells her."

"Eileen?"

"Aye. Uncle Patrick's widow."

"O'Malley, would you mind lending a hand?" Bart called out from where he stood on the other side of the cottage.

"Not at all."

They returned to Harry's bedside, Bart carrying two cups and O'Malley carrying one along with a plate of scones.

"Don't we need plates for our scones?" she asked.

"I'm too tired to be washing plates tonight, Mum. We can lean over our cups so we don't get crumbs on yer clean floor."

She frowned up at him as he handed her a cup of tea. "It's not proper. Besides, who wants to drink crumbs?"

O'Malley chuckled. "I'm not one to stand on ceremony when the scones are fresh and the tea is hot. Just don't drink to the bottom of yer cup and ye haven't a worry in the world."

HARRY LET THE men have their way, enjoying their conversation and the way the two of them seemed to get along and respect one another.

Bartholomew would be so proud of their son.

She didn't realize she was crying until O'Malley handed her another of his handkerchiefs. "Are ye in pain, lass?"

She dabbed her eyes and sniffed back the rest of her tears. "No. I'm fine."

"Why are crying, then?"

Her gaze locked on her son's as she replied, "I was listening to the two of you speaking and could not help but think how proud your father would be, Bart. I know I've told you before, but I'll tell you again—I am so proud of the man you're becoming."

He rolled his eyes. "Am, Mum. The man I am."

O'Malley shoved him with his shoulder. "Ye're getting there, lad. Ye're getting there."

They bade O'Malley goodnight and promised to send word should anything happen before he returned tomorrow evening.

Harry watched her son carefully wrap the plate of scones with one of her good linen cloths and leave it on the table. "What about the bread? How will I know it's ready to be kneaded?" he asked.

"Bring the pan over here and let me take a look at it."

"You used to holler at me whenever I peeked underneath the cloth!"

"I'm not going to lift the cloth. I'm going to see how high it has risen above the top of the pan."

He carried the pan to her.

"Hmmm…I think we'll let it finish rising while we sleep. It'll be ready to bake when the cock crows to remind us to start the day."

"Thank you, Mum."

"For?"

"Keeping your word and staying put. I worried less and could concentrate on scanning the woods near the edge of the far field, the road leading to our home, and the paths leading to the Clarkes and the Johnsons."

Harry bit her bottom lip. "Bart, I'm so sorry."

"Why?"

"I've gotten out of bed more than once today—"

His eyes blazed with anger. "You gave your word!"

"But Bart—"

"You let O'Malley believe that you kept your word!"

"If you'd only—"

"We trusted you, Mum."

She threw her water cup at his head. "I had to use the bloody chamber pot!"

His mouth dropped open, but not one word emerged.

"I was not about to ask my grown son to help me relieve myself."

He had the grace to look abashed. "I guess I never thought of that particular problem." A look of horror crossed his face. "I cannot believe I forgot to leave it next to the bed."

"Mary thought of it. It wasn't a problem. I handled it."

He lifted his shoulders and made a squeamish face. "Do I have to empty it?" He tried not to grimace, but did not quite manage. "Is it full now?"

"Mary was kind enough to leave the large bucket we use in the winter by the bed—the one we use when it's too cold to use the privy."

His relief was evident in his expression. "I'll have to thank her when I see her."

"Aye, you should. Oh, and Bart?"

"Mum?"

"Please empty the bucket for me."

His shoulders slumped. "Aye."

When he came back inside, he set the clean bucket beside the bed. "I'm sorry I hollered at you."

"And so you should be. Leaving your poor, injured mother alone without hope of relieving herself."

Hearing the teasing note in her voice, he shook his head. "Enough, Mum! I said I was sorry."

"I suppose I could forgive you. Don't let it happen again. Just so you know, I'll be getting up tomorrow, and the day after that until I'm officially allowed out of bed. You've only two more days of chamber pot duty."

He sighed. "Aye, Mum." He bent and pressed a kiss to her forehead. "Goodnight."

She yanked on his sleeve until he was close enough to kiss his cheek. "Goodnight, Bart."

He lay down on the pallet by the fire, but couldn't settle down. Guilt ate at him. "I really am sorry, Mum."

"And my temper got the better of me when you were yelling at me," she told him.

"I promise it won't happen again, Mum."

"I wouldn't make a promise that you have to break, son. Let it go. All is forgiven, isn't it?"

"Aye."

"Sleep well, son."

"You too, Mum."

# CHAPTER THIRTEEN

BART WAS WAITING for O'Malley by the edge of the Mayfield farm the following night.

"Something wrong, lad?"

The young man stared at O'Malley for a few moments before finally answering, "I was going to ask you the same thing."

O'Malley chuckled. "Not a thing that cannot be resolved by capturing the quarry I'm certain will be sent out tonight to finish the job." He dismounted and stood facing Harry's son. "Care to be more specific?"

Bart lifted one shoulder then looked away.

"Out with it, lad. Ye won't be of any use to me tonight if yer mind's muddled with worry."

"Who said I was worried?" the younger man challenged.

O'Malley nodded, approving of the fire in the boy's stance and his words. "Better. Ye'll need a fire in yer belly to face down what we both know will be coming our way—if not tonight, soon enough."

Bart frowned. "Are you ill?"

O'Malley tilted his head to one side, studying the tall youth for a clue as to why he'd ask. "Am I pale and sweating?"

"No."

"Is me face flaming with fever?"

The young man chuckled. "No."

"Well, then. 'Tis apparent I'm fine. How are you? How is yer ma?"

"But yesterday…you were pale, and sweat covered your face. I thought you'd fall off your horse—and then you did."

O'Malley sighed. "Ah…that."

"It's the plague, isn't it?"

He grabbed Bart's arms, forcing the youth to look at him. "'Tisn't the plague. I'm not ill…'tis more of a condition that happens now and again."

"You suffer from fits?"

"Nay, lad. If ye must know, 'tis more of a family curse."

Bart's jaw hung slack as his eyes rounded. "Were you the one cursed, or was it one of your ancestors? Was it a sorcerer? A witch…the devil?"

"None of those. Now quit yer questions. I may be telling ye after we catch these blackguards, *if* ye promise not to breathe a word about what happened yesterday, or what I've told ye just now." When Bart didn't answer quickly enough to suit O'Malley, he barked, "Yer word, lad!"

"Aye. You have my word!"

O'Malley nodded his head and asked after the boy's mother again. Bart answered, "Acting more like herself, though I can tell she's in pain. She'll never admit to it, though."

"And she's kept her word? She's still in bed?"

"Aye, though she reminded me she plans to return to her duties in a few days' time."

Reins in hand, O'Malley walked his horse toward the barn. "A sennight isn't enough time to recover from broken ribs! I should know."

Bart walked beside him. "How many have you broken?"

O'Malley snorted with laughter. "Too many to count."

Bart opened the gate to the corral, where the Mayfield's plow horse watched their approach. "Ever been shot?"

"Aye."

Bart closed the gate behind O'Malley's mount. "Knifed?"

"More than once."

Bart's whoosh of breath was audible—as was his admiration.

O'Malley needed to make the lad understand it wasn't something to aspire to—it was his *job* to protect the Duke of Wyndmere and his entire family. "'Tis an honor to be among me brothers and cousins protecting Their Graces, their babes, and their extended family. 'Tisn't me aim in life to have a running tally of the number of injuries I've gained working for the Duke of Wyndmere."

"Rumor has it that his lordship is related to the duke."

"'Tisn't a rumor."

Bart's face fell. "Oh."

"'Tis fact. Viscount Chattsworth is a distant cousin to the duke. Under the duke's decree, his lordship and his countess and their new babe are under the protection of the duke's guard."

Leaning against the top rail of the corral, Bart frowned. "Four adults, and three babes, is a lot to be responsible for. How do you manage it?"

O'Malley's gaze swept the perimeter, then he shifted his position to take in the rest of the land surrounding the Mayfields' farm. "'Tis more people to protect than that, lad."

"Who else is in the duke's family?"

"His brother, Earl Lippincott, and his wife and their new babe."

"That's right! I met his lordship and Lady Aurelia when they first moved into Lippincott Manor and accompanied Lady Calliope when she introduced herself to Chattsworth Manor's tenant farmers."

"Aye. Then there is the duke's sister, Lady Phoebe, who married Baron Summerfield—another distant family cousin."

"Do they have any children?"

"Not yet, though it's early days."

"Anyone else?"

"Aye, we're responsible for protecting those who work for the duke and his family—even those properties where only staff reside."

"Is that really necessary?" Bart asked.

O'Malley's gaze narrowed on the tree line to the north. Something moved among the trees. "I need ye to stay here and protect yer ma."

"What's wrong? Where are you going?"

He nodded to the spot where he'd swear he saw movement in the line of trees. "I need to be sure we aren't about to entertain guests."

Bart's brown eyes darkened as he clenched and unclenched his fists. "I'm ready."

"Sweeney's about a half an hour behind me—and should be here any minute. Otherwise I wouldn't leave ye. Where's yer weapon?"

Bart walked over to the corner of the corral and retrieved the blunderbuss and his pouch of powder.

"Did yer ma have time to mold any lead balls for ye?"

"Aye," the young man replied. "I've powder, a pouch of lead balls, as well as bits of material—"

"Ah…wadding," O'Malley remarked.

"That's what Mum called it."

O'Malley opened the gate to the corral and led his horse out. "I have faith in ye, Bart."

"And I have faith in you!"

O'Malley leapt into the saddle, then paused, cocking his head to one side. "Hear those hoofbeats?"

"Aye?"

"Sweeney's just around the bend there."

"How do you know it's him?"

"The cadence of the hoofbeats."

"They all sound the same to me," Bart grumbled.

"I'll teach ye how to recognize the difference later. I have to go!" With that, O'Malley was off like a shot, headed for whatever lay in wait for him in the darkness.

⟫⟫⟩✳⟨⟪⟪

BART WATCHED HIM leave, then turned back to wait for Sweeney to pull up beside the front of the cottage.

"Where's O'Malley? I was supposed to meet him here."

"He heard your horse, knew you were close, and left."

"He wouldn't just leave," Sweeney remarked as he dismounted.

Bart nodded toward the trees. "O'Malley saw something moving over there."

The big man's gaze swept the area, the same as O'Malley's had. "We're lucky to have a clear sky and bright moon tonight."

Bart watched him and wondered aloud, "If we can clearly see who is out there, then they can see us, too."

"Aye. Why don't we take up our positions? Did O'Malley discuss them with you before he left?"

"No, but I could hide in the lower branches of that tree over there." He pointed to a stand of oaks. "Mum's inside, but probably watching us."

"Will she stay inside?"

Bart shrugged as he opened the gate, and Sweeney led his horse inside the corral before closing it behind him.

"Mum said she would, but if she thinks we need help, she won't hesitate to join us."

Sweeney mumbled to himself about stubborn women.

Bart couldn't agree more. "Let's hope it's an animal, and Mum stays inside."

"Agreed. Think I'll go over by the back corner of your house." With a nod to the blunderbuss Bart carried, Sweeney added, "Good weapon to have. Aim for the largest part of the body."

"That's what my father always said. It's an easier target."

With a nod, they parted, heading to their respective hiding places to wait—for the return of O'Malley, and the attack they anticipated.

IT WASN'T LONG in coming. Pounding hoofbeats raced toward them. Bart thought O'Malley had been captured and the horse was riderless, until he drew closer. O'Malley was leaning against his horse's neck, trying to be less of a target.

The first shot surprised Bart. He was ready and waiting for O'Malley to ride past him before he whistled to get his attention.

Leaping from the saddle, O'Malley ran to the barn then positioned himself in the shadow of the building, rifle trained on three men racing toward them.

Before Bart or Sweeney could get off a shot, O'Malley winged the first rider. The man screamed as he dropped his weapon and leaned low in the saddle.

O'Malley reloaded and had the second rider in his sights when Sweeney squeezed off a shot that had the man flying off the back of his horse.

Bart waited for his chance. His target was too far away. As the man O'Malley had shot drew closer, a shadow lunged toward him, swinging what had to be a shovel, sweeping the man right out of his saddle!

*Mum?* She'd promised!

Before he could climb down from the tree, the third rider streaked toward him on the opposite side of the barn from O'Malley and Sweeney.

With the worry of his mother now in the thick of things, Bart took aim, watched, and waited until the man was within range. He fired and had the sickening satisfaction of watching the man's eyes widen in shock and then glaze over with pain.

Bart had winged him. Mum was safe!

He clambered down from his perch and ran toward the man in time to watch him slide off his horse.

"Good shot, lad!" O'Malley yelled as he rushed over. Instead of acknowledging Harry, who stood guard over her prisoner with a shovel, he clenched his jaw and turned his back on her.

Having collected the attacker he shot, Sweeney walked toward them. The man was draped over his horse and moaning pitifully. "Quit your whining! I winged you. You'll survive." With a gleam in his eye, he nodded to Bart. "Though if you're lucky and do not end up with lead poisoning, you'll be strong enough to face the gallows."

The man pushed himself away from the horse's side and rasped, "Gallows?"

O'Malley grinned. "Aye, did ye not know the punishment for attempting to damage a peer of the realm's properties is death?"

A loud groan from the man at Bart's feet had him frowning at the attacker. He did not feel guilty for shooting the man before the man managed to shoot him! Anger boiled deep inside of him. It wasn't right that men they didn't know were shooting at their neighbors, trampling crops, and setting fire to their barns. Whoever was behind the atrocities should have to pay.

He didn't know if what Sweeney or O'Malley said was true, but it sounded as if the men believed the penalty of death was deserved. He added his voice to their proclamation. "You'll be joining him." Meeting O'Malley's gaze, he boldly added, "Might be a day to celebrate…a double hanging!"

The man guarded by Bart's mother yelled, "You'll not be hanging me! Let me up, wench!"

Before Bart could react, O'Malley had the man by the throat and was shaking him. "Ye'll apologize to Mrs. Mayfield, or I'll snap ye in two."

Shocked at the ease with which O'Malley hauled the man up from the ground and held him by the throat, Bart could only stare and wait to see what would happen. Would O'Malley kill the man?

"Let him go."

His mother's voice was steady, but without inflection. She

must be rattled. *He* certainly was! Afraid to speak, he watched, waiting to see what O'Malley would do.

"Why?" O'Malley asked.

"You can't kill him," Harry said.

"There's where ye'd be wrong, lass."

Bart was about to interrupt when his mother spoke again. "Please, don't kill him, Michael."

O'Malley raised his eyes to the sky, punched the man in the face, and then released his quarry. The man landed in a heap on the ground.

Intrigued, Bart asked, "Why didn't you let him go the first time Mum asked?"

O'Malley shrugged. "She didn't say please."

Sweeney's snort of laughter eased the tension surrounding the group. "We'd best secure the gallows bait—and gag them."

"Brilliant suggestion, Sweeney!" O'Malley said. "Did you bring rope with you?"

"Aye. Enough to tie up my prisoner. What about you?"

O'Malley grinned. "Always carry enough for three. 'Tis me ma's favorite number."

Relieved that his new hero—O'Malley—had acquiesced to his mother's request, Bart cheerfully added, "There's a length of rope in the barn, if you need it."

"Thank ye, lad. We might at that."

Between the three of them, they made short work of securing the attackers.

"Are you planning to let us bleed to death?" one of the prisoners wailed before they were gagged.

With an exaggerated sigh, O'Malley asked for linen squares and strips to bind the men's wounds. He exchanged a look with Sweeney, who nodded and proceeded to take care of their horses. Once they'd been seen to, O'Malley returned to where the trio sat leaning against the corral fence.

Bart watched with interest as O'Malley stared at each man in turn, without uttering a word. Then he turned to Sweeney.

"Load the men in the Mayfields' wagon. Your mount is accustomed to pulling a wagon now and again. You drive. I'll guard the rear."

"Aye, O'Malley."

Bart's mother grumbled, "Aren't you going to ask if you may borrow our wagon?"

O'Malley's jaw clenched. "I could leave the prisoners here, if ye prefer."

Bart covered his mouth to keep his laughter from exploding. When he managed to swallow it, he said, "You need to thank O'Malley and Sweeney, Mum. Without their help, these men would have shot at us—mayhap even killed us before they set our barn on fire."

His mother stared at him. He felt the urge to squirm under her direct gaze, but he held on to his control, staring back at her until she admitted, "You are right, Bart. My apologies, gentlemen. Thank you for your aid tonight. If it wouldn't be too much trouble, please see that our wagon is returned tomorrow."

Without another word, she turned on her heel and marched to the door to their cottage, yanked it open—stifling a gasp of pain—stepped over the threshold, and slammed it behind her.

"Is yer ma always this difficult?" O'Malley asked.

Bart grinned. "She hardly ever admits she's wrong."

"I didn't hear her admit she was in the wrong. Did you, Sweeney?"

The viscount's man shook his head. "Nay."

Bart chuckled. "Apologizing is Mum's way of admitting when she's in the wrong." He met O'Malley's gaze. "Thank you for your help tonight. You too, Sweeney."

"Just part of the job, lad," O'Malley replied.

Bart stared at his feet. "Mum's not used to being cooped up. When she's had a chance to think it over, she'll be sorry to have challenged you instead of thanking you right off."

"Don't let it worry ye. I'm sure she's paying for her show of temper right about now."

"What do you mean?" Bart asked.

O'Malley sighed. "Don't forget I've had broken ribs, too. Yanking the door open, and then slamming it, will no doubt have caused her pain. Ye'd best see to her, lad."

Worry in his heart, Bart nodded and chased after his mother.

⟫⟩⟨⟨

O'MALLEY WAITED WHILE Sweeney hitched his horse to the wagon. "A fine night's work."

Sweeney nodded. "It must be a hard role to fill—both mother and father to a growing lad like Bart."

O'Malley looked over his shoulder at the cottage and thought *he* might be the one to apologize tomorrow. "Ye may be right."

Sweeney climbed onto the seat and released the brake. The pair made the late-night trip back to the manor house, though it would be hours before their night was over.

# CHAPTER FOURTEEN

GARAHAN GREETED THEM when they returned to the manor house. "Trouble always finds its way to ye."

It was hard for O'Malley to ignore the glaring fact that the troubles the tenant farmers were experiencing were tied to his visions. The first group of men were sent by Chellenham. Time to find out if the second were as well.

"I could say the same for yerself."

Garahan grinned. "Aye, we wouldn't have it any other way, would we?"

O'Malley dismounted and shoved his cousin out of his way with his shoulder.

Garahan cackled with laughter. "'Tis in the blood, ye cannot deny it."

"I wish I could." When his cousin stared at him, O'Malley grunted. "Leave off. I've a job to finish."

"As it was quiet patrolling my section of the estate, I'll send Hartman to fetch the constable while I guard the prisoners. Ye can have Hargrave wake his lordship."

O'Malley realized the rightness of his cousin's suggestion. He couldn't very well do it all—guard the men, send for the constable, and report to the viscount. He'd blundered the last time by not telling the viscount immediately that there had been trouble. His lordship found out *after* the constable arrived at the manor. Best not to risk the viscount's displeasure twice—if he could avoid it.

"Aye. Thank ye."

Garahan spun on his heel and strode over to the wagon. "Whose wagon did ye commandeer this time?"

O'Malley sighed. "The Mayfields'. I'm to return it tomorrow."

"We'd best get to it, then, so ye can return it first thing."

His cousin's wry smile irritated him. "Why would ye think that?"

"'Tis obvious from the distant look in yer eye, and the fact yer attention has been wandering ever since ye crossed paths with the lovely widow."

"The hell me attention has wandered! I've a lot on me mind," O'Malley said.

"Hah!"

"What in the bloody hell does that mean?" he demanded.

"Make of it what ye will," Garahan replied. "Ye have a duty to do, as do I."

Frustration bubbled dangerously close to the surface, but O'Malley knew now wasn't the time to face off with his cousin. Duty called.

Without a backward glance, he strode toward the rear entrance to the manor.

Hargrave was waiting for him. "I heard the commotion when you arrived, O'Malley. I take it there was more trouble this evening?"

O'Malley expelled a breath as he regained control of his emotions. "Aye. Garahan asked Hartman to fetch the constable. I'm to report what occurred to his lordship."

"I'll wake him."

A demanding wail had the two men staring at one another and O'Malley slowly smiling. "I'm guessing his lordship's awake already and might need a few moments to unscramble his wits."

Hargrave chuckled. "Just what Chattsworth Manor has been

missing since his lordship's brother..."

The look of horror on the older man's face prompted O'Malley to reassure the retainer, "The duke was candid with meself and the rest of the guard about all of the family situations for those we would be guarding as our turn in the rotation took us to his different estates and that of his kin."

"I see."

"I'm no stranger to loss, Hargrave. Though not as a lad, as his lordship was when he lost his brother or his ma."

"It was a devastating time for the family," Hargrave rasped.

"Now the viscount and Lady Calliope are continuing the Chattsworth line. Every member of the duke's guard will see to it that we protect them with our lives. Ye can count on us, Hargrave."

"I'm bloody glad to hear it, O'Malley," a deep voice intoned from behind them. The viscount shoved an arm through one of the sleeves of his dressing gown as he rushed toward them. His hair stood on end, as if he'd run his hands through it repeatedly. "Though if I had my druthers, I would have rather the duke hadn't felt the need to divulge our family sorrows to all and sundry."

"From His Grace's way of thinking, yer lordship, it saved ye from anyone asking after yer ma or if ye had any siblings living nearby that would require our protection," O'Malley replied.

"I suppose you're right," the viscount acquiesced. Turning to the butler, he asked, "Would you rouse Mrs. Romney and see if she could send up a glass of milk and something sweet for Calliope to nibble on while she feeds *my* son?"

The pride in the viscount's voice echoed in the hallway. For the first time, O'Malley wondered what it would feel like to know that you'd passed on not just the family name, but bits and pieces of yourself and your ancestors to your firstborn son. He nearly snickered remembering Ma's prediction that his evil temper would be his legacy to his children—and mayhap, if he was lucky, his beautiful grass-green eyes.

Pushing past the thoughts of what could never be—a marriage and family—he replied, "And a fine son ye have, yer lordship."

The viscount smiled. "He's got a pair of lungs on him, and a grip that constantly surprises me."

"Faith, ye're a lucky man, yer lordship."

"Thank you, O'Malley. I don't want to leave Calliope for too long. She tires easily. What do you have to report?"

O'Malley filled him in on what happened at the Mayfield farm. The bleak expression on the viscount's face reflected what he and Garahan had discussed, and what he knew they all hoped for—an end to Chellenham's devious plan to destroy Viscount Chattsworth's family reputation and the fortune he had been working to rebuild.

"Do you think he's gone after Lady Aurelia's uncle?" the viscount asked.

O'Malley's gut iced over as he tried to call up the image from his vision. Was the man, whose back was turned to him, as wide as Coddington's, or much thinner? Blast! He wished he had more of a clue as to the identity of the second man in his vision.

"Bugger it! Why didn't Garahan or meself think of it? Ye're right, yer lordship. Lord Coddington and his niece Lady Aurelia could be back in the madman's crosshairs!"

"And her husband Edward, Earl Lippincott, and their babe!" The viscount turned back to Hargrave. "Hargrave! I'll need to send two missives to London at once!"

"Two, your lordship?" the elderly butler asked.

"Aye, the first to Lord Coddington in London, and the second to the duke's guard stationed at his London town house."

Hargrave's brows drew together. "The guard has changed so frequently there—to whom shall I address it?"

"Address it to Emmett O'Malley and Seamus Flaherty. That way, if one man happens to be meeting with Captain Coventry, or Gavin King of the Bow Street Runners, the other will be in residence, protecting the duke's staff and his home."

"Very good, your lordship." Hargrave turned, and the viscount stopped him a second time.

"Oh, and Hargrave?"

"Your lordship?"

"Rouse Mrs. Romney first."

"At once," Hargrave replied and left to do so.

"It's good to have you back, O'Malley, if I haven't already mentioned it."

"'Tis a pleasure to be back, your lordship." O'Malley hesitated, waiting for the viscount to say what was on his mind. When he remained silent, O'Malley said, "Ye used to confide yer troubles—is there something weighing heavy on yer mind?"

"Other than the health of my wife and newborn son?"

"Aye."

"Aside from the attacks on my tenant farmers, their families, and my property?"

"I beg yer pardon, yer lordship. I should have been more specific in me question."

The viscount sighed heavily. "No. I'm the one who should apologize. I'm not the only one balancing more than one problem at a time. I know how difficult it is when you are being pulled in multiple directions at once."

"'Tis yer understanding that makes our job easier, yer lordship. Ye advise whatever *on dits* ye may have heard through yer peers, as well as local gossip from the village. It aids Garahan and meself in our decisions as to which problem needs to be tackled first and which ones require more manpower."

"Aye. Like the bloody lowlife gang of criminals Chellenham has sent to attack our tenants!" Anger radiated off the viscount in waves. "I'm afraid I'll go mad with worry that he'll send additional men to the manor house next. Good God! They could harm Calliope and our babe!"

Every ounce of color leached from the viscount's face. If O'Malley hadn't been standing beside him, he would worry that the man had been shot and was bleeding profusely.

"Ye needn't worry, yer lordship. With the addition of three of yer footmen and the lads from the village to our guard, Garahan and I have matters well in hand."

His employer nodded, regaining a bit of color he'd lost. "I cannot help but wonder if he'll up his game, sending more hardened criminals to attack our farms and my family." He paused, and his mouth hung slack for a moment before he recovered. "Bloody hell! Edward and Aurelia! Their babe is but a few months old! Send word—No!"

The viscount paced in front of O'Malley, mumbling to himself as he worked out the worry in his mind. "A verbal message is best," he finally announced. "I'd go myself, but I will not leave my wife and son alone should Chellenham send more thugs. I need you and Garahan to remain here, but send Hartman or Sweeney to Lippincott Manor at once and apprise Edward of the latest attacks and what we suspect."

Calmer now, the viscount met O'Malley's gaze. "Edward and I will be the last line of defense. No one will get past us to harm our wives or our sons!"

"Ye needed worry, yer lordship. No one will be getting past Garahan or meself." Before the viscount voiced another worry, O'Malley added, "They won't be getting past me cousins stationed at Lippincott Manor."

The viscount inclined his head in agreement.

"As to the rest, 'tis a viable worry to be sure. Ye've added to yer guard with men capable of fending off any and all attacks the bastard may send our way. Though after two failed attempts at the Mayfields' farm, I'm thinking he'll change tactics and choose a farm on the opposite side of yer estate. One without neighbors near enough to ride to the rescue, should they hear shots fired."

"Excellent thinking," the viscount said, then added, "That would be the Peters' farm."

O'Malley's jaw clenched. "Aye. Peters. I remember the man."

Chattsworth cleared his throat. "I've no doubt that you do, what with the way you brawled with the man."

"'Twasn't a brawl—'twas a half-hearted punch. He was spreading false rumors about Lady Aurelia!"

The viscount nodded. "He was, and learned his lesson to substantiate facts before passing on what others have told him is the truth. Have you been out to speak with him at all on your rounds?"

"Nay," O'Malley admitted. "For some reason, me cousin has insisted he be the one to check on the Peters family."

"Wise choice—however, the situation has changed."

"I'll see to it personally that the Peters' farm is protected, yer lordship."

"I have complete trust in you, Garahan, and your newly assembled guard."

"Ye may wish to speak to His Grace about adding more men permanently. Mayhap King can loan out one or two of his men. They've more proven their worth when the duke was under attack at Wyndmere Hall."

"Aye. In London and here in Sussex, too."

"Ye may wish to send a third missive," O'Malley said.

"I do believe I shall amend the one to London. I'll just see how Mrs. Romney is coming along with the tray for my darling wife."

The cook was coming out of the kitchen as the viscount and O'Malley were about to enter.

"Ah, Mrs. Romney, that looks wonderful. Calliope has been ravenous since our babe arrived."

"And so she should be," Mrs. Romney said. "Keeping up with feeding your heir and replenishing what she lost—"

The viscount held up a hand. "No need to continue. I know exactly what you are implying and agree. I shall take the tray to her at once. Thank you."

Hargrave arrived, and was about to return to his post, when the viscount stopped him.

"I need to add to the missive I'm sending to London."

"Of course, your lordship," Hargrave replied.

"Please ask the men to speak to King and Coventry at once about sending additional men here. We may be in for far more than we originally thought."

Hargrave's mouth thinned. "Similar to what we know happened at Wyndmere Hall?"

"I hope not, but with the continuing attacks, I'm inclined to believe it's possible."

"Yer lordship is wise to expect the worst and prepare for it," O'Malley added.

"With a fast horse," the viscount said, "and a few changes of horse along the road north to London, a messenger would be able to cover the distance in five or so hours."

"Less if he pushed his mount," O'Malley said. "The fastest I've heard of was one hundred and five miles in seven hours with eight changes of horse."

"I seem to recall my cousin mentioning that amount of time and distance."

"Best send the missive right away." O'Malley waited for the viscount's agreement, or further instructions.

"Who is the best horseman among our staff?"

"That would be Kent, your lordship."

"The oldest of the young men from the village?"

"Aye. He has a way with horses—high-spirited or a bit slow to start, all horses respond immediately to Kent."

"Very well. Hargrave, I need to deliver this tray to my wife. Please give Kent a personal message from me."

"Of course," Hargrave replied. "What is it, your lordship?"

"Time is of the essence. Please tell him that I am counting on him and have the utmost faith that he will deliver both missives with all due haste."

Hargrave was smiling as he left to rouse one of the temporary additions to the duke's guard at Chattsworth Manor.

"Walk with me, O'Malley," the viscount said.

"Aye."

As the pair ascended the staircase, the viscount said, "No

doubt you have changed plans and the rotation of the guard accordingly since the attacks."

"Aye."

"Not that I do not trust your judgment or that of Hargrave, but I would feel more confident if one or two of King's men were added to those protecting my family."

"Kent will deliver the missives as instructed. I expect to see him with at least two of King's men—mayhap one of Coventry's newest hires in his new venture for His Grace."

The viscount inclined his head. "We've never had this type of threat in all the years I've lived here—or in my father's time."

"Have faith, yer lordship. After all, ye've got men of superior strength and stamina leading yer guard."

The viscount chuckled. "You and James are among the finest men I know. Every member of my cousin's private guard has stamina and strength beyond any men that I've known. Calliope and I are deeply grateful."

"'Tis our pleasure—and our job. Think of me as yer shield, yer lordship. The lot of us took an oath to protect the duke's family with our lives. Count on us to do so."

"I shall. Send Hargrave if anything else arises tonight."

"I don't expect another wave of attackers tonight, but rest assured we will be patrolling the grounds, and the perimeter both outside and inside the manor walls."

"My thanks, O'Malley."

O'Malley bowed and retraced his steps. He needed to fill Garahan in on the change in plans and the viscount's expectations for the foreseeable future.

He'd promised to return the Mayfields' wagon tomorrow. He knew he could task one of the viscount's servants to do so, but a pair of mist-colored eyes frosting over as she commanded him to return her wagon had O'Malley looking forward to handling the minor inconvenience himself.

Garahan was speaking to the constable when O'Malley approached them. "'Tis about time ye returned. We've a slight problem concerning Mrs. Mayfield."

O'Malley nodded to the constable. "If ye'll excuse us for a moment, I need a word with Garahan." Tugging on his cousin's arm, he moved out of the constable's hearing range. "The lass hasn't reinjured her ribs, has she?"

Garahan shook his head. "Nay. The constable arrived without a wagon. He'll be borrowing her wagon but has promised to return it sometime tomorrow."

Before O'Malley could protest, Kent rushed past them, heading for the stables.

"Where's the lad going?" Garahan asked.

O'Malley's eyes never left Kent's retreating form as he replied, "I've news." He knew the tone of his voice would tip his cousin off that it was for his ears alone. Turning to the constable, he said, "Thank ye, for hauling this lot away for his lordship."

"Of course," the constable replied. "Please give Viscount Chattsworth my regards. If there is anything further to report, I shall send word."

Waiting until the constable was a safe enough distance away not to hear their conversation, Garahan grabbed his cousin by the arm, dragging him toward the stables, "What in the bloody hell is going on?"

"Kent will be delivering urgent missives to London."

"Anything else?"

"Prepare for another onslaught like we faced at Wyndmere Hall when that bloody bastard Hollingford attacked."

Garahan's face lost all expression. "Ye'll tell me the whole of it after we see Kent off."

"Count on it."

# CHAPTER FIFTEEN

THE DUKE'S LONDON staff was on tenterhooks wondering what new crisis was about to befall the duke and his family. The situation must be bleak if both Captain Coventry—the duke's London man-of-affairs—and Gavin King of the Bow Street Runners had been meeting with Flaherty and Emmett O'Malley for the last three-quarters of an hour.

The duke's butler, Jenkins, soothed the housekeeper's ruffled feathers. "I'm quite certain if Flaherty or O'Malley were at liberty to inform us ahead of time, they would have."

Mrs. Wigglesworth seemed to be digesting that last statement.

"Rest assured, they will call in reinforcements if they feel it necessary."

"You have been the stalwart sentry guarding this town house for the last three dukes," she said.

"And you, the diligent keeper of the heart of the house since the day the fourth duke hired you."

The housekeeper sighed. "Thankfully His Grace's private guard has been tasked with protecting the duke's properties whether or not he is in residence."

"It's quite brilliant, if I do say so myself," Jenkins remarked. "At any given moment, the duke may be called to London, or one of his other estates. All the while, he will be secure in the knowledge that whomsoever travels with him shall be protected en route. And their destination has been guarded in his absence."

"Nothing and no one can penetrate the web of protection the duke's guard has woven around His Grace."

"Just so, Mrs. Wigglesworth. Just so."

"VISCOUNT CHATTSWORTH'S FEARS align with our latest intelligence," King said as he stood at ease. "Chellenham has been seen frequenting the docks, and apparently those he has met with can be coaxed to share the gist of their meeting."

"The ones that ply their trade on the docks by night have little loyalty," Flaherty murmured from where he stood by the window, keeping an eye on passersby.

Emmett O'Malley's position, opposite his cousin, was deliberate. At this hour they were normally patrolling the perimeter of the duke's town house. Given the missive delivered by the ravenous lad Kent, who at the moment was being fed by the duke's cook, and the arrival of Gavin King and Captain Coventry, he'd asked two of the duke's footmen to stand guard in the alleyways on either side of the town house.

"Those bleeding blackguards will spill what they know for a pint—or less!" Emmett added.

"Although it's still unofficial," Coventry began, "I have two associates who are more than qualified to answer the viscount's call for help."

"How soon would they be able to leave?" King asked.

"Immediately," Coventry replied. "It is a requirement working as part of the team I have assembled."

"And what team is that?" Flaherty asked.

Coventry shook his head. "I'm not at liberty to say until the duke has met with the four men I plan to employ."

"I met one of yer associates while assigned to protect yer

wife—Captain David Bayfield," Emmett said. "Although she wasn't yer wife at the time."

"Miranda reminds me that you saved her from what would have been a vicious assault, and that Captain Bayfield arrived in time to alert the watch and act as backup," Coventry said.

Emmett chuckled. "Faith, when he stood in the doorway demanding to know who I was and what I did to yer wife, I sensed he would be an ally."

"You were correct," Coventry said.

"Bayfield?" Flaherty asked. "Another captain. Ye seem to know a number of them, Coventry. I'm wondering just how many the Royal Navy needs?"

"Equal in number to His Majesty's ships of the line," Coventry responded. Turning to Emmett, he said, "Bayfield remembers meeting you as well. I'm grateful to the both of you for keeping my wife safe."

"Have I met the other associate?" King asked.

"Aye—Gryffyn Tremayne, former cavalry officer in the King's Dragoons," Coventry replied.

"Ah, yes," King said. "I soundly approve of both men, Coventry. To be honest, I am relieved they are available. A few of my men should be freed up shortly from their current assignments."

"Will ye send them to Sussex when their assignments have been completed?" Emmett asked.

"It sounds as if the viscount and our cousins need all of the help ye can send," Flaherty added.

"Unless I hear otherwise," King said.

"By the by, I shall be accompanying my men to Chattsworth Manor," Coventry announced. "Was there any other pertinent information supplied?"

"Aye," Emmett rumbled. "Just one word—*Hollingford*."

"Bloody madman," Coventry growled. "He had no concern at all for the women inside Wyndmere Hall when he and his blasted band of henchmen attacked! The duchess was expecting at the time!"

"We outflanked and outfought Viscount Hollingford and his men," Emmett reminded them.

"'Twas the combination of our strategic planning and skill with a multitude of weaponry," Flaherty added.

"Unless the duke says otherwise, you cannot abandon your posts," Coventry said.

The duke's men did not bother to hide their anger at the captain's words. They shared an intense look with one another that spoke volumes.

Coventry did not apologize for what he had to know the Irishmen would take as an insult. "As long as we understand one another."

"Who have ye assigned to protect yer wife while you're in Sussex?" Emmett asked.

"Two men I trust implicitly. Daniel Hennessey, a former lieutenant in the Royal Marines, and Iain Masterson, a former colonel in the Fifth Northumberland Regiment of Foot."

King nodded. "Otherwise known as Lord Wellington's Bodyguard—the Fighting Fifth!"

Flaherty slowly smiled. "Are they to be employed by ye as well, captain?"

"Aye," Coventry said.

"Ye've taken Garahan's suggestion to heart, then," Emmett remarked.

Coventry nodded. "These men are comrades who have all been distinguished in battle at a price. Their injuries have forced them to retire from their service to the Crown—the only way of life they know. Each man put his life on the line for His Majesty and nearly perished."

"From what His Grace has said," Emmett added, "ye did the same."

"Aye," Flaherty said. "It's been our honor to work alongside of you from the day you met with the lot of us."

Coventry grinned. "That was a meeting I shall never forget."

"All sixteen of you?" King asked.

"Aye," Emmett replied. "Though we let Patrick be our spokesman, as he's the oldest of the O'Malleys."

"And the Flahertys and Garahans," Flaherty added.

It was King's turn to smile. "He seems to be the most level-headed of the bunch."

"Me brother can be," Emmett said.

"Unless he isn't," Flaherty added.

A few moments later, the meeting ended. Emmett and Flaherty escorted the men outside, going over last-minute details one last time.

"I shall keep you all informed of any scuttlebutt from the docks—"

Coventry interrupted King. "Or from Chellenham's staff. The latest *on dit* is he's treating them worse than when your cousin Sean worked for him."

Emmett's brow rose. "It might work to our advantage to hire one or two of his footmen."

"Our cousin, Sean, confided the peer only hires men strong enough to carry his lordship from his carriage to his bedchamber," Flaherty said.

"That was a requirement?" King asked.

"According to Sean, 'twas part of the nightly routine for two of the footmen, who took turns putting the peer to bed."

"It is well known throughout the bowels of London that he has not curtailed his gaming habits," King said.

"Or his preference for fresh young women from the country," Coventry added.

King supplied a detail that was unfortunately a well-known fact: "Unsuspecting country misses who travel to London with the promise of a position as a maid only to find themselves in an entirely different situation in the fleshpots in the underbelly of our city."

Flaherty cracked his knuckles. "One more reason to see that he is removed from society."

"Aye, but we'd leave him breathing," Emmett added almost

as an afterthought as King stepped into the hackney who'd answered his hail. He nodded, then gave the driver his destination.

"Why must you insist on rattling King to the point where he may wonder whether or not he can trust you?" Coventry asked.

The cousins looked at one another and shrugged. "Can't seem to stop," Flaherty said.

Emmett frowned. "If a man cannot speak his mind, he's less of a man."

"See that you do not antagonize King while I am away," Coventry said.

"Aye, aye, captain." Emmett saluted while Flaherty bowed deeply.

Coventry stifled a chuckle at their irreverence. "I should have the duke get rid of the both of you."

"Faith, wouldn't yer life be dull, then?" Flaherty remarked as Coventry mounted his horse and rode off in the opposite direction.

# CHAPTER SIXTEEN

KENT RACED PAST Garahan and O'Malley on his mission to deliver two vital missives to London.

Garahan elbowed his cousin in the side. "Out with it. What's so bloody important in those missives?"

"I spoke with his lordship while ye were dealing with the constable." O'Malley's expression was bleak as he informed Garahan of the details of his discussion with the viscount, and what the missives his lordship would send to London entailed.

"Why in the bloody hell didn't either of us remember Coddington challenged Chellenham to a duel to protect Lady Aurelia's honor?" Garahan asked.

"Seamus and I were there. *I* should have remembered."

"Did ye forget ye told me ye had yer hands full with Lady Calliope at the time?"

"I must have," O'Malley admitted. "She and Lady Aurelia were not supposed to find out about the duel—yet they did. The earl was fit to be tied when they arrived after being told *not* to attend.

"His lordship saved Coddington from getting shot in the back. The blackguard Chellenham didn't take the full twenty paces—he stopped at fifteen and fired at Lady Aurelia's uncle. He would have shot him in the back if the viscount hadn't thrown himself in front of the man."

"Seamus tells the tale better than ye," Garahan quipped.

O'Malley knew Garahan was trying to change the subject by prodding his temper. "He wasn't as close to the field as I was—"

"Which is why he tells it better than ye do," his cousin interrupted. "Seamus' perspective of the entire scene lends for a fuller tale."

O'Malley couldn't decide whether to lay his cousin out flat or turn and walk away. He settled on a verbal response. "The viscount needs us to be the last inner circle protecting his wife and babe."

"As well he should expect," Garahan said. "Was there a question we wouldn't be doing our duty?"

"Nay. His lordship needed to work it all out in his head before amending the missive he was sending to our contingent stationed at the duke's London town house."

"Have ye noticed our cousin is fiercely protective of the women in his life?"

O'Malley grinned. "Aye. Patrick would lay down his life—or bargain with the devil—to protect his wife and infant daughter. Me brother, Sean, has been hovering, anxious for his wife to deliver their babe."

Garahan nodded. "'Tis the same with His Grace, the earl, and now the viscount. Fatherhood changes a man."

"I'm thinking it merely adds to the number of people a man has sworn to protect. 'Tisn't a bad thing, but may be a bit of a distraction."

"Ye have the right of it," his cousin agreed. "Do ye think Mrs. Mayfield will be expecting ye to return her wagon before the midday meal?"

O'Malley frowned. "I'd forgotten we let the constable use her wagon last night." He stared off in the distance. "I'd best make certain to scrub down any unfortunate *stains* that may have occurred."

Garahan burst out laughing. "Ye could call blood a bit of a stain. The moon went under a cloud when ye arrived last night. I did not get a good look at the men or if they bled all over the wagon bed. If it soaked deep into the wood, and ye're worried she'll withhold her favors from ye, ye could always offer to whitewash it for her."

O'Malley's temper snapped. His right cross nearly connected with his cousin's chin, but Garahan had been expecting it and easily evaded the blow.

The glancing blow had him smiling. "Ye'd best remember to keep yer mind on yer duties, Michael—and not the fair widow."

"Bugger it!"

"Interesting suggestion, to be sure, but thank ye, no."

O'Malley flashed a grin. "Faith, ye tempt me temper and make me laugh at the same time. Thank ye, James."

"Me pleasure. We'd best be about our duties. Those on patrol will need to be vigilant taking in their surroundings. Expect trouble from every quarter."

"I'll ask the stable master to send one of the lads to the village and see about Harry's wagon."

Garahan's brows lifted in surprise. "So it's Harry now, is it?"

"She's given me leave to use her nickname. Don't be making more of it than there is."

His cousin lifted his hands in front of him and danced backward. "Wouldn't dream of it. Does she call ye Michael?"

"Only once or twice. It's usually me last name."

"Ye'll have to decide if ye want to encourage, or discourage, the lass."

O'Malley frowned. "'Tisn't an easy decision."

"We've seen enough strong, proud men struggle before they decided to take the fall."

"Fall?"

"Aye." Garahan placed his hands over his heart and batted his eyelashes. "The one that leads to love."

O'Malley snorted with laughter. "Ye'd best be watching yer step—there's a fair lass who pines for yer attention—Lady Calliope's lady's maid."

It was Garahan's turn to frown. "I don't have time to court the lass."

"Well then, just ask Mary Kate to wed."

Garahan's face paled. "Ye know I'm not ready for the strings marriage brings with it."

O'Malley laughed harder.

"Ye're an evil man, O'Malley."

"Can't help it. 'Tis the O'Grady side of our family." Satisfied he'd had the last word, he added a few more: "Think about it."

※※※

HOURS LATER, O'MALLEY slowed to a stop in front of the Mayfield cottage, pleased to note Harry was not working in the fields. He'd had a series of crises to deal with already, and did not need to butt heads with the stubborn woman again this afternoon.

He set the brake, tied off the reins, and lithely leaped to the ground. A quick glance told him Bart was alone working in the field on the other side of their barn. The lad stopped working to raise his hand.

A warmth filled O'Malley's gut as he acknowledged the greeting. He admired the lad and had to admit their farm reminded them of the one he grew up on...minus a few sheep.

Hoping to find Bart's mother resting, he knocked on the door.

It flew open, and the punch of desire nearly felled him. He stared at the vision. Bugger it, he hadn't come courting! Why in the bloody hell was he standing outside her door?

A strand of fiery silk slipped from where she'd fashioned a loose knot on top of her head. Joining the others that had escaped their pins, it added a softness that was not always evident...especially when she was being difficult. The need to reach out to wind a strand around his finger caught him off guard.

He drew in a breath, and desire tangled tighter in his gut. The subtle scent, an intoxicating combination of roses and cream scones warm from the oven, nearly had him begging. He flexed his hands before curling them into fists at his sides. The knowledge that her curves fit as if she'd been fashioned just for him had his mouth watering for a taste of her full lips.

Would her supple lips taste sweet, like meadow flower honey? Mayhap as tart as the first summer berries picked too soon.

She stared at him as if he'd lost his mind. The look in her eyes brought him up short. What in the bloody hell had happened to his formidable control? He growled low in his throat and could have kicked himself when the faint color in her cheeks faded and her guarded expression returned.

"What are ye doing out of bed?" he asked.

"It's customary to answer the door when someone knocks."

Her quick rejoinder had him tamping down the need to laugh.

She must have noticed. Her chin lifted and her mist-laden eyes iced over. "So, you finally remembered to return our wagon."

"I had not forgotten," he countered. "There were more important duties to attend to before I could get away."

Her flush of anger highlighted the crystalline gray of her eyes and the return of the flush to her cheeks.

The need to memorize the curve of her cheek with the tips of his fingers added fuel to his already simmering desire to touch her. *Out of the question!* he reminded himself. *I've no time to get involved with the feisty widow.* No matter how charming her plucky attitude and opinions, or the glimpse of sorrow he caught now and again in the depths of her changeable eyes, appealed to him.

She reached behind her to close the door and jolted.

O'Malley saw the pain etched across her lovely face. He felt for her, had been in the same position more than once—with a job to do and no time to spend in bed recovering. Moving swiftly, he caged her in his arms, expecting her to collapse, relieved when she regained her equilibrium.

"I beg your pardon," she rasped. "I twisted without thinking."

He tried to smile reassuringly and felt he had succeeded when she did not step away from him. "Normally a sign your injuries are improving, although it can ache like the very devil for longer than ye'd imagine."

"I believe I have already experienced this particular phenomenon. Though why I cannot seem to remember it will cause pain, I cannot fathom. I continue to contort my body without thinking, as if I hadn't been tackled to the ground by that behemoth."

Drawn to her strength, conscious that she had been grievously wounded, he had to fight to win the battle and firmly draw on his steely control to keep his hands—and his lips—to himself. "Ye seem to have a talent for provoking the worst in those who have been sent to demolish yer farm."

She didn't respond right away. Finally, she murmured, "I'd do anything to protect our way of life. It's all Bart and I have."

At her words, memories of home filled him—the look on Ma's face as she bent to scoop a handful of freshly turned earth and clenched it in her fist, and the conviction in Da's gruff voice as he vowed to protect his family and their land with his life's blood.

"Ye're not alone in this fight, Harry."

The look in her eyes softened to a warm, soft gray that reminded him of the early-morning mist that danced over endless fields of green. His heart and his gut ached to enfold this woman in his arms—hold her to his heart—and keep her there until they were old and gray.

He jolted back to reality and cursed beneath his breath.

She bristled, edging away from him. "There is no need to swear at me. I wasn't going to disagree with you. I know the viscount is doing all in his power to protect us. We are all part of the circle that keeps Chattsworth Manor alive and productive. He counts upon us as much as we count on him. Each doing our part."

"I beg yer pardon, lass. It was the situation I cursed, not yerself. Ye must know that I've feelings for ye. Ye're like a beacon in the night, drawing me closer against me will."

Her frown was fierce. "Like the lanterns wreckers use to draw unsuspecting ships toward the rocks so they could plunder their cargo after killing the captain and their crew?"

"'Tis hard to follow the crooked path yer mind takes, lass. Nay. 'Tisn't what I meant at all!"

"Ah, you meant like the enchanting song of a siren who lures sailors to their death upon the rocks."

"Bloody hell, Harry! That's not what I'm meaning at all."

"What *did* you mean?" she demanded.

He reached for the sunset strand that begged to be touched and savored the silken feel of it between his fingers. Lifting it to his nose, he inhaled the faint whisper of roses that clung to it. "From the first, yer hair caught me attention. Ye were standing in the late-afternoon sun. It set yer hair aglow with colors that rivaled the sunset."

Her eyes rounded as emotions swirled in their depths. The one he regretted seeing was fear, but the one he hoped to see was there, too—longing.

He closed the distance she'd put between them and traced the tip of his finger along the curve of her cheek before cradling her face in his hands. "Faith, yer eyes captivate me. Every time I see ye, lass, I crave another look, though I know 'twill never be enough."

Her cheeks flushed a lovely shade of rose, mimicking her scent, as the two tangled in his mind. Helpless to take even one step back from her, he watched the pulse at the base of her throat flutter rapidly.

"May I sip from yer lips, lass? I'm aching to discover yer taste."

"Aye," she whispered. "Please?"

He touched his lips to hers gently at first, a tentative touch that had her straining closer. He gently circled his arms around her, holding her to him, mindful of her healing ribs. She melted against him as he took his time exploring her supple mouth. The plumpness of her bottom lip enticed him to nip at it. Her soft moan of pleasure ignited the fire in his gut, encouraging him. He traced the rim of her mouth with the tip of his tongue. She stiffened for a moment, then melted against him, offering him more than he'd dared hope for.

Her mouth was a banquet of flavors. The headiest reminded him of meadow flower honey. Subtly sweet. Addictive.

He murmured against her lips, "Lass, I need to fully taste ye. I swear I won't harm yer ribs, but, by God, if I don't have more, I'll go mad!"

Her arms tightened around him in answer.

He plundered, swift and sure, sampling here, offering there, tangling them both with silken strands that promised of the pleasure that could be theirs if they were bold enough to grasp it and never let go.

Breath ragged, heart pounding, he leaned his forehead against hers. "God in Heaven, lass. Ye're lethal to a man's concentration. When we make love—"

Harry placed a hand to the middle of his chest. "No."

Shaking his head to clear it, he stared at her in disbelief. "After the way ye kissed me back, ye cannot tell me ye don't want me. I'll not be believing ye."

"We can't."

He chuckled. "Ye know 'tis a fact that we can."

"Do not push me on this, O'Malley."

Anger kindled in his gut, replacing desire. "Push ye? Ye opened to me like a flower bud feeling the first rays of the warm spring sun or soft rainfall. Ye can deny it all ye want, but I was on the receiving end of yer passion, lass."

"I'm not an innocent maid who doesn't understand desire or passion, O'Malley! I was married to a man I loved and desired. He may be gone, but the proof of our passion, our love, is walking toward us now with murder in his eyes."

O'Malley stiffened. What in the bloody hell had come over

him? He'd let down his guard and plundered her mouth against her front door for all the world to see.

He let her go and stepped back, watching her son stalk toward them.

"Take your hands off my mum!"

O'Malley raised his hands. "I already have. 'Tisn't what you think, lad."

"I grew up on a farm! It's exactly what I think."

"Bart—"

"Did you give him permission to kiss you, Mum, or did he take it without asking?"

"Young man, you have no right to speak to me like that," Harry said.

"As the man of this house, I have every right. I may be young, but I'm a man, and I know exactly where O'Malley's thoughts were headed."

"Bartholomew Tristan Mayfield! Apologize at once!"

Bart's eyes glittered with anger. "No."

O'Malley had heard enough. "I asked permission before I kissed yer ma."

Bart asked, "What about the rest?"

O'Malley knew what the boy must have seen and possibly heard. "I owe yer ma an apology, and since ye've already seen me kiss her, ye should be here when I apologize."

Confusion warred with the remnants of the boy's anger in the depths of his dark eyes, but he waited.

"Harry…Harriet," O'Malley began. "I lost me head when I kissed ye. One kiss will never be enough, lass. Ye set fire to me soul, and I'm thinking ye felt the same. But ye're right—I won't push ye, and I won't dishonor ye. I'll keep me distance, and like today, I'll ask permission before I kiss ye."

Harry's eyes filled with tears. She blinked them away, but one snuck free.

He brushed it away with the tip of his finger as he asked, "Will ye forgive me for embarrassing ye in front of yer son?"

"I trust you to keep your word, so I will forgive you. Don't let it happen again."

"Ye have to be daft if ye think I won't be asking to kiss ye again." He turned to her son. "I apologize to ye, Bart. I did not take advantage of yer ma. I was simply stating a fact she was not ready to hear."

Bart cleared his throat. "I see there is more here than what I observed. I trust you, O'Malley, and know you're a man who keeps his word. Though I understand from my father that sometimes passion can grab a man by his throat, and he will have to fight against the desires burning inside of him."

"Your father said that to you?"

"Aye, Mum."

She frowned. "Your father told me he wanted *me* to explain what happens in the marriage bed."

Bart grinned. "Father talked to me first, then said you would be speaking to me so that I would understand the woman's point of view. He told me it would be essential, once I found the woman I intended to spend the rest of my life with."

"Yer father was a wise man, Bart," O'Malley said. "He must have loved yer mother to distraction."

Harry slowly smiled. "He did, and warned that I was a distraction to him more than once."

Bart agreed, "He was wise, and he loved my mum and me."

"Never let go of that memory," O'Malley told them. "Hold it to yer heart where ye carry his love, and ye'll always have it." He bowed to Harry. "If ye'll excuse me, lass, I've new recruits to check on." To Bart he added, "I'll return later tonight to stand watch with ye."

"Thank you, O'Malley."

He unhitched his horse from the back of the wagon and mounted it. With a nod, he rode away from the woman he loved.

As he followed the road that led back to Chattsworth Manor, he wondered if *he* was the man in the vision that haunted him.

Would he live long enough to ask Harry to marry him?

Would she say yes?

Bloody hell! He'd have to ask Bart for permission.

# CHAPTER SEVENTEEN

ARRY WATCHED O'MALLEY ride away, wondering all the while what to say to her son that wouldn't unleash a torrent of questions she was not prepared to answer.

Bart didn't seem to be upset by what he'd seen or the conversation—or was it more of a confrontation?—that followed. He clicked to their plow horse and drove the wagon to the barn. There he signaled with the reins, and she watched with pride as her son had the horse and wagon ready to put away.

Once they cleared the doors, she could no longer see him. Harry knew from watching her husband teach Bart that their son would maneuver the horse and wagon into the barn with ease. He enjoyed tending to their stock but loved that horse—he would spend the time to talk to him and praise him for doing a good job for O'Malley and the constable. Nothing spooked their horse—certainly not the bed of the wagon being full of bleeding criminals.

Bart reappeared and walked swiftly to her. "Are you all right, Mum?"

"Of course. Are you?"

He nodded. "Aye. Mrs. Clarke warned me that there may come a time when you'd get lonely, missing Father."

"Did she?"

"She also said not to judge you harshly, because raising a son on your own while working the land and taking care of the both of us is a job best handled by two people."

Harry's heart filled with gratitude. Her friend had opened up a conversation she never thought to have with her son. She'd been too busy grieving silently while putting one foot in front of the other.

"I'm not looking for someone to replace your father, Bart."

He placed his hand on her shoulder. "Mary also said God is always watching over us."

"Your father and I often told you the same."

"I know. She also said He sends people who are meant to help us for a short time. If we are lucky, He'll send another special person who will be with us for the rest of our lives."

Harry tried to take in everything Mary had told Bart. It was something her own mother had promised her after Harry's father had died. Her eyes filled. Though Mother had never found a special person to fill the emptiness in her life, she seemed happy enough.

"That may be true for some people, but not everyone is destined to have more than one love in their lifetime. What your father and I had was meant to be. We were everything to one another."

Bart opened the door and held it for her. She was about to set the kettle on the cookstove to heat, but he beat her to it. "Have a seat, Mum. I'll get our tea."

"Mayhap you should wash up first."

He wiped his hands on his stomach—the only clean spot left on his shirt—and grinned. "I only touched the handle on the kettle. I'll go wash up now. I don't want to get any dirt in our tin of tea!"

His exuberance was catching. She felt lighter at heart as he dashed through their cottage, whistling as he opened and then shut the door. He was humming when he returned and held up his hands for her to inspect—just as he had when he was little. "Do I pass inspection?"

"You're in a fine mood, considering how angry you were earlier. When you stalked over toward us, I thought you'd take a swing at O'Malley."

"Mum, don't you think you could address him as Michael, seeing as how you've told him to call you Harry and already kissed the man?"

She clamped her mouth shut to keep the retort to herself. Bart wasn't a child anymore. He was right to remind her he was the man of their house. It was time she made a concerted effort to treat him with more deference—he more than pulled his weight and had earned it.

Setting her embarrassment aside to speak frankly with her son, she said, "He asked permission to kiss me, but I confess I thought it would be like kissing a member of the family."

Bart smirked. "You never kissed Uncle John on the lips."

She snorted out a laugh. "Your father's brother is—"

"A horse's *arse*," Bart supplied. "Aye, both you and Father said that more than once over the years."

"And?"

He laughed uproariously. "You're too smart to kiss a horse's *arse!*"

She laughed right along with him. "That's correct. I do hope you don't speak that way when you are helping out at the Clarkes' or the Johnsons'."

"Only when it's just Robbie, Matthew, and me."

"You are always respectful and mind your manners around their parents?"

His exaggerated sigh had her smiling. She'd asked just enough questions to remind him of the lessons she and Bartholomew had taught him. Bart was a wonderful son on the cusp of manhood.

"I'm so proud of you. Your father would be too."

"Do you think he's watching over us?"

"I know he is."

"You know what I think, Mum?"

"What?"

"God may have decided it was time to send someone special into our lives, but I'm thinking Father was the one to send O'Malley."

"What makes you think that?" she asked.

"Well, God knows that we need help, especially with the extra field Father acquired. But Father knew you'd need someone you couldn't order around all the time. Someone who would tell you when it was time to take a break and not work so hard. Someone who would kiss you until you forgot where you were…and who was watching."

Tears welled up, but she refused to cry in front of Bart. She would be the strength he could count on in their lives.

"You must have feelings for O'Malley if you let him kiss you, Mum."

"I do," she confessed.

Bart slammed his hand down on the table. "I knew it!"

Harry narrowed her eyes. "He irritates the bloody hell out of me."

Bart's mouth hung open, but not one word emerged.

Harry leaned close and, with the tip of her forefinger, tapped beneath his chin until her son closed his mouth. "The kettle's hot."

Bart grinned. "Mary said that oftentimes irritation is the prelude to attraction."

"Have you finished inspecting the field behind the barn?"

Bart poured hot water over the tea leaves in the teapot and set the kettle back on the cookstove. "I take it the other subject is closed."

"You always were a smart one, Bart."

O'MALLEY RODE LIKE the devil was nipping at his heels. His head pounded in time to his horse's hoofbeats. He'd never let his guard down. *Ever!* The very idea that one woman had the power to distract him to the point where he'd forget his duty—his vow to the duke—had his stomach churning.

By the time he reached the stables, he was certain of one thing: he could not afford to kiss the lovely Widow Mayfield again. He refused to let himself be tempted if it meant he would forget those under his protection. His lordship, Lady Calliope, and their babe depended upon him!

He would not let them down. Mayhap he should send another to stand watch with Bart this evening.

Before he could decide which man would go in his stead, his cousin strode toward him and stopped in his tracks.

"Did the widow feed ye tainted meat?"

O'Malley stared at Garahan.

"Poison ye?"

That got a rise out of O'Malley. "She did nothing of the kind, and ye'll not be suggesting it again."

"Bugger it," Garahan grumbled. "Either ye ate something tainted, or ye're about to cast up yer accounts all over yer favorite pair of boots."

A cold sweat broke out on the back of O'Malley's neck. Before he fulfilled Garahan's prediction, he ran around the back of the stables, where he could empty his stomach in peace. Bent over, hands braced to his thighs, he reached into his pocket for his handkerchief and came up empty. *Blast!* He'd given it to Harry.

A linen square appeared before his face. He wiped his mouth and slowly stood. "I didn't eat anything."

"What ails ye, then?"

"Nothing wrong with me."

Garahan snickered. "Ye can fetch yer own bucket of water to get rid of the 'nothing,' so no one comes around the corner of the stables and slips in yer vomit!"

O'Malley didn't move, even when he heard his cousin grumbling about someone—*probably me*—being a stubborn *arse—aye, definitely me.*

When the bucket was shoved at his gut, he caught it. He stepped around the reminder that a woman had nearly made him forsake his vow and filled the bucket at the pump. Garahan had a shovel and a small pile of dirt beside him, waiting.

"Empty the bucket over it. I'll toss on the dirt." He didn't say another word until the task was done. "Spit out whatever is on yer mind. Did ye come upon a wounded animal on the way home and have to shoot it?"

O'Malley knew Garahan would continue to come up with what he would consider reasons to turn his own stomach. He'd wager what he had to confide in his cousin would be added to the list. "'Tis something else entirely."

"Is it now?"

"I kissed Harry."

Garahan slowly nodded. "'Tis best if ye use her given name, else someone who isn't acquainted with the lovely widow might think ye prefer kissing men." O'Malley swung at him, but Garahan was expecting it and sidestepped the blow. "Did she kiss ye back? Are her lips sweet or tart? Firm or soft?"

This time when O'Malley threw a punch, he hit his target.

Garahan drew in a breath and slowly exhaled, rubbing his jaw. "I may have deserved that, *if* ye're thinking of courting the lass. But if ye're not..."

"I won't be kissing her again."

"Ah." Garahan's knowing look irritated O'Malley. "She didn't kiss ye back. The widow may not be ready to be kissing another man. Ye may have to give her time."

O'Malley grabbed his cousin by the front of his shirt and shook him hard. "She bloody well kissed me until me eyes crossed and the part of me that's been too long without a woman stood up and cheered."

Garahan grinned. "Well now, seeing's how yer stomach may be a bit raw, if ye let go...I just refilled me flask."

O'Malley let go and held out his hand.

Garahan reached in his frockcoat pocket and retrieved his

flask. "Seeing as how ye just lost the lining of yer stomach, why don't ye keep me flask and hand me yer empty one?"

"How do ye know it's empty?"

"Ye've never been stingy about sharing the Irish. Ye probably forgot to refill it before ye left to return the widow's wagon, else ye'd have never cast up yer accounts behind the stables when ye had the cure in yer pocket."

O'Malley took a long sip, wiped his mouth with his sleeve, and took another deep pull of Irish whiskey. "I was distracted. 'Tis why I'll not be kissing Widow Mayfield again."

Garahan's expression was bleak. "If ye must know, 'tis why I've been ignoring Mary Kate. I cannot think straight when she looks at me as if I'm a bloody hero like *Cú Chulainn* or *Brian Boru* stepping out of the pages of history to sweep her off her feet."

"I'm thinking Mary Kate might not want a demigod or warrior king, but I get yer meaning."

"So that's why ye've been avoiding her?"

"Aye. Me mind wanders to"—Garahan paused and grinned at O'Malley—"other things when she smiles at me."

"'Tis what happened when I kissed Harry. She kissed me back, and I lost me head entirely."

"Did ye now?"

"Aye, in the heat of the moment, I *may* have mentioned making love, and she *may* have put her hand to me chest and said no."

"Even I could have told ye she's the marrying kind."

"Well, of course she is, but me brain was so fuddled, I didn't get that part out. 'Twas in me heart the whole time we were kissing. That's when her son came over and demanded to know what I was doing."

"Even a blind man would know what ye were about—it must have been the shock of seeing someone kissing his ma that had him asking."

"He asked me straight out if I asked for permission to kiss her, or if I just grabbed hold and had me way about it," O'Malley said.

"Bart is wise for his years. He's got the makings of a fine

man—and nearly there!"

"I'm thinking Harry's the one who is angry with me."

"Give her time, and she'll come around to speaking to ye again," Garahan said. "The two of ye seemed to hit it off, and it's hard to lose a friend—someone who understands ye."

"What makes ye think she's a friend?"

"The way ye speak of her—and the way ye stare off into space when I know ye're thinking about her."

"Ye know me too well," O'Malley admitted. "'Tis why I haven't harped on ye about Mary Kate, although anyone with eyes can see she worships the ground ye walk on. Ye saved her, James. The day she was booted out of Lady Kittrick's home onto the sidewalk as if she mattered no more than a pile of rags, ye were there. Ye helped her to her feet and convinced her to go with ye to the duke's town house."

"Between meself and cousin Sean, we were able to. I cannot forsake me vow to His Grace."

"Neither can I."

"Then we'll bolster one another when we're missing the pair of lassies and sulking into a mug of ale or glass of the Irish."

"That we will," O'Malley said.

"O'Malley!"

The cousins turned as one.

"Aye, MacReady? Is there trouble?" O'Malley asked.

"Not sure as yet," MacReady replied. "Captain Coventry just rode up flanked by two men."

"Where is his lordship?"

"With Lady Calliope. I thought you could speak with the captain and find out who the men are before I let Hargrave know they've arrived."

With a glance at his cousin, Garahan said, "Ye're taking a big risk keeping Hargrave in the dark."

O'Malley shrugged and said, "Lead the way, MacReady."

As soon as they rounded the corner of the stables, O'Malley hailed Coventry. "'Tis good to see ye, captain. Who have ye brought with ye—Bayfield! How are ye?"

"Looking forward to catching up with yourself and Garahan before we meet with the viscount," Captain Bayfield replied.

"His lordship was expecting two of King's men," Garahan said.

"His men are currently on assignment," Coventry said. "We agreed you needed assistance immediately. I'm pleased to introduce Gryffyn Tremayne. Tremayne, meet Michael O'Malley and his cousin James Garahan, two of the duke's personal guard."

"Men, Tremayne is a former Cavalry officer with the King's Dragoons," Bayfield added.

"'Tis a pleasure to meet ye, Tremayne," O'Malley replied.

"Are ye going to be joining Bayfield as part of Coventry's new venture?" Garahan asked.

"I've heard a lot about the two of you," Tremayne said before answering Garahan's question. "Aye, I've been hired on by Coventry and am looking forward to meeting His Grace."

O'Malley grinned.

"Is the prospect of meeting the duke humorous?" Tremayne asked.

"Well, now that depends," O'Malley answered.

"On?"

"How many brothers and cousins ye have that will be working alongside of ye. Coventry was there and can attest that His Grace more than held his own meeting meself and me kin the day he hired us on."

"I see. Is it true there are sixteen of you?"

"Aye," Garahan responded. "Eight O'Malleys, four Garahans, and four Flahertys."

The other man slowly smiled. "I do believe I'm going to enjoy meeting the rest of your clan."

"If you're going into a situation where you need a man to guard your back, you cannot ask for better than one of the duke's guard," Bayfield told him.

"'Tis good of you to say so," O'Malley said.

"I'd best let Hargrave know you've arrived, gentlemen," MacReady told them before he strode off toward the manor house.

"Who is Hargrave?" Tremayne asked.

"His lordship's butler," Coventry replied.

The stable master and two of his stable hands took the reins of their mounts, promising to take care of them and see that they were brushed and fed an extra cupful of oats.

The group followed Coventry to the rear entrance, and Tremayne asked, "Is there somewhere we can wash before we meet with his lordship?"

"Aye," O'Malley replied. "Mrs. Romney keeps a pitcher of water, soap, and fresh linens in the pantry for just that purpose."

"Coventry, do you need to warn Mrs. Romney before she meets me?" Tremayne said.

"Warn her about what?" O'Malley asked, while Garahan shrugged.

Tremayne stared at the Irishmen for a moment before he cleared his throat. "Most females are put off by my scar. Surely you noticed."

O'Malley *had* noticed the slashing scar from the man's forehead to his chin. "Aye. Though from yer serious tone, for a moment I thought it was something else entirely. A scar earned serving yer country is a badge of honor."

"Aye," Garahan agreed. "As to a more serious topic, I was thinking I might have competition charming the cook into baking fresh scones daily—and having to share them with ye."

O'Malley snorted with laughter as he shoved his cousin with his shoulder. "Faith, ye're the bold one who has charmed Mrs. Romney into doing just that since the day the duke assigned ye to yer post here at Chattsworth Manor."

The hesitation left Tremayne's eyes. "I used to be known for charming the fairer sex...but that was before I received my *badge of honor* in the name of His Majesty."

O'Malley glanced at Bayfield, who gave a slight shake of his head, as if to let him know it was best to drop the subject. "The viscount's staff are loyal to a fault, the salt of the earth, and made of sterner stuff," O'Malley said. "I don't think ye'll have anything to worry about. Lady Calliope may take exception to ye charming one member of her staff in particular."

"Oh." Tremayne straightened his shoulders as if bracing himself. "Who might that be?"

"Her lady's maid—"

Garahan interrupted, "There isn't anyone ye need to be concerned with, *especially* Mary Kate."

Tremayne looked from one man to the other and back. "I see. Mayhap this Mary Kate's heart is already engaged?"

"That it is," Garahan said.

"Tremayne and I shall keep that in mind. We'd best do a cursory wash of face and hands before meeting the viscount," Bayfield said.

"Lead the way." Tremayne swept out his hand.

Coventry paused next to O'Malley. "Until this situation either presents itself—with Chellenham sending more men—or resolves itself, I think it wise to stop antagonizing one another."

Duly warned, the cousins agreed, waiting for Coventry and the others to enter the manor house first.

"What are ye about, bringing up Mary Kate's name when I've just told ye I was not going to be letting her winsome ways and dimpled smile turn me head?" Garahan asked.

O'Malley shrugged.

"'Tisn't a proper answer," Garahan growled. "See if I don't warn Tremayne and Bayfield that yer lovely widow is off-limits as well."

"I'd be grateful if ye would," O'Malley admitted.

"Are ye daft? Ye just told me..." Garahan's eyes widened as he realized his cousin's intent. "Thank ye for looking out for me best interests."

"I'll be thanking ye as soon as ye do the same for me," O'Malley said.

"Do ye think they'll be stationed here long enough to capture a few hearts?" Garahan asked.

"How long did it take ye to capture Mary Kate's?"

Garahan grinned. "At least five minutes…mayhap a half more, but Coventry's men lack our Irish charm."

"And our roguish ways," O'Malley added. They walked, side by side, ready to face the latest crisis.

✦ ❖ ✦

# CHAPTER EIGHTEEN

"Captains Coventry and Bayfield, and Lieutenant Tremayne, your lordship," Hargrave announced with appropriate reverence.

Viscount Chattsworth rose from where he was seated behind his desk, extending his hand in greeting. "Coventry! I'm surprised to see you."

"I was meeting with King when your missive arrived," Coventry said. "Unfortunately, King's men are all currently on assignment."

They shook hands. "Then I'm relieved you're here." Turning to the men, the viscount waited for the captain to do the introductions.

"Captain David Bayfield, Lieutenant Gryffyn Tremayne," Coventry said, "may I present Viscount Chattsworth."

"Thank you for coming in response to my urgent missive. Gentlemen." With a broad sweep of his hand, the viscount invited them to sit. "My housekeeper, Mrs. Meadowsweet, should be along momentarily with our tea. Hargrave, please remind O'Malley and Garahan that we are waiting for them."

His butler's lips twitched, though he did not smile. "They are on their way—momentarily distr...er...detained, your lordship."

The viscount suspected Garahan was at fault. The man was always trying to charm an extra scone or two out of his cook.

"Hurry them along, if you would."

"At once."

"Allow me to thank you in advance for your assistance, gentlemen," the viscount said to the men gathered in the room. "When O'Malley and Garahan arrive, I'll let them fill you in on the recent attacks my tenant farmers have suffered. Hopefully after a tour of my estate, you will be able to add to the protection plan the duke's guard already has in place."

"I noticed a few new faces have been added to the guard," Coventry remarked.

"It had been my plan to do so—however, a happy event required my full attention, and thankfully O'Malley and Garahan took care of that for me."

"May I offer my sincere congratulations, Chattsworth," Coventry said. "I trust Lady Calliope and your new babe are well."

The viscount smiled. "Aye. I've insisted that she rest, but apparently, my countess has other ideas regarding how much rest she requires."

"I have a similar situation at home," Coventry said with a knowing smile.

"How are your wife and son?"

"Miranda is healing and has regained more dexterity and strength in her hands. Michael looks taller every morning. It's quite astounding."

"I'm pleased to hear the news about them both. I've already noticed our son seems to be gaining weight daily. It's a marvel how quickly he's growing."

The men were quietly talking when Hargrave knocked on the open door. "O'Malley and Garahan, your lordship."

O'Malley shook his head. "I tried to tell him ye were expecting us and didn't need to be escorted."

"Aye, but Hargrave is ever the proper servant," Garahan said.

"Your tea, your lordship." Hargrave stepped to the side to allow Mrs. Meadowsweet and two footmen to enter. The first footman carried a large tray with the silver tea service. The other footman carried a tray with serving dishes piled high with sandwiches, scones, and a selection of tarts.

"Mrs. Meadowsweet, would you do the honors?" the viscount asked.

"I'd be delighted." She directed the servants on the placement of the trays. When she was satisfied, she thanked the footmen and dismissed them. After pouring and serving tea to the viscount's guests, she served plates with generous helpings from the selection of savory and sweet offerings.

"I believe Mrs. Romney is sending another pot of tea, ah, and here it is." She motioned to the footman to remove the empty pot and leave the full one. "Shall I remain and pour, your lordship?"

"We shall endeavor to manage. Thank you," the viscount said.

"Ring if you change your mind."

"I shall. Thank you, Mrs. Meadowsweet."

As the door clicked shut, he nodded to the group. "Now then, O'Malley will inform you of the nature and frequency of the attacks, while Garahan can explain what they have done to counter them."

By the time the duke's men finished their report, the viscount was pleased to note Coventry and his men were sitting on the edges of their seats.

"Questions?" he asked.

Coventry frowned. "Have the prisoners been transported to London?"

"The first group has," O'Malley replied.

"And the second?" Bayfield asked.

"The constable plans to transport them later today," Garahan said.

"Any further questions? Tremayne?" the viscount asked.

"None at the moment, your lordship," Tremayne replied. "Though I am quite certain I shall have a few after we tour the estate. I'm especially interested in the land and wooded areas surrounding your tenant farms."

"I'm interested in the roads leading to and from the village," Bayfield added. "Are your farmers equipped and adept at defending themselves?"

"Aye, most of them," the viscount answered. "Two families suffered injuries during the first and second attacks. O'Malley and Garahan have been taking turns at these farms during the overnight watch."

"Any attacks during the day?" Tremayne asked.

"Not as yet," the viscount said. "However, the attacks have increased in severity, so I suspect that too may change."

"I'd like to visit the families with injuries first," Tremayne said.

"Excellent notion," Bayfield remarked.

O'Malley rose. "We'll be needing fresh mounts for the men."

Garahan quickly followed suit, as did the others, ready to follow O'Malley's lead.

"Though I'm certain the stable master has been caring for yer horses," Garahan said, "'twould be wise to let them rest a bit longer."

Coventry's eyes gleamed. "Chattsworth, I have a favor to ask of you."

"Whatever you wish, captain," the viscount said.

"That was far easier than I'd heard it was rumored to be."

The viscount frowned. "Just what *is* this favor?"

O'Malley leaned toward his cousin. "I'll wager he's wanting to ride his lordship's beautiful black stallion."

"Who wouldn't want to ride Maximus?" Garahan asked. "Ye'll have to come up with another wager."

"Give me time," O'Malley said. "I'll think of one."

"The honor of riding Maximus," Coventry told the viscount.

"I'll have to confer with my stallion and allow him to meet you before agreeing," the viscount replied. "If Maximus takes to you, then you may of course ride him."

IN THE DIM light of the stables, Coventry waited for the viscount to speak to his stallion before introducing him to the beautiful black beast.

When Maximus turned to stare at the captain, everyone fell silent. After a few moments, the horse gently nudged the captain's eyepatch and then snorted, blowing a breath in his face. It was love at first sight for both man and horse.

"Saddle those three geldings for the captain and his men," the stable master said. "I'll let O'Malley and Garahan saddle their horses, while his lordship has another word with Maximus."

The viscount murmured softly in his stallion's ear. Instructions given, he patted his horse's neck and held him by the bridle while Coventry mounted. "A light hand on the reins is all you need. Max is quick to respond to a press of the knees as well."

"Thank you, Chattsworth," Coventry said. "I shall take excellent care of Maximus for you."

The other men were mounted on fresh horses and on their way in short order. O'Malley led them on the road that looped around the manor house before taking them on the path that wound through the vast estate, leading them to the first of viscount's tenant farms—the Clarkes' and the Mayfields'.

"Ethan Clarke was shot defending his farm," O'Malley told the group as they reined in their horses. "They were able to stop the miscreants from setting their barn on fire—"

"It appears the miscreants returned...and succeeded," Bayfield countered, pointing to the pile of ash as he dismounted. He walked his horse to the corral and tied off the reins.

"They returned the following night," Garahan told them. "That's when their son Matthew was struck in the head while standing watch."

"Expecting the attackers to return and finish the job," Tremayne added, as he dismounted and secured his reins to the top rail of the corral.

"Is there a Mrs. Clarke?" Bayfield asked.

The door to the cottage opened and a slender woman raised her hand in greeting. "Mr. O'Malley, Mr. Garahan, what brings you here?" The worry in her voice was sharply evident.

Clarke and his son appeared from the back of the cottage. "Thought I heard voices," Ethan remarked. Taking in the serious expressions around him, he asked, "More trouble on the way?"

"Aye," O'Malley responded. He didn't want to worry the family unnecessarily. "I'd like to introduce Captain Coventry and his men, Captain Bayfield, and Lieutenant Tremayne. Coventry and Bayfield are retired from His Majesty's Royal Navy. Tremayne retired from His Majesty's Royal Dragoons. They've arrived to lend a hand with the recent rash of attacks plaguing his lordship's tenants."

He watched Mrs. Clarke's curious gaze sweep from one man to the next, as she took note of Coventry's black eyepatch and Tremayne's slashing scar. A gust of wind blew the lace at Bayfield's cuffs, revealing his badly scarred wrists.

"Would you care for tea?" she asked. "The kettle is always hot."

"No thank you, Mrs. Clarke," Coventry responded. "O'Malley tells me we've more ground to cover before we head back to meet with his lordship."

"I've just taken a currant cake out of the oven, Captain Coventry. I'd be happy to send you off with a few slices."

"That's kind of you, but—"

"Mrs. Clarke's currant cake melts in yer mouth," Garahan told the men.

"I haven't tasted better," O'Malley added, then elbowed Garahan. "Don't be telling me ma."

"And risk her whacking me with her rolling pin? Ye have no worry of that."

Coventry chuckled. "Then I'd be delighted to accept on behalf of my men."

"I'll just be a moment," she called as she spun around to go back inside.

"It distresses Mary to speak about the attacks," Ethan told the men. "What would you like to know?"

By the time Mary returned with the promised cake, the men had discussed the numbers in the band of attackers, what weapons they used, and what time of day the attack occurred.

It was a solemn group that arrived at the Mayfield farm. Bart was on hand to greet them. "O'Malley? Garahan? Have you come to warn us about an imminent attack?"

"Nay, Bart," O'Malley replied. "Captain Coventry and his men have come to lend a hand fending off further attacks."

"Let me get my mum. She'll want to meet you." His hand was reaching for the door as it swung open. "Oh, there you are, Mum. O'Malley and Garahan have brought reinforcements to meet us."

"Allow me to introduce ye to Captain Coventry and his men," O'Malley said. After introducing the men, he introduced Harry and her son.

"A pleasure, Mrs. Mayfield, Bart," Coventry said. "We have some questions about the attacks and have just come from speaking to the Clarke family."

"We heard the shots the night they were attacked," Bart told them.

"Then what happened?" Tremayne asked.

"I told Mum to stay put"—Bart frowned at her—"but she didn't."

"I'm the one skilled with herbs and a needle and thread," she reminded her son.

"Aye, but—"

"No buts. We both had a duty to be there for our neighbors. Mary needed my help removing the pistol ball from Ethan's shoulder, and Matthew needed your help standing guard until the Johnsons arrived."

O'Malley clenched his jaw, noting the way Bayfield and

Tremayne openly admired the lovely Widow Mayfield. He nudged his cousin, who hadn't held up his part of the bargain—to let the two men know Mrs. Mayfield was spoken for. At least, that was O'Malley's intention sometime in the future.

"Have ye any fresh scones, Mrs. Mayfield?" Garahan asked. "Mrs. Clarke is sending the men home with a bit of her currant cake."

She smiled. "How did you know I just took a batch from the oven?"

"The scent, for one." Garahan beamed. "Yours are delicious."

"Aye," O'Malley agreed. "Though for me cousin's sake, don't be telling Mrs. Romney, or she may cut off our ready supply of scones."

Harry was laughing as she retreated into the cottage.

Tremayne's gaze clashed with O'Malley's. At the unspoken warning in the Irishman's direct gaze, Tremayne sighed. "As no one referred to a Mr. Mayfield, I take it she is a widow?"

"Aye," O'Malley said.

"Do you have an understanding with the lovely Mrs. May-field?"

"Aye. Of a sort," O'Malley responded while Garahan snorted with laughter.

"Interesting and evasive answer to a direct question," Tremayne said. "If I asked Mrs. Mayfield, would she give a similar answer?"

O'Malley curled his hands into fists, then slowly relaxed them.

The retired dragoon slowly smiled. "I believe I'll ask her."

"Ye'll not be asking her anything!" O'Malley bit out.

HARRY STOOD IN the open doorway, a linen sack filled with scones clutched to in her hand. "Would you care to explain that last statement, O'Malley?"

Green eyes blazing with anger pinned her to the spot, while the hint of desire behind the anger pulled at her, tempting her to brave the flames and taste the passion barely held in check.

"Nay," O'Malley replied.

Coventry cleared his throat, while Tremayne and Bayfield continued to stare at her.

"Have I missed an important part of your conversation, gentlemen? If I have, please do enlighten me."

The three men from London remained silent.

Garahan, dear man, spoke up. "Well now, lass, it appears as if Lieutenant Tremayne would like to ask ye a question." Turning to his cousin, he continued, "And me darling cousin does not wish to let him."

Incensed at the very idea that any man would hinder her right to speak, Harry shoved the bag of scones at Garahan. "Since you do not seem to be involved in their ridiculous argument about something neither dunderhead has a right to decide for me, you may have the entire bag of scones, Garahan."

He snagged the bag with one hand and pulled Harry into his arms with the other. Pressing a kiss to her cheek, he laughed. "Thank ye, lass. I believe I'll be heading on back to the manor house. Take care of yer ma, Bart."

"I will, Garahan!" When no one moved, Bart announced, "My mum and I have chores to do. If you have any more questions regarding the attack, you may come back tomorrow. Mum's still healing from her injuries and needs to rest."

Without another word, he put his arm around her waist and led her back inside.

With the closing of the door, her anger dissipated. She pressed her back against the door and blew out a breath. "Thank you for taking over, Bart. I was about to say something that would put me beyond the pale and find the both of us out on our *arses* with nowhere to live...and nowhere to go."

"We could always go live with Uncle John...you know, *the*

*horse's arse."*

Harry's mouth hung open for a moment before she dissolved into a fit of laughter, clutching her aching side. When she finally came up for air, she brushed a lock of hair out of his eyes. "You are your father's son, Bart. In every way. Thank you for being the voice of reason just now. I certainly wouldn't have been reasonable after hearing those two buffoons posturing."

"Even a blind man could see the lieutenant was taken with you."

"He doesn't even know me!" Harry protested.

"Sometimes you just know. Isn't that what you said after seeing Father for the first time?"

"You're right, and I did. However, the feeling is not mutual. Besides, I have too much to do working with you to keep our farm profitable, tending our stock, keeping our home, and feeding you."

The rhythmic beat of horses' hooves hitting the dry dirt road was oddly soothing. Mayhap it had more to do with the fact that the group of uninvited guests were leaving than the cadence.

Harry walked over to the table and sank onto a chair.

Bart followed and sat beside her. He reached for her hand and grasped it. "We're doing all right, aren't we, Mum?"

She patted his hand before releasing it. "We are doing just fine." When her son looked down and then away, she knew something plagued him. "What is it? You know you can ask me anything."

He sighed and met her questioning gaze. "I think O'Malley's ill."

She frowned. "He seemed fine to me. Has he said something to you, or acted in such a manner, to have you reach that conclusion?"

Bart nodded. "He had a death grip on his horse's mane and his face was pale and sweating."

Worry filled her. *A fever that comes and goes...* That was how her husband's virulent fever started! One day he was fine, the next a little warm. A few days later, his fever raged, and before she could get it under control, he slipped away. "When was this? Did he say anything to lead you to believe he was ill?"

"Not that he was aware of," Bart hedged.

"You'd best tell me."

"He was looking in my direction, but not at me—more like *through* me."

"Go on."

"O'Malley was murmuring about a duel, blood, someone being shot in the back."

"He must have snapped out of it, and whatever caused him to act as if he were having a fit."

"Aye. When I asked him about it, he brushed it off. It was almost as if he were in a trance...*ensorcelled*."

"It seems I may have to speak to the man before I've forgiven him for overstepping boundaries by telling me what to do," Harry said.

Bart's worry was evident. "We need to help him, even if he doesn't want it."

"Agreed. We owe the man for the help he's given us."

"Then you'll forgive him long enough to get him to tell you what's wrong with him?"

"I will do my best, Bart."

"I cannot ask for more. Thanks, Mum."

# CHAPTER NINETEEN

T HE TENSION BETWEEN Tremayne and O'Malley simmered during the remainder of the tour of the viscount's estate. Clouds gathered, and the temperature had dropped by the time they returned to the manor house.

The stable master and his hands were there to greet the men. "The viscount expected you to return a while ago. Was there a problem?"

O'Malley shot Tremayne a hard glare, which was returned with the subtle lift of the lieutenant's eyebrow. The former dragoon was the epitome of cool under fire. O'Malley longed to blast the man into next week but couldn't. Wouldn't. He'd given his word.

"Nay," he replied. "There were more than a few farmers that needed assurance we'd be able to protect their families and their farms."

Garahan grinned. "It must have been baking day. We've quite a haul from the grateful wives of his lordship's tenants." He held up a linen sack. "A gift from Mrs. Mayfield."

The stable master's face showed his surprise. "O'Malley trusted you to carry baked goods?"

"Oh, this sack's not to share. 'Tis for meself," Garahan said, preening.

O'Malley shifted his attention to his cousin. "'Tis a greedy man who would think only of himself and how many scones he could shove down his gullet."

Garahan bristled but didn't respond as O'Malley expected him to. The *eedjit* held his gaze for a few moments, then turned his back on him!

Before O'Malley could taunt his cousin into an all-out brawl, relieving the knot of anger and frustration in his aching gut, the viscount appeared.

"Ah, gentlemen, you've returned. Any news to report?" The first one to answer was the stallion. Maximus' greeting had the viscount laughing. "I can see that you've enjoyed your time away, Max. Care for an apple?"

His horse whinnied in reply, nudging the pocket of the viscount's frockcoat. The laughter in the viscount's eyes had guilt slamming into O'Malley. It shamed him. Protecting the viscount and his family mattered far more than his own bruised pride and battered heart. Truth be told, Bart and his mother did too.

Hoping to ease the tension he'd caused for the latter part of the tour, O'Malley said, "Mayhap me cousin will share one of his scones."

"Aye, with Max," Garahan gleefully replied. "Not you."

The men chuckled watching the exchange between the Irishmen.

The viscount cut to the chase. "My wife will be joining us for supper. We can meet and go over your questions afterward."

O'Malley asked, "Would you like our report before you eat?"

The viscount declined. "The invitation included the five of you, O'Malley. Lady Calliope is longing for company and news of our tenants—especially the Clarkes and the Mayfields. As you have been assigned to those two families in particular, she is looking forward to speaking with you."

Chattsworth turned to the newcomers. "My wife is anticipating meeting you, Tremayne...Bayfield." He slowly smiled. "Apparently, I've given too little information for her to form an opinion. Calliope is anxious to return to her duties as chatelaine of the estate. She thrives on helping others. I would caution you not to discuss the attacks or the threat that looms over this household. I'll not have her peace of mind disturbed more than it already is."

"Of course," Tremayne replied.

"Wouldn't dream of it," Bayfield added.

"I shall be happy to distract her ladyship with tales of the happy disruption that one lad of three and ten and his mother, the love of my life, have made to my formerly staid bachelor household," Coventry offered.

The men were in a far better frame of mind as they followed the viscount to the manor house. "Have I mentioned, Coventry, just how grateful I am that you are here?" the viscount asked.

The captain inclined his head. "Aye, Chattsworth. I have a feeling we shall not have long to wait before we are put to the test, protecting those you hold dear."

The viscount's hands clenched into fists. "I intend to be there on the front lines to defend my wife, our son, and those whose very livelihood depend upon us."

O'Malley was close enough to hear the conversation. "His Grace would not want ye there. He'd want ye with yer family."

"I understand the duke was in the thick of things when Hollingford and his men attacked Wyndmere Hall."

O'Malley frowned. "Aye, at first 'twas because of the fire from the lightning strike, and then when Hollingford's men—"

"I shall be wherever I am needed," the viscount interrupted. "I know you and Garahan will protect my wife."

O'Malley glanced at his cousin, but neither spoke.

"The earl rode over while you were showing the men around the estate," the viscount said. "He's made an excellent suggestion."

O'Malley knew before the viscount continued what the suggestion would be. "Safety in numbers."

The relief in the viscount's expression was evident. "Aye. Edward will be bringing Aurelia and their son to stay until this whole bloody business is finished."

Garahan smiled. "Three more of the duke's guard will be a welcome addition to our ranks."

"Friends of yours?" Bayfield asked.

"Aiden's me brother," Garahan explained. "Sean is brother to O'Malley here, and Emmett is one of our cousins."

"That will add to our number sufficiently," Coventry said. "With the addition of three more of the duke's guard, plus the combined experience of the lot of you—"

"Don't be forgetting yerself, captain," O'Malley reminded him.

Coventry nodded. "With myself and the men temporarily assigned as part of the guard, we shall have the advantage!"

"The key will be making it appear as if we do not," Tremayne added.

O'Malley had to give credit where credit was due. "Ye have the right of it, Tremayne. I'd like to hear yer thoughts on that and add a few of me own."

"Excellent notion, O'Malley. I look forward to it."

The rear door swung open as Hargrave announced, "Her ladyship requires your immediate assistance, your lordship."

The viscount's face paled as he bolted past the butler into his home. "Is anything wrong, Hargrave?"

The butler frowned. "Nay. I did not mean to alarm his lordship. Her ladyship was quite insistent that I fetch him the moment he returned."

"Lady Calliope and the babe are well?" Coventry asked.

"Aye. Captain, if you and your men will follow me, his lordship has asked that the three of you take the guest rooms."

Tremayne frowned. "Where are O'Malley and Garahan staying?"

"We have our own quarters in one of the outbuildings," O'Malley replied. "Suits our purpose and doesn't disturb the household with our odd hours coming and going while on patrol."

"If you don't mind, captain," Tremayne said, "I'd like to bunk with the duke's guard."

"I would as well," Bayfield added. "We have much to plan, and from the feeling in my bones, not as much time as we had hoped."

"I'm quite sure his lordship will agree to whatever you require," Hargrave said.

"Is there enough room in your quarters for the earl's guards and two more?" Coventry asked.

"Aye," Garahan replied. "His lordship added a larger bunk area at our request."

"You expected trouble and the need to house more of your guard?" Bayfield asked.

O'Malley's voice was bleak when he responded, "We always expect trouble. Making room for the entire guard at each of His Grace's estates made sense. Any family gatherings would include the necessary addition of their personal guard."

"His Grace is a man who enjoys planning for all possibilities," Coventry said.

Garahan grinned. "I'm thinking he wasn't planning on twins."

Their shared laughter eased the rest of the earlier tension. Coventry's men were shown to the rooms assigned to them to clean up before the meal. All agreed that the men would move their belongings to O'Malley and Garahan's quarters after they ate and had their meeting with the viscount.

O'Malley didn't have to tell Garahan that he intended to return to the Mayfield farm to stand watch after the meeting. It had been added to his nightly routine since the first attack.

He didn't know whether to anticipate speaking with Harry, or to dread it. A wise man, as his ma liked to remind him, would carry a little bit of both in his heart.

Before he let himself get too tangled in conflicting emotions, he had a dinner and a meeting afterward to get through without letting the blasted lieutenant needle him about Widow Mayfield. Bloody confident bugger better not try to charm her away from him!

An emotion O'Malley hadn't felt in far too long to remember reared its ugly green head. 'Twasn't the same as when his cousins would charm one of the buxom serving lasses away from him over a tankard of ale. The realization that his heart had never been fully engaged until now was a surprise. She'd slipped under his guard and remained front and center in his thoughts.

He nodded to Garahan as his cousin jogged along the path to their quarters to catch up to him.

"Are ye still worried about keeping yer vow to protect the duke and his family?" Garahan asked.

"Nay."

"Ye've more than a tinge green about yer gills."

O'Malley didn't want to confide in anyone, let alone his cousin, who would torment him to no end. "Going over plans in me head. Considering the variables."

"Such as?" Garahan asked.

"What are the chances this new lot of dregs from the docks will be more skilled with weapons than the last?"

"If their aim were truer," Garahan mused aloud, "'twould be to their advantage. The last group had rifles, but not the skill to use them."

"Aye," O'Malley agreed as they made their way along the path. "Mind if we stop in the stables for a minute?"

His cousin shrugged. "We have a bit of time. Are we meeting an informant there on the sly?"

O'Malley shook his head, then slowly smiled. "Just thought of some encouragement for the lads."

Garahan shoved his cousin with his shoulder. "Ye're a bloody *eedjit*! The geldings haven't any more hope of charming a willing filly—given their lack of certain attributes—than ye do with the prickly but beautiful widow."

"Even those of us without hope could use a spot of it to cheer us," O'Malley countered. "Don't ye remember that fine gelded Irish pony the Flahertys had?"

Garahan paused, gripping the knob to the side door of the stables. "Bloody hell! I'd forgotten all about him. He'd start running around the corral—building up steam, no doubt—and then try to cover any mare in season."

O'Malley nodded. "Aye. He'd been castrated, but his other parts—and that bit of his brain that would go haywire scenting a mare in season—were still in impressive working order."

Garahan chuckled. "Whisper encouragement to the lads, then. I'll distract the stable master, so he won't catch ye making promises that'll have the stable lads chasing after the geldings in vain."

"If it were me," O'Malley said, "I'd let the gelding make the most of their time with the mares. The stable master won't be letting them graze among the ladies after the lads had their fun."

Lighter in heart, he whispered to the geldings…a fine tale of an Irish pony with a stallion's heart.

A few minutes later, O'Malley heard Garahan and the stable master's voices drawing closer.

"Remember what I've told ye, lads. 'Twill be a day to re-member," O'Mally promised. The horses' whickering and whinnying warmed his heart.

"We'd best hurry," Garahan said as he approached his cousin. "We don't want to disappoint the countess by being late."

O'Malley gave one last pat to each of the geldings, bade the stable master goodbye, and followed his cousin to the door. Once they were outside, he raised his eyebrows and grinned. "The lads invited ye to watch."

Garahan doubled over with laughter. When he could catch his breath, he punched O'Malley in the arm. "Ye're a wicked, wicked man, Michael. Faith, I love that about ye."

# CHAPTER TWENTY

O'MALLEY AND GARAHAN stood at attention just inside the dining room doors.

"'Tisn't right," O'Malley grumbled. "We're the duke's personal guard—not dinner guests."

Garahan tugged at his cravat. "I hate this bloody thing! We always stuff them in our pockets after teatime."

"Only because the viscount doesn't mind that we're not dressed to the nines, as the duke would have us at all hours of the day."

"It feels like a noose about me neck."

O'Malley pitched his voice low so as not to be heard. "How would ye know?"

Garahan's bleak gaze hinted that he had a secret he'd never shared.

"Tell me which bloody bugger tried to hang ye, and I'll gut the bastard!"

Tremayne appeared out of nowhere. "Wouldn't that jeopardize your position within the duke's guard?"

O'Malley stiffened. "'Twas a private conversation."

Bayfield joined the trio. "What did I miss?"

"If it was private," Coventry said, "you wouldn't be having it in Viscount Chattsworth's dining room where the footmen stationed about the room would hear it."

"Excellent point," Tremayne said. "Mayhap we can continue this conversation before our meeting."

O'Malley clamped his jaw shut.

Tremayne acknowledged the action with a smirk. "As you mentioned, it was private. Though if we are to be fighting alongside one another for the same cause, you may reconsider your position and include Bayfield and me."

O'Malley snickered. "Ye remind me of Da's prized bull—"

"Lady Calliope!" Coventry's voice covered the inappropriate remark O'Malley had been about to make. "Thank you for including my men in your gracious invitation to dine with you this evening."

"Captain Coventry, how wonderful to see you." As it had since the first day O'Malley met Lady Calliope, her warm, sweet smile and soothing tone eased whatever tension existed prior to her entering a room.

"I assure you, the pleasure is all mine," Coventry replied.

She turned to greet Coventry's men, her smile widening. "I've heard tales already of how your men have charmed Mrs. Romney into baking additional cream tarts. They are a favorite of mine."

"Lady Calliope, may I present Captain David Bayfield and Lieutenant Gryffyn Tremayne," Coventry said.

O'Malley marveled that the countess did not bat an eyelash at Tremayne's slashing scar—nor the scars Bayfield endeavored to hide with the froth of lace at his cuffs and height of his cravat. "It's a pleasure to meet you, gentlemen. Thank you for agreeing to accompany Captain Coventry and help protect our family and our home."

The viscount drew her closer to his side. "My dear, we agreed not to bring up any unpleasant topics this evening."

Her eyes narrowed, and she frowned at her husband. "I believe the attacks on our tenant farmers should not be referred to as unpleasant. Mayhap calamitous, or diabolical, not merely unpleasant."

The viscount seemed to have developed a tic under one eye, but his wife's next comment appeared to soothe him.

"However, as I did promise, I shall not bring up the subject again—whether or not I agree with your description of our tenants' plight."

Tremayne snorted, trying to cover his laughter, which had Bayfield covering his mouth with his hand and coughing.

O'Malley and Garahan did not bother to try to cover their laughter. "Ah, Lady Calliope, 'tis always a pleasure to see yer ladyship," O'Malley said.

"Aye," Garahan agreed. "Ye're a vision of loveliness."

The viscount frowned at Garahan and cleared his throat. "If you would all be seated, dinner is ready to be served."

As soon as the viscount turned his back to escort his wife to the table, O'Malley leaned close and warned his cousin, "Mind yer manners where Lady Calliope is concerned."

"I was only giving her ladyship a compliment."

"If ye don't want to end up on yer *arse*, ye'll not be embarrassing her ladyship with yer compliments."

"She didn't mind," Garahan protested as they moved to their seats at the other end of the table from the couple.

"Aye," O'Malley agreed. "But his lordship bloody well did."

"Problem, O'Malley?" Coventry asked as he paused behind him to find his seat at the table.

"Nay."

From the way the captain stared at him, O'Malley knew the meal was going to be more of a trial than a pleasure.

He didn't relax until the meal ended and the viscount rose and offered his hand to Lady Calliope. She placed her hand in his and beamed at him. As she rose from her seat, the men did as well.

"Thank you for your company, gentlemen."

"I know I speak for everyone here when I say that it was our pleasure," Coventry responded.

The men bowed as the couple left the room.

Coventry addressed those remaining. "His lordship has asked that we meet with him in his downstairs library in half an hour."

"That gives me time to check in with the men patrolling the perimeter," O'Malley replied.

"I'd like to accompany you," Tremayne said.

O'Malley was about to refuse when he saw the look in Coventry's single-eyed gaze. Bloody hell! Refusal was not an option. "Very well."

GARAHAN WATCHED THE two men leave and sighed. "Oil and water, Coventry. Are ye sure ye know what ye're about?"

"If you value your position within the duke's guard," Coventry warned, "you'll remember that her ladyship deserves your utmost respect."

Garahan bristled. "Are ye suggesting I disrespected her?"

"I'm asking you to refrain from personal comments. It distresses his lordship."

Garahan glared at the captain but did not contradict his edict. Coventry was part of the chain of command between His Grace, the Duke of Wyndmere, and their immediate employer, Viscount Chattsworth.

"You and Bayfield check with the contingent from the village. I understand they should be arriving momentarily from their patrol of the outer grounds."

"Aye," Garahan grumbled as he strode from the room, with Bayfield hot on his heels.

AT HALF ELEVEN, O'Malley was back in the saddle heading to the Mayfield farm, but he wasn't alone. Tremayne rode beside him, and both urged their horses from a canter to a brisk trot. The horses easily covered the distance, their gait smooth as they traversed the familiar road by the light of the waning moon.

Confident in his horse—and that of the man beside him—he wondered if the predictions discussed during the meeting just a short while ago would come true.

*Are Chellenham's latest dregs from the docks en route to Chattsworth Manor?*

O'Malley had no doubt this next group of men would be more skilled—and tenacious—than the last. With the temporary additions to the guard, Coventry and his men, and the anticipated arrival of three additional members of the duke's guard stationed at Lippincott Manor, O'Malley looked forward to Chellenham's latest horde descending upon them.

Bart was standing guard by the barn when they arrived. "O'Malley, Tremayne! I'm glad you're here," the young man said. "I've got a bad feeling in the pit of my stomach. I tried to tell Mum, but she brushed it aside, telling me it was nerves."

"Let's hope she's right," Tremayne said. Keeping his voice low, he added, "As every warrior readies himself for the battle ahead, he mentally calculates the odds against him, the cunning of his enemy, and the enemy's ability to draw him out of hiding."

O'Malley agreed. "If it puts ye on edge, then ye know ye're ready to do battle."

Bart glanced at the house and to the two men on either side of him. "I'm worried about Mum."

"You're smart to worry, though we'll keep her safe," O'Malley assured him.

"When was the last time you checked in with her?" Tremayne asked.

"An hour ago. There has been no movement from the tree line over there." Bart pointed to the north. "Just a feeling as if someone's just walked across my grave."

"You'll be on the alert, then," O'Malley said. "Don't fight it, lad."

"Embrace it," Tremayne added.

The young man's relief was palpable. "You don't think I'm imagining it?"

"Nay. Trust yer gut." Turning to Coventry's man, O'Malley said, "Tremayne, stay here. I want to have a closer look at that tree line. It's where the blackguards launched their attack the last time." Thankfully, the man agreed.

"What about me?" Bart asked.

"Check on yer ma and stick close to her."

"If she's all right, I'll lean out the door and wave."

"That's fine. I'll signal if I see anything."

"The owl?" Bart asked.

"Aye. Two hoots in a row—trouble. One hoot—all is well."

He waited until Bart stuck his head out of the door and waved before he rode off at a fast clip toward the trees. He trusted the lad's instincts but needed to get a closer look. Chellenham's men may have set up camp under the cover of the dense trees.

A shot rang out. O'Malley veered sharply to the left as heat from the lead ball grazed his upper arm. He leaned forward as if he'd been hit and rode like the devil, galloping toward the Mayfields' barn.

Tremayne returned fire as O'Malley thundered past him.

The lone rider chasing O'Malley reined in his mount and rode back to the cover of the trees.

O'Malley reined in his horse and jumped off—rifle in hand— to run back to the cover of the barn. Rifle trained on the retreating horseman, he ignored the annoying pain in his upper arm and the warmth of the blood trickling from the wound.

"How many did you see?" Tremayne asked.

"Blackguard shot at me before I could get close enough."

Tremayne did not move from his vantage point. "Any chance of the patrol swinging by in the next hour or so?"

"Aye. The lads from the village are due by shortly."

"Behind you!" Tremayne swung around at the faint sound of footfalls approaching.

"Don't shoot!"

"Bart? I thought I told you to stick by yer ma," O'Malley said.

"She sent me outside to check on you. We heard the shot and your horse galloping like the hounds of hell were nipping at your heels."

"Close enough, lad. The man who shot at me nearly hit me."

"Mum will be happy that she won't have to use her needle and thread on you tonight."

O'Malley hesitated. "I didn't say that."

"He hit you?" Bart's voice cracked, and he suddenly sounded all of his four and ten years.

"Winged me, lad. Not to worry."

"Are you bleeding?"

"Just a wee bit."

"Mum will have my head if I don't let her know you've been shot so she can take care of your wound."

"Winged," O'Malley corrected him. "Not shot. No pistol ball in me arm. Just took a bit of me jacket and meself with it."

"No sign of movement," Tremayne said. "Why don't you have Mrs. Mayfield take a look at your arm? Bart will stand watch with me. Eh, Bart?"

"Aye, lieutenant!" the lad replied, shouldering the gun he held.

"We'll alert the patrol to what happened," Tremayne said, "if you are not back in position by the time they arrive."

"I won't be a moment," O'Malley promised.

He ran from shadow to shadow to the cottage and rapped on the door twice.

"'Tis me, Harry. Let me in!"

The door swung open. Harry grabbed him by the cravat, yanked him inside, and pulled him toward the table. "Here. Sit. Where did you get shot?"

"Nowhere," he replied.

"Then why are you here?"

"Bart insisted I let you look at me arm."

"I thought you said you weren't shot."

O'Malley gritted his teeth. "I wasn't shot."

Harry raised one eyebrow in silent question.

"The pistol ball grazed me upper arm."

She'd already pulled the kettle off the heat and poured it into the large bowl she had lined up along with linen squares, a bowl of herbs, and another of threads.

Two low hoots sounded close by. Trouble!

"The lad has yer blunderbuss. Do ye have a pistol?" O'Malley asked.

"Just the blunderbuss." When he didn't move, she urged, "Go! I'll be fine. Don't let them shoot my son!"

O'Malley eased out of the door and ran hunched over toward Tremayne and Bart.

"How many?" he asked when he got there.

"Four," Tremayne replied.

O'Malley drew in a breath and slowly exhaled. This was it, then. They'd have to make a stand here against the latest wave of Chellenham's bloody bastards! "Are they on foot?"

"Aye," Tremayne replied. "Two tall shadows just separated from that stand of trees."

"I saw two more over there." Bart pointed in the opposite direction.

"They're thinking to outflank us," Tremayne murmured. "How fast can you climb up into the loft, Bart?"

"Tree's closer."

"Go, then—we'll cover you."

"Quietly now, lad," O'Malley urged.

Bart shimmied up the base of the tree, grabbed hold of a branch, and pulled himself up and into position. Once there, he heard a faint hoot.

"All's well?" Tremayne asked.

O'Malley nodded. "Aye. He's in position and a crack shot."

A tall shadow separated from the trees and ran toward the barn, yelling, swinging a lantern.

Tremayne took aim and hit the lantern and his target. Both crashed to the ground, unmoving.

Another shadow rushed at them from the other side of the barn. A faint hoot sounded before the echo of Bart's blunderbuss and a scream of pain.

Two men ran toward the barn, lanterns raised above their heads. O'Malley shot one intruder in the wrist. Tremayne shot the other in the hand. Twin screams of agony echoed through the night.

"We'd best be collecting our prisoners," O'Malley said.

Tremayne said, "For a moment I was back on the peninsula and forgot you wanted the men captured alive. You only need to worry about three of them."

O'Malley placed a hand on the other man's shoulder. "Ye'll get no complaint from meself or any of the others. In case I forgot earlier, thank ye for yer service to king and country. We're in yer debt."

Tremayne nodded. "Let's go. I don't want Bart to see the man I shot. Hit him dead center."

"We'll start with the one Bart shot and work our way over to the others. I'll guard yer back in case they have pistols or blades tucked into their pockets."

They doused the patches of dry grass that had ignited from the flaming lanterns with dirt first. Then, one by one, they tied up their prisoners, hauled them over to the corral, and leaned them against the fence.

The sound of hoofbeats drawing closer had O'Malley relaxing. Tremayne swung around, his rifle trained on the approaching horsemen. O'Malley knocked it away. "'Tis our patrol."

"How do you know? I cannot recognize a single horseman."

"The sound of their hoofbeats. I know me horseflesh. Anderson!" O'Malley yelled.

"Aye. Was there trouble?" Anderson replied.

"Ye could say that."

"Where are Bart and his mum?"

"Over here!" Bart called out. "Mum's putting a field dressing on those two over there."

"I didn't want them bleeding all over our wagon," Harry grumbled loudly.

O'Malley sighed. "I already apologized and told ye I'd paint over the stain, Harry."

Tremayne stared at the widow. "Did O'Malley just call you Harry?"

"It's my name," she replied.

Bart chuckled. "It's Father's nickname for you, Mum."

"Ah, is it Harriet, then?" Tremayne asked.

She glanced at O'Malley before answering, "Aye. Harry to my close friends."

The patrol sent two men to the tree line to root out any other intruders. The remainder helped load the bandaged and trussed-up prisoners into the bed of the Mayfields' wagon.

"His lordship needs me report," O'Malley told the patrol. "Thank ye for yer help. I can take it from here."

Harry stepped in front of him. "You'll not set foot off this farm until I see to your arm."

"I thought you did that earlier," Bart said.

"There wasn't time," O'Malley told him.

"You'd better let Mum clean it out. Infection could lead to wound fever," the young man warned.

O'Malley heard the worry in Bart's voice and was about to protest, but he knew the lad would be thinking of the virulent fever that took his father's life. "I can probably spare a few minutes more."

"You'll spare as long as it takes to clean your wound and bind it," Harry said.

Tremayne stared at her with open admiration. "Is she always this forthright?"

O'Malley chuckled. "She's a bossy bit of goods."

Bart leaned close. "Be glad Mum's outside and doesn't have her rolling pin or cast iron pan handy."

O'Malley smiled. "Faith, I grew up dodging the same. Your ma's a woman after me own heart."

"We'll stand watch over the men. Let Mrs. Mayfield see to your arm," Tremayne told him.

"I won't be long," O'Malley assured them for the second time, following Harry inside the cottage.

He only had a moment to react to the closing of the door before finding his arms filled with the curvaceous widow.

"I heard the shots," she mumbled against his chest. "I had to look! I had to see if Bart was injured."

"I gave ye me word to protect him."

She burrowed closer. "When I heard you'd been shot, I couldn't think, couldn't move…couldn't breathe," she whispered.

"'Tis an insignificant nick, lass. Not even a wound."

She pressed her lips to the hollow of O'Malley's throat, and he moaned.

"Ye shouldn't be kissing me like that. I've just been in a fight. Me blood's up, lass, and with it the need to burn off the frustration sizzling through me veins."

"Kiss me, O'Malley."

His lips met hers as fire exploded in his gut and raw need had him by the throat. He plundered her willing lips until she sagged against him.

He ended the kiss abruptly, pulled back, and stared into her eyes. "Ye'd be smart to be afraid of me."

Her wicked laughter had him by the bollocks. "I'm not afraid of you, O'Malley."

He dipped his head and trailed the tip of his tongue along her collarbone, nipping and kissing his way back to her lips. "I could eat ye alive," he rasped. "Ye'd be a banquet I'll never tire of sampling."

"Mum?" Bart called from the other side of the door. "Do you need help with O'Malley?"

Harry's look of horror had O'Malley snickering. "Ye want me to answer for ye?"

"Don't you dare!" she said, tugging him toward the table.

⇒⟫⟩✕⟨⟪⇐

THEY WERE SEATED when Bart opened the door. "Tremayne's offering to hold his arm still for you."

"No thank you, Bart." She hoped her son didn't look beyond what was in front of him—his mother tending to one of the duke's men and O'Malley patiently waiting for her to finish. "It will take me longer to get his frockcoat off," she explained. "The blood dried and is stuck to his wound."

"All right, Mum." Bart's gaze settled on O'Malley, and an unspoken communication seemed to flow from the man to her son. He turned toward her and, with one last look charged with meaning, said, "Let me know if you need our help, Mum."

The door closed quietly behind him.

O'Malley leaned toward her and captured her lips in a succulent kiss. Drawing back, he blew out a breath. "I'd best let ye care for the scratch on me arm." He put the tip of his finger beneath her chin and tilted her head until his gaze captured hers. "Else I'll be barring the door and tossing ye on the bed and making love with ye till our eyes cross." He kissed her again, as if she were delicate...fragile. "Once we do, lass, I'll never let ye go."

# CHAPTER TWENTY-ONE

HARRY'S HEART HAMMERED in her breast. Emotions she'd closed off the day she buried her husband threatened to break free from the tidy little box she'd shoved them into.

As if he knew he'd overstepped his bounds—and that of society—O'Malley fell silent. Watching her. *Waiting.*

Rather than incite him, fanning the flames still flickering between them, she had to douse the fire, calm them both. She owed it to the man who'd stood between an unknown enemy and herself and her son, shielding them as surely as she knew he'd done for the duke and his family.

He'd been honest about his feelings—and his duty to the duke. She would not encourage him to forsake his vow. It would crush that part of him she revered—his integrity. He was so much like the man she married.

Honest and trustworthy.

Brave and strong.

She willed her hands to stop trembling, reached for the sleeve of his frockcoat, and helped him remove it. The jagged tear across the upper arm of his black coat reminded her that it could have just as easily been along the line of his jaw, or across his temple.

Her stomach flipped over at the sight of his blood-soaked sleeve. Her gaze locked with his, and though she tried, she could not conceal her worry.

"'Tisn't as bad as it seems, lass. Trust me, 'tis all bluster," he rumbled. "I've been winged before."

She squared her shoulders, stiffened her spine and her resolve, not willing to show the man she admired, and deeply cared for, any other weakness. He needed her to tend to his wound—not ease the ache of unfulfilled passion between them.

She reached for the cuff of his cambric shirt. It was too snug a fit to roll up his sleeve. Dear God, the power in his arms was a distraction! She swallowed to ease the dryness in her throat.

Silently, she admonished her wayward thoughts. *Ignore the span of his shoulders, the bulging muscles of his biceps! You need to stop the bleeding!*

Thoughts and feelings she dare not give voice to filled her to bursting. Pinpricks of awareness tingled the palms of her hands. His scent—a virile, healthy male with a hint of crushed autumn leaves and evergreens—mingled with the fire in the hearth, surrounding her.

The need to hug him to her breast and never let go no longer shocked her. She no longer denied the attraction—she reveled in it. Drawing in a fortifying breath, she rebuilt the walls of her defenses against this man who'd challenged her on every level. She had to think of Bart and their livelihood—their farm. Her neighbors, and acquaintances from the village, would shun her if she gave in to the overwhelming need to comfort O'Malley with her body…her heart…her soul.

But she wanted him to know…*needed* him to know the battle she'd been waging not to throw herself at him.

His hand brushing her cheek surprised her. "Ye're killing me with the hunger in yer eyes, lass. Later…when we are free to speak of what is in our hearts, we'll have the luxury of time to learn the secret places where the press of questing lips, tip of the tongue, or nip of the teeth, will unlock the shackles ye've had to wrap around yer heart."

The intensity in his glittering green gaze seared through her.

"Ye will trust me with yer body, lass."

She was torn. The need to do as he asked tempted her to toss aside her pride. Was she brave enough to flaunt convention? Could she lay aside her worries to lose herself in the sizzling passion radiating off the man she tended?

"Ye'll know when the time is right. Same as meself. I'll not compromise me vow to make love with ye, though I'd wager me life ye'd be worth losing it to have ye in me arms, if only for one night."

Tears welled in her eyes. She was powerless to hold them back.

"Don't cry, Harry. Not for me."

She wiped her eyes with the backs of her hands. "Let's get this shirt off you, so I can see how deep the wound is."

"Just take a knife to the sleeve and cut it off. Ye'll see well enough then. I don't want to keep Tremayne and Bart waiting."

"I can do that." She slid a sharp knife into his fine lawn shirt, removed the sleeve, and set it on the table. "It's not as deep as I feared."

In a bid to counter the strong pull he had on her, she searched her mind for something, *anything* to talk about that wouldn't have her leaning forward to press her lips to his cheek, his jaw, his beautifully sculpted lips. Bart's worry popped into her mind.

"May I ask you something?"

He wrapped his fingers around her wrist, holding her to him. "Aye."

She let her gaze shift to his hand and then back to his eyes. He understood her silent question and let go. Walking over to the table, she washed her hands thoroughly with a sliver of lye soap. "I'll have to set aside the time to make more—our supply is dwindling."

Confusion marred his handsome face. "Supply?"

She reached for the worn linen cloth to dry her hands. "Sorry, I was thinking aloud. Soap—I need to make more."

"'Tis no small task. I can help ye with that after we apprehend the devil behind these deeds." When she remained silent, he prompted her, "Ye had a question, lass?"

She poured hot water from the kettle into a large bowl, then added the bit of soap until she was satisfied that it would be enough to begin cleansing his wound. After dipping a clean cloth in the soapy water, she gently washed around the wound. "I'll try to be as careful as possible, but this may pain you."

O'Malley grunted as the soap seeped into the raw gouge in his arm. "Ask yer blasted question!"

She bit her lip. Bart's worry had become her own. "Did you have another of your fits tonight? Is that why you were slumped over in your saddle?"

His eyes blazed, though he tempered his words with more patience than she'd given him credit for having. "I do not suffer from fits. Who told ye that lie?"

She dipped the cloth in the second bowl of water to rinse it. When she was satisfied there was no residue or dirt, she immersed it in the soapy water once more. "Bart confided what he'd seen the other night, and your reaction when he asked a similar question. We aren't trying to have you removed from the duke's guard because of this weakness. We want to ensure that more people are aware of your condition so that we can be prepared to aid you in every way possible."

He grabbed hold of her hand and the dripping cloth. Danger rippled off the man in waves. "I do not suffer fits. I do not speak of my..." His voice trailed off, and she suspected he did indeed suffer—greatly.

"Everyone has a weakness they learn to deal with, whether it be poor eyesight, difficulty speaking, mayhap a limb that is shorter than the other. Megrims, tender skin that is easily irritated by—"

He yanked on her arm. She fell against him and was about to struggle to free herself, but there was something in the depths of his eyes that urged her to listen. Whatever he was about to confide would be hard to swallow.

"Tell me, Michael," she urged. "I won't break your confidence or trust by speaking of it to anyone, save Bart. It is for him that I ask. He admires you, has listened to your advice, from sharpening his hunting skills to aiming a rifle from the boughs of a tree."

"'Tis one of the O'Malley curses."

Her eyes widened in shock. "Your family has more than one?"

"Aye. Well, the one 'tisn't a curse—unless the jealous or feeble-minded among us see it as such and paint it that way when they pass it to another over their morning tea."

She placed a hand on his shoulder and eased back. "Bart will be back if I don't finish tending to your injury. Please tell me of these curses."

"Every generation, a new healer is born. One with the gift of sensing pain in another and the knowledge of which herbs and tinctures will ease the pain or cure the malady. A gift that has at times carried a heavy price—even death."

Her mind raced. She could not fathom anyone being sentenced to death for using the gift of healing, but knew those that healed were also called another name—witches. "I am so sorry to hear what must have been a horrific time for your family." With great care, she removed a few singed bits of fabric from his shirt sleeve, and that of his frockcoat from his arm. He winced, and she paused. "I'm sorry to hurt you. There is just a little bit more stuck to the dried blood."

"Do what ye need to. I'm grateful for yer care, lass."

"Who is this generation's healer?"

"Me cousin, Emmett. He's stationed at the duke's town house in London."

Satisfied when the trickle of blood ran true to color—not tainted with black powder, dirt, or foreign objects—she handed him a folded linen bandage. "Press this against your arm for me. I need to fetch a linen strip to hold it in place." As she selected, and discarded, a number of lengths of linen, she asked, "What of the second curse?"

"Just as there is a healer born to every generation of O'Malleys, there is another born with the bloody gift of visions."

She spun around, a length of pale pink linen dangling from the hands clutched to her heart. "Visions? Like Cassandra?"

"Ye studied the ancient Greek pantheon?"

"My father encouraged my mother to teach me to read. He never minded that he had no heir—he saw to it that I was educated as if I had been his son. So do you prophesize events and no one believes you?"

He looked away from her. "'Tis more like the *banshee*—in Gaelic, 'twould be *bean-sidhe*...meaning woman of the faery. Ma was an O'Grady before she married Da. They're one of the five ancient families honored to have a *banshee*—a spirit, sometimes in the flesh—who warns of coming death to the family they serve by wailing."

"Have you sent word to your brothers and cousins? Are you able to see whom the *banshee* is wailing for?"

"Aye...and nay. Me visions don't work that way." He lifted the other end of the linen strip. "'Tis pink."

"And it's clean. It's a serviceable weight of cotton...percale."

"The weight and type of cotton doesn't change the fact that the bloody thing is pink!"

She knew he was distracting her from the sensitive topic they discussed, and she let him. "Are you going to be difficult about the fabric I used to hold the bandage in place? If I don't secure the bandage, you will continue to bleed. What a sight it would be— the great O'Malley succumbing to a scratch, as you put it. Fainting and falling off his horse into Lieutenant Tremayne's arms!"

"Bloody hell, lass. Do yer worst, but mind what ye say."

She couldn't resist one more taunt. "The color brings out the green of your eyes."

O'Malley shot to his feet, wavered for the briefest of moments, then glared at her. His eyes flashed with irritation.

"Let me help you with your frockcoat."

"I'll not be needing it."

"If you're continuing on your patrol, the moonlight will illuminate your shirt beautifully," she reminded him. "If you don't mind being seen…" She let her words hang.

O'Malley wasn't a fool. He knew his temper was preventing him from thinking clearly. He blew out a breath, mumbling. *Probably cursing.* "You're welcome, Michael."

He raised his eyes to the ceiling and sighed—loudly. "Thank ye for tending to the insignificant scratch on me arm, lass."

She beamed at him. "Try not to get shot again tonight. You may not be close enough for me to tend you…but if you are, I have more strips in that lovely shade of pink."

His snort of laughter eased the bit of worry twisting inside of her. "Faith, ye're a treasure, lass. With the extra men, we'll be increasing our patrols. Someone will be by tomorrow. If there's trouble—go to the Clarkes' or the Johnsons'. There's safety in numbers."

"I'll think about it."

"Don't," he warned, "I'll have yer word now that ye'll do as I say."

"O'Malley, I do not need to listen—"

"His lordship trusts that I will do what I think is best for all concerned. I can have ye forcibly removed from yer land until the danger passes, or ye can do as I say. The choice is yers."

"Fine! I will acquiesce this one time."

The door swung open and Bart and Tremayne entered the cottage.

"What's keeping you, O'Malley?" the lieutenant asked. "We need to deliver the prisoners to the manor house, report to this lordship, and continue on our rounds."

"Just leaving instructions with Mrs. Mayfield."

The laughter in Tremayne's voice hinted that he'd overheard the last bit of their conversation. "Excellent. The safety of *all* of the viscount's tenants is paramount."

Bart pointed to the frockcoat draped over the back of a chair.

"Need help with your coat?"

"Nay, lad. I've got it." O'Malley struggled but managed to pull it on. "Send word if there's trouble—after yer ma and yerself have sought refuge at the Clarkes' or the Johnsons'."

"You have my word, O'Malley," Bart replied.

"That's fine, then, lad. The patrol will be by again in a few hours."

"Mum and I are indebted to you both."

"'Tis part of the job, lad."

Harry watched Bart lead the men outside, accepting the fact that although O'Malley may not realize it, he did not leave empty-handed—she'd willingly given him her heart.

# CHAPTER TWENTY-TWO

TREMAYNE SHOOK HIS head. "Why did you not demand the men tell you who sent them?"

O'Malley watched until the constable and his men drove the borrowed wagonload of thugs around the bend in the road that led to the village. He didn't have time for explanations and didn't feel he owed one to the lieutenant. Earl Lippincott's carriage was due at any time, and with it, a world of chaos.

He glared at the lieutenant in answer.

"The viscount or the duke may have to put up with your arrogant attitude, O'Malley, but I do not. I demand you answer my question!"

O'Malley spun around. "Garahan and I already know who is behind this latest attack! This is the third wave of men who have struck at the viscount's tenant farmers, shooting at them, destroying their crops, and torching their barns. 'Tis but one man with twisted notions of revenge against the viscount. I do not have the time to give you the reasons why. You'll just bloody well have to trust me!"

Tremayne raised one eyebrow as if to question O'Malley's conclusion.

O'Malley's temper simmered. The sound of more than one carriage approaching had him drawing in a deep breath and tamping down his anger—and the need to punch the smug former dragoon in the face.

"That'll be Earl Lippincott, Lady Aurelia, and their babe."

"If they only live a few miles away," Tremayne said, following O'Malley around to the front of the manor house, "why do they need so many carriages? Do they expect this attack to turn into a siege?"

"Why don't ye ask his lordship? I'm sure the earl would love to chat with ye while his wife and infant son are in firing range from a sharpshooter!"

Tremayne's stony expression pleased O'Malley no end. He'd hit a nerve. The man did not flinch, but there was a trace of anger in his eyes.

When the lieutenant remained silent, O'Malley said, "We can settle this later, in the far outbuilding. Me cousin and I keep our bare-knuckle skills sharp by practicing on one another."

"Name the time," Tremayne rasped. "I'll be there."

The viscount and Captain Coventry noted their approach, while Hargrave and a half-dozen footmen waited for the occupants of the caravan of carriages to disembark.

The carriages slowed as they approached the front steps. O'Malley stared at the coat of arms on the third carriage. "Bloody hell!"

"Problem, O'Malley?" Tremayne asked.

"'Tis Lady Aurelia's uncle, Lord Coddington."

"If he's family, what is the issue?"

"Coddington challenged Chellenham to a duel—I'll fill in the particulars as to why later. Chellenham cheated. The viscount leapt onto the field, taking the bullet aimed at Coddington's back."

"Chellenham?"

O'Malley noted the lieutenant's rigid posture, the tightening of his jaw, the intensity of his gaze, and approved of the man's anger. It was appreciated.

"He's the bloody bastard behind these attacks," Tremayne said.

"Aye. Now move yer *arse*, Tremayne. 'Tis me duty—and for the moment yers—to protect the duke's brother and his family."

Bayfield joined the viscount and Captain Coventry. O'Malley observed Bayfield moved to stand on the captain's blind side to protect him.

O'Malley scanned the perimeter, knowing Tremayne and Coventry would be doing the same. Satisfied there was no imminent threat, he turned to observe Hargrave and the footmen standing at the ready to assist the occupants of the caravan in disembarking. Mrs. Meadowsweet and a trio of maids waited behind them.

O'Malley overheard the viscount murmur, "Bloody hell, what's Coddington doing here? Chellenham will have even more reason to launch a full-scale attack when he gets wind that his nemesis is here at Chattsworth Manor."

Coventry said, "If I were you, I'd be more concerned that Chellenham's men lie in wait with their rifles trained on your back."

The viscount nodded toward the first carriage. "Pardon me while I greet my cousin and Lady Aurelia."

O'Malley knew the viscount would not respond. Lady Calliope had cautioned him not to speak of the threats while the earl and his family were guests in their home. Additional duties and patrols had been discussed and assigned. Though he and Garahan balked at not heading up one of the patrols, they understood the viscount's—and the earl's—need to have them as the last circle of defense protecting their families.

O'Malley's gut churned as his mind tallied the similarities and differences between Chellenham and Hollingford. Chellenham was more predictable than Hollingford had been, while the filth he hired from the docks was just as lawless and cruel as those Hollingford had hired.

Both peers were outspoken, prone to wagering falsehoods against the good name of ladies and gentlemen of the *ton* without discretion.

Hollingford had set his sights on the Duke of Wyndmere, his duchess, and family, whereas Chellenham's sights were set on Coddington, Chattsworth, Lippincott, and their families—*as well as* the Duke of Wyndmere and his family.

As before, there were sixteen men ready to defend those targeted by a madman—though only five of them were elite members of the duke's personal guard. O'Malley would feel more confident if his other brothers and the rest of his cousins were standing beside him, ready to face down the bloody bugger.

If only there was time to assemble the rest of the duke's guard... But time, distance, and the urgent need to protect the duke and his estates were against them.

O'Malley's brother, Sean, dismounted and handed the reins to the waiting stable hand. He nodded to a footman, who assisted a petite, heavily pregnant woman from the carriage, then waited for the servant to step aside before he slipped his arm around her back, supporting her.

O'Malley grinned at the smile on his brother's face and the look of adoration the woman returned. The pair were well matched.

"Who is the petite beauty with the blue-black hair married to?" Tremayne asked.

The couple slowly approached them. "Me brother, Sean," O'Malley replied.

"Do they live at Lippincott Manor?"

"Aye. Given the threats, I would not take the chance and leave her behind either."

"I should say not. Are many of the duke's guard married?" Tremayne leveled his questioning gaze on O'Malley. "I would think that would hinder their ability to carry out their duties for the duke."

"Just two—the eldest of both branches of the O'Malley clan." O'Malley grinned as the couple paused beside him. "Sean, I'd like ye to meet Lieutenant Gryffyn Tremayne."

Sean extended his free hand, smiling. "Yer reputation proceeds ye, Tremayne. May I introduce me wife, Mignonette."

The lieutenant bowed. "Mrs. O'Malley, a pleasure to meet you."

Her warm brown eyes studied him for a moment before her smile bloomed, "And you, lieutenant."

O'Malley was not surprised his sister-in-law did not show any reaction to Tremayne's scar. Mignonette had bravely nursed his brother when Sean was badly injured—dug in, refusing to leave his side when he faced the possibility of losing his arm.

Her face paled, and Tremayne said, "You must be exhausted, Mrs. O'Malley. Please do not linger on my account."

"I do tire more quickly as of late. It is the motion of the carriage—" She paused, blinked, and seemed to wilt before their eyes.

Sean swept her off her feet. "Easy, lass. Allow me to escort ye inside."

O'Malley watched his brother stride purposefully toward the open door. If his brother could marry—and from the looks of it, happily juggle his position within the duke's guard with a wife and a babe on the way—then mayhap *he* could too.

He scanned the perimeter again. The servants were the last to emerge from the carriages and would be shown to their temporary quarters. Trunks were offloaded, and the remainder of the guard handed their mounts off to the stable master and his hands.

Tremayne stared after the couple. "Your brother is a lucky man. Like Mrs. Mayfield, Mrs. O'Malley was not offended by the livid scar on my face."

O'Malley's gut clenched at the mention of Harry's name, but he ignored it. "Ye'll find those connected with the duke and his family are grateful for those who've fought for the Crown. Even more so those that protect them from blackguards who would seek to harm them. Though I cannot say the same for the high-flyers of society, ye'll be treated with the respect ye deserve here at Chattsworth Manor."

"It will be a welcome change."

Earl Lippincott, Lady Aurelia, and the bundle in her arms slowly approached. "O'Malley, good to see you again," the earl said.

"'Tis a pleasure, yer lordship, Lady Aurelia, and Master Edward."

Lady Aurelia beamed at him. "Isn't he a beautiful babe?"

"Aye, that he is, yer ladyship." O'Malley lowered his voice to confide to the earl, "'Tis good that ye've arrived. We had another *visit* last night."

"Chattsworth sent word," the earl replied. "And is the reason we arrived before tea."

"Yerself and yer family are in good hands, yer lordship. We'll guard ye with our lives."

"We count on it, O'Malley." Turning to the man by his side, the earl addressed the other man. "Tremayne, thank you for joining Coventry and the rest of the men."

"It's an honor, your lordship."

Lady Aurelia lifted her gaze from the babe in her arms long enough to meet Tremayne's gaze and softly smile. "Thank you for your service to the Crown, lieutenant, and thank you for coming here to protect our son and our extended family."

Tremayne bowed gallantly. "It is my pleasure, your ladyship."

"If you'll excuse us," the earl said, "I do believe the viscount just chased his wife back inside."

"My cousin-in-law has much to learn about women," Lady Aurelia murmured. "We'd best hurry, Edward, else William may end up spending then night sleeping in an armchair in his study."

O'Malley did not say a word. Knowing Lady Calliope, she would stand her ground and win! She'd been at Wyndmere Hall when it was under attack. Her Grace had bravely rallied the women around her. Along with the duchess, ladies Phoebe, Aurelia, and Calliope were divided into shifts. The housekeeper had the ladies cut linen into strips and squares of varying sizes. Then they would sort them and refill essential supplies to care for the injured. The cook had them constantly chopping and stirring huge pots of stew and soup, and making batches of scones, biscuits, and bread to keep the men fed.

Someone would have to enlighten the viscount as to just what his countess was capable of handling. O'Malley would prefer if it was not himself, but would if no one else volunteered.

As the earl and his wife were greeted on the steps by the viscount's butler and housekeeper and escorted inside, O'Malley heard a deep voice behind him. "Michael!"

He turned and grinned. "Dermott, I'd like to introduce ye to Lieutenant—"

"Tremayne," his cousin said. "I've been waiting to meet ye, as Coventry's sung yer praises."

O'Malley wondered how his brother and cousin knew of Tremayne as he finished the introduction, "Me cousin, Dermott O'Malley."

Tremayne chuckled. "Captain Coventry can be overly effusive in his praise. The pleasure is mine. It is an honor to work with the duke's guard. Coventry has spoken highly of you as well."

"Coventry's the best of men," Garahan announced, striding toward them. "Tremayne, meet me brother, Aiden."

The lieutenant turned to greet them. "O'Malley's informed me the rest of His Grace's personal guard are not available."

"Aye," Garahan said. "Four of our kin guard Their Graces and their twins at Wyndmere Hall. Three guard His Grace's sister and her husband at their estate on the Borderlands."

"Two each are stationed at the duke's London town house, and Penwith Tower on the coast of Cornwall," O'Malley added.

"It must be a logistical challenge to keep track of everyone," Tremayne said.

"Proof of that is the latest one, removing the married members of the guard from the quarterly rotation among the duke's family's estates," Coventry informed him as he joined the men.

"By now, we've all spent time at His Grace's estates,"

O'Malley said.

"'Tis Baron Summerfield's estate, Summerfield Chase, the most recent addition to our rotation that not all of us have had the opportunity to guard," Garahan added.

"In the next rotation, I'll be guarding the baron and Lady Phoebe," Aiden said. "Looking forward to it. Beautiful country, the borderlands."

O'Malley signaled to Garahan. "Men, we have the next few days' assignments to hand out."

"Rather than have the rest of our contingent meet us in front of the house, they're waiting by the stables. If ye'd follow me," Garahan said.

The men were assembled standing at attention, waiting for Garahan and O'Malley.

"Hartman, are yer men ready?" O'Malley asked.

"Aye, O'Malley."

"Kent, are yers?" Garahan asked.

"Aye, Garahan."

Introductions were made as the men were divided into four groups. "The viscount has requested that Garahan and meself protect the inside perimeter, but there's been a change since they arrived," O'Malley explained. "Me brother will be taking me place, and I'll take his on the outside perimeter."

"Why the change?" Dermott asked.

"The earl suggested that with Sean's wife just a few months away from delivering, his concentration may be divided unless they are under the same roof."

"Ah," Aiden murmured. "Wise decision."

"We'll be changing out two men constantly so that we have a constant exchange of vital information regarding our patrols," O'Malley continued.

"That way, no one will be leaving their post for more than the time it takes to change positions," Garahan added.

O'Malley cleared his throat to get everyone's attention. "The patrols are as follows: first patrol—under meself—will be responsible for the outside perimeter. Deacon, Ryerson, and Tremayne, that will be yer assignment.

"Second patrol—under Dermott O'Malley—will be responsible for the tenant farms to the north. Hartman, Flanders, and Gilbey.

"Third patrol—under Aiden Garahan—will be responsible for the tenant farms to the south. Hornsby, Kent, and Gordon.

"And the fourth patrol—under Captain Coventry—will be responsible for the road to the village. Sweeney, Anderson, and Bayfield."

"We'll meet in shifts when we can, but as of this moment, consider these yer assignments until informed otherwise," Garahan said. "We've arranged for able-bodied stable hands and under-gardeners to take four-hour shifts at a time, to allow ye men to sleep."

A deep rumbling had O'Malley smiling at the youngest of their recruits—Ryerson. "Ye forgot to mention when the men can expect to be fed."

Garahan chuckled. "We aren't after starving ye men. Food will be delivered to various checkpoints along the way."

"Checkpoints?" Ryerson asked.

"Aye," O'Malley replied. "For those patrolling the farms to the north and the south, three meals a day will be delivered to one of the farms on yer route."

Ryerson's stomach growled again, and Garahan shook his head. "Don't worry, lad, we'll feed ye."

"I wasn't worried," Ryerson replied.

"Nay," Kent said, "but your gurgling guts are!"

"What of the rest of the patrols?" Anderson asked.

"We have a footman designated to deliver food to those on the outside perimeter patrol," O'Malley replied.

"And the men on my patrol?" Coventry asked.

"That was actually the easiest to arrange with the inn in the village. Three meals, lads," O'Malley said.

"Any questions?" Garahan asked the group.

"We may have our own weapons, but only have a small supply of lead balls at the ready," Kent informed them.

"The viscount and the earl have had men assigned to the task of melting the lead and using molds in different sizes to create the variety of lead balls ye men require," O'Malley said.

"And powder?" Flanders asked.

"Aye. Not to worry, lads; ye'll not be expected to wield yer rifles like a club—though if it comes down to that"—Garahan's gaze swept across the men—"we know ye'll rise to the challenge and do whatever it takes to protect *everyone* under their lordships' care and that of the duke."

"Which in turn protects those in the village, should the attackers decide to draw attention away from their primary target—Chattsworth Manor," O'Malley added.

Tremayne locked gazes with O'Malley. "A sound plan of action."

Relieved that the former dragoon approved of the plans they'd gone over in detail, Garahan asked, "Any further questions or worries?"

"Will whoever is responsible for providing our meals have hay and oats available for our horses?"

Garahan grinned. "Excellent question, Anderson. Aye, they will, along with a fresh supply of water."

Anderson looked relieved.

"For those of ye without yer own mounts," O'Malley announced, "horses will be provided to ye."

"Thank ye all for volunteering to be a part of the duke's guard," Garahan said. "We need each and every one of ye to be ready for the onslaught O'Malley, Coventry, and I believe is but a few hours away."

"One last thing, men," Coventry said. "Raise your right hands." The group complied. "Swear that you will protect the duke, his family, and extended family with integrity and honesty. You are both shield and weapon. Guard them with every weapon in your arsenal—no matter the cost to you."

O'Malley noted with pride that every man's expression blazed with conviction as the group chorused, "I swear!"

"We've a fine bunch of raw recruits," Garahan declared.

"I've a feeling they won't be raw come morning," O'Malley said.

He had no idea how prophetic his words would be.

# CHAPTER TWENTY-THREE

Harry was not surprised when one of the viscount's stable hands approached their farm with their wagon. O'Malley had told her the duke's guard would be busy with patrols. Rumors of a large-scale attack swept through the neighboring farms.

Worry eroded her confidence in the man she loved.

*Loved?*

Was she mad? O'Malley's position within the duke's guard put him in harm's way daily. Unscrupulous knaves constantly launched verbal and physical attacks against the duke and his family. Like the knights of old, he would fight to the death to protect his liege lord.

Instead of giving her heart to him, she should have guarded her heart more fiercely! Bart delighted in each and every tale of bravery, with details of each and every injury O'Malley and Garahan had received since swearing allegiance to the duke—never once realizing each tale scored another slash to her heart.

Given the number of attacks they'd rallied against, and that of the farms to the south of the manor house, her heart would be in shreds in a fortnight. There was no protecting what she no longer guarded. She'd given it freely with each searching gaze, each protestation that she did not need his help. Lord help her, each time he held her to his heart, every press of his lips, battered against her defenses until she'd been helpless to resist.

Fear's razor-sharp talons tore through her hard-won composure. Bowing her head, she prayed the rumored attack would be the last. If not, she had no idea how she would survive another onslaught.

⤜⟫⟫⟫⟪⟪⟪⤛

"WILLIAM HAS ABSOLUTELY no idea how capable I am," Calliope protested as she settled her babe in his cradle. "He keeps me wrapped so tightly with cotton batting in his bid to protect me, I could scream!"

Aurelia smiled. "Edward and I had quite the discussion—"

Calliope's eyes lit with amusement. "Argument?"

"Call it what you will," Aurelia said, "the fact remains, I had to remind him of what he wishes to forget."

"Oh, and what might that be?" Calliope asked.

"You know very well." Aurelia frowned. "Persephone, Phoebe, you, and I were instrumental in keeping the men who fought to protect us fed and patched up!"

"Has he admitted to anyone that you're a crack shot?" Calliope asked.

Aurelia tucked her son in the cradle opposite Calliope's son. "Not that I know of. I plan to have Uncle Phineas remind Edward of that fact, if I could get Uncle alone for more than five moments at a time."

"Has Edward confided what they have been discussing behind closed doors?"

Aurelia blew out a frustrated breath. "Not even a hint."

"It must have to do with our situation here," Calliope said.

"Or the contents of the latest intelligence from Mr. King."

"I would venture to say both are distinct possibilities." Calliope worried her lip. "The problem remains, how will we convince our husbands to confide what they know?"

"I have one or two suggestions, my love."

Calliope swung around. "How long have you been listening to our private conversation, William?"

"Long enough." The viscount brushed a lock of hair from her cheek. "You will cease worrying about that over which you have no control."

"You as well, Aurelia," Edward said from where he stood in the doorway to the nursery. "We'll not have either of you involved."

"But we can help!" Calliope protested.

William's face lost all expression as he closed the distance between them. "Our babe's life depends upon your doing exactly as I say." When she did not respond, he pulled her into the shelter of his embrace and repeated, "Our babe's life depends on you...as does mine."

Edward stepped around the couple to where his wife stood between the cradles. "Would you jeopardize our son's life to satisfy your pride?"

Aurelia lifted her chin and asked, "Would you?"

"As Edward's mother, you are more important at this stage of his life."

"You are, too," Aurelia said.

Edward pulled her close and rasped, "You feed him. I cannot."

"A wet nurse could—"

"Enough! This discussion is over. We have discussed the imminent danger to you and Calliope—and our sons."

"Aye," William agreed. "Neither one of you will set foot outside the manor house until the culprits currently swarming toward us have been captured and escorted by the constable to London."

Calliope's gaze locked with William's. "Will we?"

"I have taught Calliope to handle a pistol. She's as adept at handling one as I," Aurelia boasted.

"The two of you are more than welcome to set up broken

crockery on the herb garden wall for target practice—when this is all over," Edward told her.

William's eyes bored into his wife's. "Edward and I have been discussing a number of prizes suitable for obliterating Mrs. Romney's cast-off crockery."

"Your lordship," Hargrave intoned from the open doorway. "An urgent missive just arrived."

The viscount's gaze hardened. "Written?"

"Messenger?" the earl asked.

"A messenger is waiting to speak to you by the stables."

The viscount pressed his lips to his wife's forehead. "Stay inside, Calliope. My heart cannot take the worry that you would seek out danger, when you could be protected."

She met his concerned gaze and sighed. "Until you return to share the news."

The earl lifted his wife's hand to his lips. "Stay here, Aurelia. William and I have spent an inordinate amount of time shoring up our defenses."

Aurelia glanced at her friend before agreeing, "If you promise to share whatever news the messenger brings."

The butler cleared his throat. "Your lordship?"

"Coming!" the viscount replied.

"Behave!" Edward warned Aurelia.

With the departure of the men, Calliope slowly smiled. "Well, that went far better than we anticipated, don't you agree?"

Aurelia's soft laughter lightened the forbidding gloom their husbands had left behind with their unnecessary warnings.

"I'll ring for Mrs. Meadowsweet," Calliope said. "She'll know who the messenger is if he's from the village."

"Better yet, ask for Mary Kate," Aurelia suggested. "Your maid has been a godsend as far as bringing bits and pieces of gossip and helping us put them together."

"Which would not be necessary—" Calliope began.

"If our husbands were more forthcoming with news," Aurelia finished. "Jenny, too, has been helpful. Our maids will have a very clear picture of what is happening by now."

"I'll include our request for a tea tray," Calliope said. "We may as well fortify ourselves while we wait."

"Excellent notion. I shall ask Uncle Phineas to take tea with us—in the upstairs sitting room. He's not as comfortable in the nursery."

A few hours later, Lady Calliope and Lady Aurelia had digested the urgent news and sought the advice of Lord Coddington. He was more inclined to listen to their ideas than their husbands had been, but agreed that they should not leave the protection of the manor house for any reason. He urged them to meet with the housekeeper and the cook to begin preparing for war!

# CHAPTER TWENTY-FOUR

O'MALLEY AND THE rest of his men patrolled as planned. Word went out to the other patrols to do the same. None of the men in the temporarily assembled guard were to show any sign that they were braced for the attack they knew was coming.

If there were eyes and ears watching and waiting to see if the duke's guard acted as if they were on edge, they were doomed to disappointment. Not one of the men would show hesitation. No one would show apprehension that may reside side by side with their unflagging courage.

The duke, with the help of Captain Coventry, had chosen his men wisely. They in turn chose from within the rank and file at whichever of the duke's homes—or family's homes—they protected as necessary.

Word had reached Coventry by special messenger half an hour ago—Chellenham's band of cutthroats were approaching from the south. It was the least expected route, and therefore the one O'Malley and Tremayne had wagered would see the first wave of attacks.

O'Malley was torn—the Mayfield farm was to the south of Chattsworth Manor and in direct line of attack. Mayhap because of the failed attempts to decimate the farm, intelligence indicated their farm would be the first point of impact.

Dear God, he wanted to be standing beside the brave woman

who'd captured his heart from the first time she'd stood toe to toe arguing with him. He could not change their carefully orchestrated plans because of his heart. Like a dutiful soldier, he would do his part, thereby bringing a swift but forceful end to Chellenham's treachery.

Tremayne urged his horse to ride up alongside O'Malley. "Garahan assures me his brother is more than capable of leading his recruits into the fray. The devious peer will not succeed in his first bid to destroy the foundation of his lordship's estate—his tenant farms."

O'Malley spared him a glance but did not speak. His voice would give away the emotions clawing through him—as if the devil himself whispered in his ear, demanding he abandon his post as head of the perimeter patrol.

"Aiden Garahan's patrol will not let harm befall the Mayfields or their neighbors," Tremayne continued. "Coventry ordered one man from each of the other three patrols to assist the patrol guarding the farms to the south."

Unease slithered from the base of O'Malley's spine to the nape of his neck. Icy chills threatened, but he controlled them. Tremayne had fought in the King's Dragoons. He was as adept at planning campaigns as he was carrying out those plans, and O'Malley would put his trust in him.

"We've sharpshooters and weapons enough to protect the viscount and the earl and their families. 'Tis the ones on the farms…" O'Malley began. "They're not trained to defend against what they've been battling. The recruits in the guard have either been trained by their sires to hunt or are those who've retired from service to His Majesty, such as yerself."

"Time to clear your mind of everything save one fact—*we* are responsible for the lives of those within the walls of Chattsworth Manor," Tremayne said. "The viscount and his family, the earl and his family, and every man and woman serving on the viscount's staff."

"Don't be forgetting the four-legged ones," O'Malley reminded him.

Tremayne ran a hand along his mount's neck. "A dragoon never forgets the partner who carries him bravely into battle."

The men were nearing the manor house when they heard the sound of pounding hooves—a horse at full gallop. O'Malley held up his hand for his men to hold their positions. He intercepted the rider. "State yer business!"

The messenger pulled to a stop and stared at the men. "I'm a special messenger from London."

"Delivering a missive to Viscount Chattsworth?"

The young man nodded.

Tremayne asked, "From Gavin King?"

Again, the young man nodded.

"And ye've an urgent reply to deliver to King?" O'Malley asked.

"I need to keep moving," the messenger said.

The determined gaze pleased O'Malley. "Watch yer back," he warned. Then watched as the messenger rode away.

O'Malley and Tremayne paused at a hail from Garahan, who rode out to intercept them. "Ten men from the dregs of the underworld should have reached the southern tenant farms by now."

"'Tis old news, cousin," O'Malley replied.

"Ten from the docks will be lying in wait until the dregs arrive after they destroy the tenant farms to the south—twenty in all will storm the manor house!"

"King's messenger told you this?"

"Aye. Their lordships have asked that ye station yer men strategically as Tremayne suggested, should it come to this."

Tremayne's eyes narrowed as he surveyed their surroundings. "Time to move."

"Does King suspect any others will be joining Chellenham?" O'Malley asked.

"Nay," Garahan replied. "Chellenham, the bloody bugger, has boasted—and wagered heavily—that his band of thugs will triumph, taking Chattsworth Manor and holding the viscount and his family prisoners."

"Then he has not heard that Coddington and the earl are sequestered here," Tremayne said.

Garahan agreed.

O'Malley wasn't about to challenge the plans in place, but had to ask, "Has the viscount sent messengers to Dermott O'Malley and Coventry?"

"Aye," Garahan replied. "The viscount and the earl expect the reinforcements to head directly to their assigned positions.

O'Malley sent up a quick prayer to his Maker to protect Harry and her son until he could get to them.

It was going to be a long night.

⟫⟨⟨

CALLIOPE RUSHED INTO the kitchen. "My sweet little William has been changed and fed. Put me to work. I'm yours to command until Mary Kate sends word that he's awake and hungry again."

Aurelia looked up from the stack of linens she'd been sorting. "Is my son still asleep?"

"Aye, knock on wood," Calliope said, laughing when Aurelia complied.

"Why don't you take over for me sorting and preparing bandages? Mrs. Romney, are there any more vegetables to chop?"

The cook pointed to a large bowl. "Please start with those, your ladyship. Once those have been added to the meat mixture, we can start rolling out the dough I've prepared for the meat pies."

"Won't that be time-consuming to slice and serve half a dozen pies?" Calliope asked.

Mrs. Romney smiled. "Aye, which is why we'll be making ones to fit in a man's grasp."

Calliope beamed at her cook. "What a wonderful notion!"

Aurelia paused in her chopping to ask, "Could we do the same with a fruit filling? That way the men would get a boost from the sweet after they fill their bellies with the savory pies." Tears welled in Calliope's eyes, and her friend was quick to admonish her, "No time for that now. We can cry buckets later—just as we did after the duke and his men put an end to that blackguard Hollingford's attack."

"We did, didn't we?" Calliope asked.

"Much to the dismay of the men defending His Grace," Aurelia added.

The sound of several shots fired nearby had Hargrave rushing into the kitchen and putting his back to the door. "Your ladyships, I have the strictest orders from their lordships to see that you do not leave this sanctuary!"

The grim tone of the butler's voice and his dramatic pose—spread-eagle against the back door—had the women setting aside their worry over the shots they'd heard, grumbling to the butler.

"We already promised, Hargrave," Calliope reminded him.

"I gave my word," Aurelia added.

"I am here to see that you keep your promise, Lady Calliope," Hargrave said. "And to see to it that you keep your word, Lady Aurelia."

The women shared a telling glance before going back to their assigned tasks. Once Hargrave ascertained that they would indeed keep their word, he relaxed his stance and said, "I need to relay your assurances to their lordships, but I will return."

More shots echoed—closer this time. Calliope's hands shook, but she dutifully finished folding and stacking the bandages, checked to see if the pot of threads had come to a boil, and gathered her supply of tinctures and salves. "That's done," she murmured. "Do you think any of the duke's guard have been injured?"

Mrs. Romney must have detected the fear in her voice. "We shall be ready if anyone has been. Right now, I'll need you to roll out more dough for the fruit hand pies for the men, your ladyship."

Another task was just what Calliope needed to keep her hands busy.

"Do not fret, your ladyship—you'll curdle your milk."

Calliope's mouth hung open at the cook's warning. Looking to Aurelia, who nodded, she turned back to the cook. "Have you ever known that to happen?"

"Aye, to my cousin. Her husband had to send word to the local midwife, asking for a wet nurse."

Calliope silently began a litany of prayers to not let her fears overwhelm her so that she could continue to serve wherever she was needed in between feeding her babe. A soothing calm filled her as her prayers were answered.

$$\diamond$$

# CHAPTER TWENTY-FIVE

HARRY STARED AT the people crammed into their cottage. Robert, Cynthia, and Robbie Johnson. Ethan, Mary, and Matthew Clarke, and Bart. "We have more weapons than windows to fire them from."

Bart grinned. "We could take turns. One person shoots, steps aside to reload, while the second person is shooting."

Robert and Ethan were in agreement, but she wasn't sure it would be their best defense. "We don't for certain know which direction to expect the attack from. To the west would be the easier route because of the open fields leading up to our farm. The east has more wooded area—and places to hide—but to reach them, our attackers would be within our sights long enough for us to gain the upper hand."

"I had no idea you had a head for strategic planning," Mary remarked.

"Did your husband teach you of such things?" Cynthia asked.

Harry didn't have time for explanations, so she ignored the question. They had to be in position, and she still had to decide how to protect their livestock. "I don't know what to do with our milk cow, our chickens—what of our plow horse? They could be in the line of fire. I don't want any harm to come to them. What did you do with your livestock?" she asked Robert.

"We set the chickens loose before we came here. They'll be

more interested in hunting up what few bugs they can find this time of year."

"And your cow?" Harry asked.

"I had Robbie shepherd her into the woods. Our horses are hitched to our wagons. Ethan and I drove them over to the tree line. They're hidden from view," Robert told her.

She didn't like the thought of the attackers coming upon their defenseless cow, but what other option did she have? If the cow was in the barn, the attackers may set it on fire with the cow inside!

Worry consumed her. Would there be enough time to have Bart take their cow to the woods as well?

Mary grabbed hold of her arm, jolting Harry back to the present and their situation. "Harry, did you hear what Ethan suggested?"

"Nay. I'm sorry, I was wondering if there's time to hide our cow in the woods, too."

Ethan's brow was furrowed. He must have been mulling it over. "All we know is that attack is imminent. Given that the attackers have set fire to more than one barn, we should remain here in the cottage, using Bart's suggestion. Let your chickens loose."

"What about our cow and plow horse?"

"Turn them out of the barn, point them toward the tree line, and slap their flanks to get them moving toward the shelter of the woods."

"We're out of time, Mum," Bart said. "I think we should do as Mr. Clarke suggests."

"Should we wait for the duke's patrol?" Cynthia asked.

"They said they're making the loop of his lordship's farms near us," Mary added.

"I don't think we should wait. Do you, Robert?" Harry asked.

"Nay."

"Ethan?"

"Nay."

"Then we make our stand here and now! Ladies, help me set out the lead balls and extra powder you brought with you. We'll need to have ready access to both once the shooting starts."

"What about a lookout, Mrs. Mayfield?" Robbie asked.

"You've got the perfect tree by your barn," Matthew added.

"No one knew I was there until I fired Father's blunderbuss," Bart said with pride.

"A sound notion, Robbie," Robert said.

"Who'll volunteer?" Ethan asked.

"I will!" Bart said. "I'll turn out the cow and our horse and climb the tree and wait."

"Bart, I—"

"I can do this, Mum. Trust me."

She pulled him into a hard hug. "Take the blunderbuss and ammunition with you."

His grin was infectious. "I won't need it. O'Malley had his cousin deliver two rifles and ammunition early this morning."

"They dropped off rifles to us as well," Ethan said.

"We're ready for a siege, Harry," Robert told her.

"Well then, let's get started," Harry said. "Bart, wait!"

Her son paused with his hand on the edge of the open door. "Mum?"

"Use the signal O'Malley taught you to let us know you are in position in the tree."

"One hoot, I'm in the tree," he told those gathered. "Two hoots, I've spotted the attackers."

"Be safe!"

"Always, Mum," Bart answered.

"Mary, Cynthia, is everything in order?"

"Aye, Harry," Mary replied.

"I think we should have the powder and lead balls within reach," Robert suggested.

Harry readily agreed.

"Ethan, how's your shoulder?" Robert asked. "Will it stand up to the recoil?"

"I'll let you know when it starts to affect my aim," Ethan replied.

"Ladies, please distribute the powder and ammunition between Ethan and me."

"What about us?" Robbie asked.

"We're here to help," Matthew said.

"You two are responsible for loading the weapons we hand off to you," Harry said. "With the additional rifles and ammunition supplied by the duke's guard, we will have more than enough to keep up a constant barrage of fire."

"I'll wager the thugs from London won't be expecting any resistance," Ethan murmured.

She was helping to dole out the ammunition when a thought occurred to her. "We could use our wagon as a decoy," she suggested. "If we push it over on its side, the attackers may think we are behind it and waste a lot of lead balls shooting it."

Robert grinned at her. "That is a good idea. Away from the cottage and the tree."

"Aye."

"What of the possible damage to your wagon?" Cynthia asked.

"That is the least of my concerns right now," Harry said.

A low hoot sounded, and she breathed a sigh of relief. Bart had taken care of the animals and climbed into position.

"Never mind the wagon. Everyone ready?"

The answering chorus of ayes filled her with relief. They were stronger together. They would defend their farms and their families. The duke's guard would be on hand to help, but if the attack came before the guard returned, the Johnsons, Clarkes, and Mayfields would stand their ground.

Harry would not give up her husband's dream!

She would go down fighting!

HARRY STRETCHED HER arms over her head to loosen the stiffness in her muscles. She was used to working outside, whether it be never-ending chores or working in their fields. Anything physical…inactivity was wearing on her nerves. "Why haven't we heard anything? Do you think the information was wrong? Mayhap the attackers changed their mind."

"I doubt it," Robert replied, keeping an eye on the scene outside his window.

"From the rumors running rampant in the village, the man behind these continued assaults has boasted and wagered heavily on the outcome," Ethan reminded them. "The attack will come."

Two low hoots had Harry's belly twisting into one large knot. "They're coming!"

"To your stations!" Robert rasped.

The first shots were too far away to do any damage.

"They must believe they are already victorious, wasting ammunition with warning shots," Harry said.

"Wait until they are close," Ethan cautioned. "Then fire!"

The next series of shots sounded closer. "They're coming directly from the south!" Harry said. "Bart's tree is right in harm's way."

"He'll be fine as long as he doesn't shoot until they are within range," Robert responded.

"But he's just—" Harry bit her tongue to keep from uttering *too young*. Bart had proven himself many times over since her husband died.

Before she could think of something else to say, a barrage of bullets peppered the front of the cottage.

"They must have one or two of those rifles O'Malley talked about," Robbie said.

"From Kentucky," Matthew added.

"Wish we had one of those," Robbie said.

"Come on, you bloody bastards," Robert growled low in his throat. "Just a little bit closer."

The sound of two rifles firing simultaneously was louder than

Harry expected. She jolted, then quickly tried to hide the fact that the sound unnerved her. She needn't have worried—no one was looking at her, as they were handing off weapons, reloading them, and returning fire.

Between herself, Mary, and Cynthia, they kept a steady supply of powder and lead balls flowing.

Robbie and Matthew never slowed down their repetitious movements: powder, wadding, pistol ball, ramrod—reloading every time a rifle was handed to them.

The scent of burned gunpowder filled the cottage, but Harry ignored it. She couldn't let her mind get stuck on one thing. She had to move constantly, or she'd scream. She hadn't been able to sneak a peek at the tree Bart was perched in. Even if she had been able to, the smoke from the black powder outside—and inside— was too thick.

A man's high-pitched scream had her drawing in a breath and holding it, afraid to exhale for fear that she'd hear Bart calling to her. Had her son been shot? Had the lead ball felled him from his perch in the tree?

Dear Lord, the need to rush out of the cottage and into certain death overwhelmed her. She had to know. She had to see!

"Don't," Matthew rasped, tugging on her sleeve to stop her. "Bart'll let us know if he's been hit."

Harry rounded on the young man. "What if he's been seriously wounded and cannot speak? How will he let us know?"

"He's smart," Robbie told her. "He'll find a way. Have faith in him, Mrs. Mayfield."

Encouraged by the boys' faith in her son, she drew on her reserves. She straightened her spine and squared her shoulders. She could do this. She *would* do this!

# CHAPTER TWENTY-SIX

TEN MEN ON horseback rode toward the three farms. "We split up here," the one in the lead said. "Three of you men come with me—there's unfinished business with this farm. We've a barn to burn and a house to raze."

With a nod, he indicated the next three men in line. "Ride on to the next farm. The rest of you head to the one beyond that far field."

"What do we do if we meet resistance?"

"Squash it like a bug! Move out!"

The group separated. Six men rode off to the east, while four rode north—straight for the farm Chellenham had nearly foamed at the mouth demanding they destroy. The black-hearted thug leading the way vowed he would not rest until not one scorched stone was left standing of the cottage or barn. He had no problem eliminating anyone—or anything, for that matter—that stood in his way.

BART'S HEART NEARLY stopped beating when he saw ten men riding toward their farm. Though there were still leaves on the trees, a few had already started to fall. There were some thin spots among the branches where he would easily be spotted—if one was looking for a young man perched in a tree aiming a rifle with the intent to shoot. And shoot he would, if it meant protecting his mother and their farm.

He hooted twice, the signal that the attackers had arrived.

The sound of shots being fired in the distance had him drawing in a breath and slowly exhaling it. He needed to stay calm. His father had reminded him of that when they were hunting. And O'Malley had warned him of that the night they had been lying in wait for the previous gang to attack.

An explosion of sound close by jarred him from his thoughts. The four men riding toward the cottage had fired simultaneously. Answering fire from inside the cottage had him silently cheering on Mr. Clarke and Mr. Johnson. They would fend off the attack now that the group had divided and split themselves between the three farms. Divide and conquer wasn't always the answer, Bart reasoned. Safety in numbers would win the day!

Shots fired from inside the cottage kept the men from getting any closer. Every time one of the men moved to the side, a shot fired at their horse's hooves stayed their movement.

Bart frowned. He wished he was inside, where the action was happening. But Robbie and Matthew could load as fast as he could. His friends were the reason their fathers were able to keep up the steady stream of lead balls holding off a devastating attack.

He bided his time, hoping that the duke's men would arrive soon. If they were within shouting distance, they would have had to hear the gunfire.

A hiss of sound caught his attention. The men separated, two moving to the left and two to the right. The frontal attack advantage would shift in the favor of the four men.

Should he fire at one of them? They were too far away...out of range. If he fired now, it wouldn't do more than give away his position.

"I wish you were here, O'Malley," Bart murmured.

"THEY'VE SHIFTED THEIR position," Ethan warned.

"Aye," Robert agreed. "Smart move. They'll have the advantage now that they've moved closer."

"Close enough that you're well within their sights," Harry said. Her heart ached for the men who bravely defended her home and thereby their farms. It bled for her son. She had not heard another hoot to tell her that he was unharmed.

"We can't just let them shoot at us without returning fire," Ethan replied.

"I thought we heard more than four horses," Harry said.

"Probably split up," Ethan said. "Heading to our farms."

"Thank goodness we moved our livestock," Robert remarked.

Two shots were fired in quick succession, splintering a piece of the window. Ethan moved just in time to avoid getting hit.

Robert shot but missed the two men with their rifles trained on him. They returned fire, nicking another piece of wood from the window frame—this time too close to Robert. A large splinter embedded itself in his shoulder.

His sharp intake of breath had Harry moving toward him. "Hand me your rifle. Let Cynthia pull that out." She passed the rifle to Robbie, who handed her the one he'd just loaded. She took aim and fired at the ground between the horses. Both shied at the sound. A good distraction, she thought.

Without saying a word, she passed the empty rifle to Robbie, who handed her one primed and ready to fire.

This time, she aimed at the larger man's left hand. If her aim was true—and she rarely missed—he wouldn't be able to hold his rifle to fire it. A glancing shot would still accomplish her goal…one less weapon aiming at her family and friends. She prayed the lead ball would hit her target as she fired.

The man's look of shock, followed by his scream of anger and pain, had her standing in the middle of the window, waiting for him to notice that a woman had bested him!

Then her pride suffered a mighty blow—the breath was knocked out of her as she was tackled to the floor. She would have suffered a blow to more than her pride if the shot that shattered the water pitcher behind her had pierced her breast.

She struggled but couldn't catch her breath. Her vision was shrinking until all she could see was a tiny pinprick of light surrounded by the fathomless black that claimed her, dragging her under.

AIDEN GARAHAN AND his patrol heard the shots as they rounded the long bend in the road. They were too far away to shoot and hit their target. He told his men to gallop, with the order to fire as soon as they were within range.

"Ye bloody bastards!" Aiden fired off a shot as he charged toward the Mayfields' cottage. His target grabbed a hold of his arm and fell off his horse, joining a man who howled in pain, holding his bloody hand. "Hornsby, Kent, aim for their hands or their weapons!" Aiden said.

Shots echoed his command as the other attackers were hit. The sound of horses approaching had him wheeling his mount around to see six men galloping toward them! He took aim and shot the man in the lead. The man's look of shock would have been comical if five others weren't still charging, almost in range to shoot at Aiden.

His men flanked him before he could shout the order. Simultaneous shots were fired, hitting four of the men, who dropped their weapons as they cried out in pain. He nearly smiled.

Before he could reload, the last man was winged. Aiden looked in the direction the shot came from and knew without a doubt the widow's son had fired it. "Bart?" he called out.

"Aye! You got here just in time!"

"Secure them!" he ordered his men before dismounting.

Bart jumped out of the tree and ran to meet him halfway. "I wasn't sure how much longer we could hold them off," the young man confided. He sprinted to the cottage door, calling over his shoulder, "I think they may have hit someone inside."

"We've got to secure the prisoners," Aiden said. "I'll be in as soon as I can."

Bart didn't answer. He opened the door and disappeared inside.

Aiden and his men made short work of the job. After ordering his patrol to stand guard, he entered the cottage to find Bart on his knees beside a woman with hair the color of sunset. His heart clenched in fear. O'Malley had sung the woman's praises just a few hours earlier. His cousin's litany had touched a part buried deep in Aiden's heart—he yearned for someone to care for. O'Malley had grinned, confiding he was captivated by her obstinate, stubborn personality, excellent aim with kitchen utensils, eyes the color of morning mist, and hair that rivaled the setting sun.

He would do all within his power to help the woman his cousin loved. He fell to his knees beside Bart. "Where was she hit, lad? I don't see any blood."

"It was my fault." A young man stepped forward. "She'd just shot and hit one of the attackers but stood unprotected in the middle of the window! I couldn't let her get shot."

Aiden met the lad's tortured gaze and felt for him but needed to know what happened to the widow so he could fix it. "Did ye hit her over the head?"

Bart wasn't paying any attention—he was patting the side of his mother's face and urging her to open her eyes.

It was then Aiden saw what he'd hoped for—the subtle inhale and exhale. "She's breathing!"

"I tackled her from the side," the lad protested. "I didn't kill her."

"Ah. Brilliant choice, given the situation. What's yer name, lad? Mine's Garahan. *Aiden* Garahan—James is me older brother."

"Robbie Johnson. My mum is taking a nasty splinter out of my father's arm."

Aiden glanced toward the couple seated at the table and the bloody mess the wood had made of the man's shoulder. "While yer actions were just what I would have done, there is the possibility that she hit her head when she landed. Did ye notice?"

Concern filled Robbie's eyes, and he quickly said, "Don't worry. I've heard tales of Mrs. Mayfield. She's made of sterner stuff. Has the making of a true Irishwoman—just like me ma."

Bart glanced at the man beside him. "That's what O'Malley told Mum."

Aiden's eyes widened a fraction. "Well now, that's telling."

The door burst open. "Aiden! We're needed at the manor house!"

"Have half the men get ready to ride," Aiden instructed.

"Go!" a man he hadn't noticed before told him. "We can guard the prisoners."

"Thank ye. What is yer name, should me cousins ask?"

"Clarke—Ethan. My wife Mary and son Matthew."

"Thank ye, Ethan." Aiden laid a hand on Bart's shoulder.

Before he could speak, Ethan told him, "Don't worry—we'll take care of Harry."

Aiden stood and glanced at the man at the table. The look of relief on his face and the wad of linen pressed against his injury told him all he needed to know. The wood had been removed. "I'm thinking he'll be okay once the stitching's done."

Bart snorted and shook his head. "That's Mr. Johnson, remember?"

Aiden frowned. "Who in the bloody hell is Harry, and what happened to him?"

"Harriet...Harry for short," Bart replied, "is my mum."

All the pieces of the situation fell into place. "In that case, we'll take yer offer. Though we've secured them, a rifle trained on them would ensure they won't try to escape."

"We've done this before," Bart told him. "Recently. Go, we know what to do."

"Thank ye."

Aiden spun around and bolted out the door.

"Mount up, men! The armed reinforcements inside will guard these bloody bastards until we get back."

"Not if Chellenham hits his target," one of the prisoners said.

Aiden had the man by the throat before he could blink. "What do ye know?"

The man's face turned red, but he refused to speak. Aiden didn't have the time to extract the potentially vital information.

"I'll be back for ye," he warned. "And when ye tell me what I'm wanting to know, ye'll wish to God that I'd killed ye."

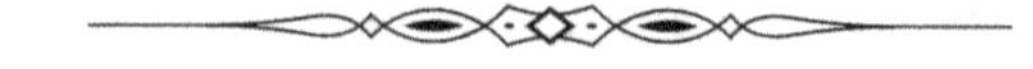

# CHAPTER TWENTY-SEVEN

"A HAIRSBREADTH TO the left," Sean murmured as he aimed his Kentucky long rifle on the man hiding in the copse of trees at the edge of the herb garden.

"Aim for his extremities—not his head or his heart," Garahan said. "His Grace and their lordships will have enough to contend with. Ye'll not be adding charges of murder to it."

"'Tisn't murder," Sean growled, "if he's the one who set this band of bloodthirsty thugs on the viscount and the earl!"

"Hand over the rifle!"

"Bollocks to that!" Sean fired, and heard a satisfying scream of pain drift toward them.

Garahan shoved his cousin, grabbing for the weapon. "I ordered ye to hand over yer rifle!"

Sean snorted with laughter. "When, in this bloody lifetime, have I ever listened to the likes of ye?"

"The viscount put me in charge of the inside perimeter! Ye should listen—"

Sean sighed. "Faith, yer a royal pain in the *arse*, Jamie-lad. But ye're family, so I won't knock yer head off until after we collect the prisoners and see them carted off to London to stand trial."

Garahan glowered at him.

"Mayhap the man I shot is a relative of the bloody lord behind this evil campaign against the viscount," Sean suggested.

They switched positions in the viscount's library, the only room with windows facing south and west. The viscount, the earl, and Lord Coddington were spread out, stationed on the opposite side of the house.

"It's gone quiet," Garahan observed. "Have one of the footmen standing guard find Coventry. It may be time to rally our troops and sweep the grounds. Though it pains me to do so, we'll have to care for the blackguard's wounded."

"With luck, 'twas Chellenham I winged," Sean remarked.

The footman pounded on the door, exclaiming, "Garahan! Aiden and his patrol have arrived!"

Garahan opened the door and stepped into the hallway. "What do ye know of the situation outside?" he asked.

"It's gone deathly quiet," the footman told them. "Tremayne and O'Malley rode off like the devil was on their heels."

"Which direction?" Sean demanded.

"East—just beyond the stables."

The viscount strode toward them, yelling, "Coddington! Lippincott! Stay here and guard our families! That bloody bastard will not escape justice a second time!" Chattsworth tucked a brace of pistols in his waistband and ran to the door at the end of the hallway.

Sean started to follow after the viscount, but Garahan stopped him, saying, "Stay put, Sean! Ye've a wife and babe on the way. Guard their lordships' backs and their families. I've nothing to lose."

Garahan spun around and plowed into soft curves. "What in the bloody hell!" He braced his hands on the young woman's shoulders and stared into her summer-blue eyes. "Mary Kate? Are ye hurt, lass?"

Her eyes welled with tears, but she shook her head. He didn't have time to get her to tell him where he'd hurt her. He was nearly thrice her size.

"Sean! See to Mary Kate. I've got to protect the viscount!"

SEAN WAS ALREADY rushing forward. He slipped his arm around her waist and noticed her wince of discomfort. *Likely bruised a few ribs.* "Here now, lass. Come with me. I'll have Mrs. Meadowsweet take a look and see where me bull of a cousin damaged ye." Lady Calliope's maid murmured something, but he didn't quite hear her. "What was that ye said, lass?"

Tear-drenched blue eyes lifted to meet his gaze. "My heart."

Unease speared through him. He hoped he'd misheard her. "What did ye say?"

"He's broken it." Shoulders slumped, she limped a few steps and stumbled.

Sean swore beneath his breath and scooped the woman into his arms. "Ye'll be fine now—just let Mrs. Meadowsweet and Mrs. Romney take care of ye." He carried her in the direction his *eedjit* cousin had gone.

He burst into the kitchen. Lady Calliope was the first to spot him. "Mary Kate! What happened? Did you go outside even after we were told not to?"

Sean set her onto one of the chairs against the wall. "Me cousin turned and bumped into the lass—he's built like a bull, so no doubt he's damaged the poor thing."

"Thank you, Sean."

Calliope turned from him, but he mumbled, "A word, yer ladyship?"

She followed him toward the pantry.

"Ye should have seen her face before me cousin plowed into her. I'm thinking 'twas something he said."

"What did he say? What were you speaking of?"

"Garahan's gone after Tremayne and O'Malley. 'Tis me duty to guard their lordships and yer ladyships."

Tears welled in Lady Calliope's eyes, but she blinked them away. "They've gone after Chellenham. My husband set off after

O'Malley and Garahan. Why would William follow them? Did he intend to face down the man who's already shot him? Does he value his life so little?" A sob escaped before she drew in a calming breath. Exhaling slowly, she met Sean's gaze. "What will I do without him?"

"Ye're strong, stronger than his lordship realizes, yer ladyship. Don't be thinking doom and gloom. He needs yer strength and yer faith in him. 'Tis likely me cousins have already cornered Chellenham. Yer husband will arrive in time to question him. They'll see to it Chellenham doesn't win!"

He bowed, intending to get back to his post, but her hand on his arm made him pause.

"You're absolutely right, Sean. Thank you for reminding me. Go! Their lordships are on the second-floor landing—there are two windows there that face the stables."

Sean ran for the stairs while she turned back to take care of one more wounded soul.

O'MALLEY AND TREMAYNE cornered the bloody bugger behind the elaborate plot to destroy the viscount. O'Malley had him in his sights, aiming for his black heart.

"Do not kill him," the lieutenant said.

"Chellenham!" a voice called out from behind them.

"Bloody hell," O'Malley swore "'tis the viscount!"

Their nemesis walked slowly toward them.

The man was mad! O'Malley could not believe Chellenham smiled, all the while walking toward himself and Tremayne, who still had their pistols aimed at his heart.

Chattsworth's voice cut through the tension. "I demand satisfaction!"

Chellenham laughed in reply.

"You'll not escape justice this time, Chellenham," the viscount said. "There is nowhere for you to hide."

Chellenham closed the distance between them. "There is nothing you can threaten me with, Chattsworth. I have a far more powerful ally who has promised *his* protection."

O'Malley and Tremayne were immediately on guard, watching the lord's reaction to the viscount's proclamation, and moved to flank him.

Despair flickered for a moment before the viscount's emotions were hidden once more under a neutral expression. "You are a coward!" he declared. He turned his back on the man and walked away.

Chellenham lifted his pistol and took aim at the viscount's back.

Tremayne yelled, "Duck, Chattsworth!"

O'Malley dove toward the viscount, using his body as a shield, protecting the viscount from Chellenham's lead ball. He felt the impact of the ball and knew he'd fulfilled his vow.

Relief tangled with the pain. Circumstances had changed his unwanted vision...the viscount did not take a lead ball in the back.

O'Malley wobbled and fell to his knees, pain radiating from his biceps. Clapping a hand to the wound was agony, but he needed to stop the bleeding.

His mind replayed the second vision he'd had, and he realized it had changed in location as well—they were not at the Mayfields' farm.

The echo of a second shot surprised him. Tremayne wouldn't have fired. He was the one who'd ordered O'Malley *not* to shoot Chellenham.

His gaze swept the area to look for the shooter in time to see Chellenham fall to the ground with a hand to his side. Bright red crimson oozed around the hand that moments before held his pistol.

Yet another aspect of O'Malley's vision changed— Chellenham would not be able to take aim and shoot while wounded…the viscount was safe!

Satisfied he'd protected his charge and that Chellenham would not have the opportunity to commit murder, he drew in a breath and looked at his bleeding arm. "Bollocks, that hurts."

A man stepped from behind the cover of a stand of trees, bringing him back to the present.

"You ruined my daughter," the man growled. He lifted his pistol, aiming for the bleeding lord's forehead. "Prepare to die!"

Tremayne appeared, shot the pistol out of the man's hand, and wrestled him to the ground. "Don't you know the penalty for killing a peer of the realm is death?"

"He isn't dead and likely won't die from a paltry wound to his side. He's got enough flesh not to miss what my lead ball removed from his sorry hide," the man added without remorse.

"You'll have to come with me," Tremayne said. "The constable will want to speak with you."

"I have nothing to say," the man said.

"O'Malley?" Garahan rushed toward the blood-soaked scene. "Ye're not dead, then."

O'Malley snorted. "As ye can see."

Garahan noticed the viscount getting to his feet, and asked, "Are ye hurt, yer lordship?"

"My pride is sorely bruised, Garahan," Chattsworth answered. "What do you intend to do about it?"

"I'll have to speak with me cousin and Tremayne to get to the bottom of the situation. I promise yer lordship, yer pride will be avenged—no matter if it be me cousin that did the bruising."

"Ye're all heart, Garahan," O'Malley grumbled.

The viscount inclined his head. "My thanks, Garahan. Now then. Unfortunately, we need to attend to our prisoner. It would not be well done of me to let the bastard bleed to death while I watched, would it?"

"Not at all," Garahan agreed. "Lady Calliope will be pleased when we tell her the rumors are false—yer lordship is *not* a bloodthirsty man."

O'Malley and Tremayne snorted with laughter.

When O'Malley groaned, Garahan knelt beside him to examine his wound. "'Tis only a flesh wound—and from what we've been told, the one Sean suffered a few months ago was far worse than yers."

"True. Would ye mind slicing off me sleeve? I need to bind the paltry scratch, as I can't bind it meself."

Working quickly, Garahan slit his cousin's sleeve and wrapped it around O'Malley's arm. "That should hold ye for a bit."

"What about me, you *stupid* Irishman?" Chellenham said.

"Faith, do me ears deceive me, Michael?"

O'Malley's face lost all expression. "Ye've ears like a cat, James."

"'Tisn't right to insult the man who intended to bind yer wound and take ye to the manor house to have it tended to properly," Garahan said. "I may have changed me mind." He turned to glare at Chellenham. "Mayhap I'll let ye bleed while I drag ye back."

The older peer looked worried.

"We have wounded to tend to at the manor. You are wasting our time, Chellenham," Tremayne said. "If I were you, I'd apologize to Garahan."

"I spoke in haste," Chellenham said.

Garahan ignored the peer and addressed the lieutenant and the man standing beside him. "Ye'll have to fill me in on what happened here on our way. Apparently, I'm not to have the pleasure of watching the bloody bugger bleed while I drag his *arse* back."

Tremayne's lips twitched, as if he was about to smile. "Aye, neither of us will allow him to bleed. I'll bind the man's wound if you'll escort our other prisoner back." With a glance at the lord still lying on the ground, he said, "I may need more than one sleeve to bind his wound. You'll owe me a boon, Garahan."

That Chellenham was thick through his middle was obvious

to the men.

"Use me other sleeve—I'll not be needing it," O'Malley said.

Garahan used his knife to slice through the fabric before handing it to Tremayne. The lieutenant frowned, and Garahan said, "Fine, then—I'll give ye both me sleeves, too. If it's not enough, use Chellenham's blasted sleeves!" He handed his knife to Tremayne then asked the viscount, "Would ye help O'Malley walk back? I'll be escorting this other prisoner—we'll be finding out his name and why he shot Chellenham. Tremayne's got guard duty on the other one."

"Of course." The viscount helped O'Malley to stand. "Lean on me, O'Malley."

"Thank ye, yer lordship."

"You saved my life, O'Malley."

O'Malley grinned. "'Tis me duty—and a pleasure. Yer lordship's life is one worth saving."

✦ ══════◈◇◈══════ ✦

# CHAPTER TWENTY-EIGHT

"O'MALLEY!" AIDEN CALLED as the group approached with their prisoners. "As soon as ye're finished here, I've urgent news for ye…troubling news."

O'Malley looked to Tremayne, who said, "We can handle these two—and the others as well." Tremayne looked to the viscount and Coventry for confirmation before adding, "We've willing hands enough to care for the wounded. The rest of the guard will handle the perimeter protection. We'll expect you when we see the whites of your eyes."

Relief and understanding filled O'Malley. He turned to his cousin. "Any injuries at the tenant farms?"

Aiden frowned. "Aye, a few—nothing serious, excepting the one."

Dread obliterated the relief from moments before. "Bart or Harry?"

"'Tis Harry." Aiden's hand shot out, forcing O'Malley to a stop. "She wasn't shot. Nearly was, from what young Robbie told me. She'd just fired her rifle and stood in plain sight in front of the window instead of seeking cover."

"Pride," O'Malley rasped, understanding the need to discover if you'd hit your target. "What happened?"

"Robbie said he threw himself toward her, knocked her off her feet."

Worry filled him at the prospect of his Harry adding injuries on top of her injuries. "Did she crack her head on something?"

"The lad didn't seem to think so, but it happened so fast he couldn't be sure. He was worried he'd reinjured her ribs."

"Was she conscious when ye left?"

"Her eyes were closed, and she was breathing. From the way her son was trying to rouse her, I'm thinking mayhap she had the wind knocked out of her at first. If she was lightheaded—"

O'Malley picked up on the thought. "She wouldn't be wanting to open her eyes to watch the room spin. She hates to appear weak before her son—and her neighbors. She's as strong as me ma. Strong as yers."

He turned to go, but the viscount ordered him, "Have someone tend to your arm. Unless you want company on your ride to the Mayfield farm to ensure you do not pass out and fall off your horse."

O'Malley narrowed his eyes at the viscount, who slowly smiled.

"Thought that might convince you," Chattsworth said. "By the by, did the lead ball pass through your arm, or is it embedded?"

O'Malley grumbled, "Felt it hit the back of me arm and tear through the front. I won't be sitting still long enough for anyone to stitch me back together."

The viscount and Coventry exchanged glances. "Have one of the women add a thick bandage around your arm before they tie it off," Coventry said. "Mayhap by the time you reach the farm, Mrs. Mayfield will be well enough to stitch it for you."

"Lord willing," O'Malley mumbled as he dragged his feet to the kitchen.

Harry peered through her lashes, hoping this time the room

would cease to spin. Satisfied that it would, she opened her eyes.

Bart jumped to his feet and shouted, "Mum's awake!" He reached for her hands and held them tightly. "Does your head pain you? Did you smack it on the floor when Robbie tackled you?"

She took mental stock, starting with her head. "I think I may have bumped the back of it on the floor. Don't be mad at Robbie—your friend saved my life."

"I know, Mum. Already thanked him, after…"

"After?"

"I punched him."

"Bartholomew Tristan Mayfield!"

"Bloody hell, Mum! You were struggling to breathe. I didn't know if O'Malley's prediction had come true—and one of your ribs poked through a lung!"

Robbie walked over to stand on the other side of the bed. "I didn't mean to hit you so hard, Mrs. Mayfield, but I wasn't close enough to grab your hand and tug you out of the way."

"As I just told my hotheaded son here, you saved my life, Robbie. Thank you." She studied the fist-sized bruise on his jaw. Turning to her son, she said, "Ask Mary to soak the poultice we use to reduce swelling in warm water—not boiling, mind. When it's ready, Robbie, please sit down and place it on your jaw."

Bart's eyes blazed. "You would have done the same."

Harry sighed. "I'm not given to hauling off and clobbering anyone in the face. That would have been your father."

Her son's abashed expression satisfied her need to let him know how displeased she was, while at the same time reminding him that he was on the cusp of manhood and would be held to a higher standard.

He acquiesced and walked over to where Mary was pouring hot water into their tea kettle, doing as his mother requested.

Harry turned her attention to Robbie, who said, "You've done so much for my family and the Clarkes. I couldn't just stand there."

"Harry?" Mary joined them. "You're finally awake."

"I have been for a little while, but whenever I tried to open my eyes, the room spun. I was afraid to move for fear I'd embarrass myself by casting up my accounts."

"Lack of air from having the wind knocked out of you," her friend remarked. "Mayhap a result of the bump on the back of your head. Does it pain you?"

"Not unduly. Bart, would you help me sit up? Mary, would you mind seeing if the bump on my head is swelling?"

Bart slipped his arm beneath her back and carefully lifted her. Mary put a few pillows behind her to prop her up. "How's that, Mum?"

"Better, thank you. I'm sure I can stand—" A chorus of *nos* had her frowning. "I know my own strength."

"Not all the time," Mary countered. "I'm going to gently touch the back of your head. Let me know when it hurts and if you become dizzy or nauseated."

"I will."

Mary touched a few spots before Harry drew in a sharp breath. "Ah, that's quite a bump."

"It wouldn't pain me as much if it were insignificant," Harry grumbled.

"Nausea?"

"No."

"Dizzy?"

"Not now."

"Well then, I think it's safe to say after a day or two in bed, you should be able to resume your normal activities, as long as you mind your ribs and don't overdo."

"I will not be staying in bed. I've supper to see to, and—"

Hoofbeats pounded toward the house.

"Bart! The window. See who's coming."

Bart did as she asked. When he turned around, he was grinning.

"Well, who is it?"

The door to the cottage swung open and O'Malley stepped over the threshold. Harry watched as he took note of the room's occupants. She waited for him to notice her. Their gazes met, and he walked toward her. The need to feel his arms around her nearly overwhelmed her. He stood before her, his gaze sweeping from the top of her head to the tips of her toes. "Ye're awake, lass! How do ye feel?"

"I've felt better."

He acknowledged everyone with a brief greeting, then turned back to Harry. "Aiden wasn't certain if you'd done more damage to yer ribs. Before ye ask, I told him about yer prior injuries. He thought ye may have smacked yer head on the floor. Do ye remember what happened?"

"Most of it." Harry described the scene, as best she remembered, of Robbie and Matthew reloading rifles for their fathers, of Ethan and Robert aiming their lead balls strategically to keep the attackers at bay. She told how Mary and Cynthia kept level heads, not quailing over the bloody mess when a splintered bit of wood from one of the window frames got embedded in Robert Johnson's arm.

"Ye've been busy," O'Malley murmured, reaching for her hand. "Does yer head pain ye?"

"Not overmuch."

His steady gaze soothed the worry she'd held close to her heart. She knew the danger he faced as one of the duke's guard. He had been honest with her from the first, spoken of the times when words were not sufficient, and action was required— whether it be with fists or weapons. She accepted his staunch conviction to honor his vow to the duke.

She gazed into his grass-green eyes, then looked deeper…into the very heart of the man. The man she loved. It was time to stop hiding from the possibility of a second chance.

Harry had not asked to have her heart yanked from her breast and offered to the man who had butted heads with her from the start. He'd tried to change her mind about protecting her son and their farm, but she had stood firm in *her* convictions. Doing what she felt was right had unintentionally proven O'Malley to be right...she *did* need him. Together they would stand stronger. O'Malley would take some of the burden of running the farm from Bart's shoulders and her own.

But without Bart's consent, she would hold O'Malley off until her son was ready to give it.

A flicker of emotion caught her eye. She looked deeper still and noticed what O'Malley had been keeping from her—a hint of fear that she would rebuff him. Bloody hell—she never had a chance of refusing what he boldly claimed the other night...*when* they made love, as if it were a foregone conclusion. It may have been in his mind, but not in hers.

And now...now, she knew why she had obstinately refused to listen to her heart—she too was afraid. Afraid to love again. To love with her whole heart was a risk she had willingly taken when she was young, and so in love with Bartholomew, she felt as if she would perish without him by her side. His death had left a gaping hole in her life, and with it the realization she would have to face the trials and tribulations of helping their son become the man he was destined to be alone.

Fear opened her eyes. Fear that she would never see Bart come into his own, live his life, find his place, and marry a young woman who would hold his heart carefully...tenderly. She accepted the fact that she would put herself in the line of fire to protect her son—even if it meant giving her life to do so. That acceptance brought a clarity and helped her untangle her feelings for O'Malley.

Harry was ready to accept the gift of a second love in her life—along with all of the trimmings, the intimacy O'Malley spoke of. Someone to confide her worries to; someone who would have her back. She would offer her heart and her body. Listen to his worries...if the hardheaded Irishman would deign to let her. She would have *his* back.

"Are ye in pain, lass?"

His softly spoken words, and the way he trailed the tips of his fingers across her cheek, had her sighing. "Not any longer."

When he sat on the chair beside her bed, she scooted over to lean against O'Malley's broad chest. Contentment filled her as the rightness of her momentous decision settled her quivering stomach.

He flinched, and she noticed the sleeve of his frockcoat had been slit from shoulder to wrist, hiding the fact that a thick bandage had been wrapped around his upper arm. She sat up straight. "You're hurt!"

"'Tis nothing."

"Let me see," she demanded.

"It's been seen to."

She narrowed her eyes at him. He was not going to give an inch. "Take it off and let me see."

His lightning-fast grin had her smiling in return. "I admire boldness in me woman, but wouldn't ye rather wait until we're alone before ye demand I take off me clothes?"

A snort of laughter from behind them her face flaming. "You are a rogue! I did nothing of the sort."

He leaned close, his lips a breath from hers, and pitched his voice low so only she could hear. "I see the want in yer mist-laden eyes, lass. Ye cannot help yerself."

Angry with herself, for being tempted, and with O'Malley for fanning the flames of her desire, she countered, "You flatter yourself, O'Malley."

His deep, rumbling laughter filled the cottage. She'd missed the sound of her husband's laughter…his prompting her to anger, only to cajole her to laugh again.

The fever had taken her husband so quickly that they never had a chance to say goodbye or speak of a future without him in it. In her heart she knew Bartholomew would not want her to struggle as she had had. Nor would he want her to agonize over her decision to allow Bart to shoulder more of the workload now that he was old enough to do so.

Bart's voice brought her sharply back to the present. "Mum, O'Malley's bleeding."

# CHAPTER TWENTY-NINE

O'MALLEY KEPT HIS counsel while Harry barked orders to the women. Mary had more threads boiling, while Cynthia had once more spread out a selection of linen squares…and more of that damned pink fabric cut into long strips, waiting to secure whatever bandages the widow intended to use on him after she put the needle to his flesh.

He shuddered just thinking about it. He did not mind watching someone have their wounds repaired with needle and thread, but he did mind when the wound and the flesh were *his*.

"I don't understand why Lady Calliope didn't insist—" Harry began.

"She tried," O'Malley interrupted. "I politely refused."

Harry shook her head and tied off the last knot. Cynthia held out a wad of linen. "Hold this on the inside of your arm," the widow ordered him while holding a thick bandage on the opposite side of the wound. "Cynthia, please hand me that first strip—"

"I'll not be wearing any more of yer pink frock on me arm."

Bart's chuckle was echoed by that of his friends. Wisely, their fathers kept their silence, but the laughter in the men's eyes gave them away.

"A smart man would not refuse proper care for his wounds, O'Malley," Harry said.

His temper flared. "Are ye saying I'm not smart?"

Harry's lips lifted into a soft, sweet smile, tempting him to kiss her.

"Not at all," she soothed. "You are highly intelligent. It is the stubborn part of you that shoves the intelligent side of you aside to have its way—whether it is right or wrong." She tied off the pale pink linen strip and tucked in the ends. "There. Now you will not continue to bleed. You must be lightheaded yourself."

He was but would go to blazes before he admitted it to the woman calmly waiting for him to agree. "Nay."

"How is your stomach?" Mary asked as she removed the bowl of extra threads and the ones filled with bloody water.

"Fine," he lied, willing the churning in his gut to stop.

"A slice of the day-old bread will sop up the bile in your belly," Bart said.

O'Malley wondered, would the Mayfields always insist they were right?

Robert and Ethan walked over to sit with him at the table. "Trust me," Robert said, "it worked after my wife yanked—"

"Carefully extracted," Cynthia corrected him. "I did not yank."

O'Malley's good humor returned. "I take it ye're referring to the huge hunk of wood in yer arm."

Robert nodded, and his wife laughed. "It was a sliver, albeit a thick one, but a sliver just the same. And I did not *yank* it free. If I had, you would have completely lost your breakfast."

"Woman—"

Robbie interrupted his father, "Day-old bread works wonders settling an uneasy stomach. Mine threatened to erupt when Mrs. Mayfield didn't immediately rise to her feet."

"Now, Robbie," Harry said, "remember what I said."

"Aye, Mrs. Mayfield, but the memory of it still has my stomach churning with worry."

"Hand me a slice of that bread, Robbie," his father said.

O'Malley watched the scene with interest before realizing

what Bart and the others were up to. He acquiesced but did not intend to admit his stomach was uneasy. "If there is enough, I could use a slice meself."

The women had already cleared off the table and were setting out a simple meal—it had been hours since anyone had eaten. Bread, fresh and day-old, along with sweet butter and the hearty stew Mary and Cynthia had set to simmering before the first shot was fired. The savory scent wafted toward the men as bowls of stew were set before them.

O'Malley watched Harry with her neighbors and liked what he saw. They were close friends—more like family, drawn closer by the events of the last few weeks. It would be a good place to settle down, he mused before shock had him checking that thought. If anyone had told him he would even *consider* tying himself down to one place, and one woman—with a son of four and ten, no less—he would have laughed in their face.

Now as he sat among them, treated as one of them from the first, he felt a kinship that rivaled what he shared with his brothers and cousins. One of his ma's favorite sayings filled his head and nudged his heart: *Family, it's the glue.*

When the meal was over, Harry turned to the others, who with a glance seemed to be in silent agreement with whatever the widow wanted.

"What is it, lass?"

"Is it over?"

He drew in a deep breath and slowly exhaled, relieved to be able to assure them. "Aye, for the moment. We've rounded up Chellenham and his band of thugs."

"Will they be transported to London?" Robbie asked.

"Aye, though I've a feeling someone higher up than the Duke of Wyndmere will have a say in what happens to Chellenham."

Ethan frowned and nudged Robert. They shared a black look, and Ethan spat out one word: "*Prinny.*"

"Ridiculous name for a grown man—and the prince regent at that," Harry mumbled.

"Aye, but there ye have it," O'Malley said. "His word supersedes that of those beneath him."

"The dukes and viscounts on down to the lesser nobles and gentry," Mary added.

O'Malley frowned. "He was the royal behind Chellenham's canny escape from justice when he attempted to murder Lord Coddington."

"The viscount was a hero that day," Bart said.

"That he was, lad."

Matthew looked at his friends. Bart prodded him until he asked, "Who shot you, O'Malley?"

"Was it one of the attackers?" Robbie said.

"Did he shoot you off your horse?" Bart asked.

"No to both questions," O'Malley replied.

Harry set her teacup on the table and reached for his hand. "Was it an accident? Did one of your own men shoot you?"

O'Malley shot to his feet. "Me brother and me cousins have never shot anyone by *accident*. We've skills far beyond what ye can imagine, *Mrs.* Mayfield."

Harry rose to stand beside him, placing her hand on his arm. "I apologize if I offended you. That was not my intention at all."

He nodded.

Bart asked, "Then why won't you answer the question?"

O'Malley's knees threatened to give way as the loss of blood and submitting to the dreaded needle and thread caught up to him. Before he disgraced himself and fell down, he sat. "If ye must know, Chellenham."

"You were that close to him?" Ethan asked.

"Aye."

Harry slipped her arm through O'Malley's. "You are hiding something from us. Are more men coming? Will they succeed where the others failed?"

Robert rose to his feet. "Will the bloody bastards salt our fields after they destroy our crops? Burn down our barns? Our homes?"

O'Malley knew then that he would have to tell them the truth. "No. Chellenham's evil plot has been foiled. He lost in his bid to destroy the viscount…though not without one last parting shot."

Harry's eyes welled with tears. With his free hand, he swept them away and cupped her cheek.

"You truly are the Duke's Shield, Michael. Protecting the duke and his family, and extended family."

"'Tis a moniker any one of me cousins or brothers could have earned."

"I thought I was mistaken as I stitched your wounds, but now I realize my instincts were correct."

"Oh, and what might that be, lass?"

"The exit wound is usually larger."

His gaze locked on hers. "Aye."

"The lead ball struck the back of your arm first, penetrating through to the front."

Bart's face paled. "He tried to shoot you in the back?"

O'Malley knew he would have to finish his explanation. "The viscount challenged Chellenham to a duel to end the madness."

"Bet he refused," Robbie piped up.

"That he did, lad. The coward laughed at the viscount, who mistakenly thought that would be the end of it and turned to go. I saw Chellenham take aim and did what I had to do."

"Used your body as a shield," Harry rasped.

"I took an oath to protect the duke and his family—immediate and extended."

Her eyes filled, and this time her tears spilled over. "You could have been shot through the heart!"

O'Malley pulled her chair close to his and put his arm around her. "I wasn't. Dry yer eyes, lass. I won't have ye crying over the likes of me."

She wiped her eyes with the backs of her hands. "I hate to cry."

"Mum hardly ever cries. But since the first attack, she's making up for it," Bart said.

"I'm fine," O'Malley said. "Don't worry about me. 'Tis yerself I worry about. I'll have yer word now that ye'll not be up and working the fields for a day or two, lass. I've got to report back and settle a few loose ends and won't be able to help ye until 'tis finished." He was not about to confide that one of those loose ends included her—and their future.

"If they let you leave, why can't you stay?" Bart asked.

"Aiden reported that yer ma had been severely injured. He wasn't sure if ye'd regained consciousness. Robbie's a fine, sturdy young lad. Was it the impact that had ye passing out?"

Harry frowned. "It all happened so fast."

Robbie explained, "All I could think was knocking her out of the way. I apologized, but I can tell you I'm sorry every day for the next week if you need me to."

Harry met Robbie's gaze. "You have nothing to apologize for. You saved my life. Pride blinded my better judgment and had me standing there waiting to see if I had hit my target. I will never be able to thank you enough."

"Aiden knew…" O'Malley began. He let his words trail off. He did not intend to discuss how he felt about the widow with an audience. The need to confess what was in his heart swept through him. He needed to hear what was in hers. When his throat tightened, he willed it to relax.

"What did he know, Michael?" Harry asked.

O'Malley knew the hardheaded woman felt as he did, though he would have to press her to admit her feelings. The lass was stubborn to the bone…they both were.

"I'll be thanking ye for the rest of *our* lives. Robbie." O'Malley never broke eye contact with her. "Harry—Harriet Mayfield, ye fill a hole in me I didn't know was there. Would ye do me the honor of becoming me wife?"

When she did not answer right away, he added, "Faith, I know ye're a strong woman, more than capable of living without the likes of me, but ye fill me heart to bursting." He looked at

Bart and rasped, "I'm not after replacing yer da, lad. I'd be proud if ye'd consider me yer friend. Anything I can do to help ye achieve yer goals, I'll gladly do."

Worry was a double-edged knife flaying his guts wide open. He needed to be sure the stunned look in his love's eyes was a good thing. Acting on instinct, he drew her off her seat and onto his lap. Pulling her close, he pressed his lips to hers. Softly, gently at first.

When she kissed him back with passion, he answered in kind. Lost in the wonder of the woman in his arms, he felt the room and its occupants fade until it was only the two of them.

Somewhere far off, someone cleared their throat, but he ignored it. Kissing Harry was all that mattered. She had to agree. They would wed, or he would toss her over his shoulder and cart her off and have his way with her. She would have to accept him then!

He tore his lips from hers and stared into the soft gray of her eyes.

*Nay.* He would never dishonor her. From the moment he'd arrived at Chattsworth Manor, he had watched her take on whatever life tossed in her path. She was honest, brave, and strong—a woman who knew her own mind. She had friends enough to help, should their union bless them with a babe. He had not wanted to marry, but Harry changed his mind. If he could not have her as his wife, he would never marry. She was the one. There would never be another like her. He did not know what he would do if she turned him down.

"Marry me, Harry—put me out of me misery."

She stared into his eyes and finally said, "One question, O'Malley."

"Whatever it is, ask, and I'll do me best to answer."

"Are you miserable with me or without me?"

His snort of laughter had her narrowing her eyes. "Without ye! Faith, but ye're a hardheaded woman, lass."

She beamed at him. "I do try."

O'Malley was not about to let her evade his question and let it go unanswered. He held her gaze captive as he called over his shoulder, "Bart, have the lads give ye a hand digging a hole in yer field."

Bart's mouth opened and closed twice, before he replied, "A hole? How big?"

"Let's see now. I'm over six feet tall—ye're tall enough to pace that off and add a bit to the length. As to the depth—at least a good six feet deep will do, as I'm not after being dug up after I'm dead and buried."

Harry's mouth gaped open. He closed it for her.

She finally found her voice to ask, "Are you ill? Suffering from a malady you have not told me about?"

He did not want her temper to flare again, so he kissed her thoroughly, deeply. When he could bring himself to end the kiss, he told her, "Lass, either say aye ye'll marry me, or nay. If ye answer aye, then we won't be needing the hole. Answer nay"— he leveled his gaze at Bart—"the lads best not be skimping on the depth."

Harry threw her arms around his neck and kissed him until his eyes crossed. When he came up for air, he rasped, "Well now, lass. We've witnesses enough who will attest that ye're more than a bit partial to the idea of marrying me. Just say the word, and I'll be asking his lordship to obtain a Special License."

She frowned at him. "You haven't asked Bart for permission yet."

"Stubborn as me ma, and hardheaded to boot. 'Tis a wonder I thought I could live me life without ye, lass. 'Tis clear ye're the only one for me. If me brother and me cousin can manage marriage, and starting a family, while working for the duke, then so can I!"

Harry poked him in the chest. "Mayhap I don't want to marry again."

"Ah, lass, ye wound me to the core. I love ye, and know I don't deserve ye, but I'm hoping ye'll marry me anyway."

She smacked him on the back of the head.

"Bloody hell, woman! What did ye do that for?"

"Ask Bart's permission so I can say yes, you hardheaded Irishman."

"Admit ye love me first, lass."

Harry rolled her eyes. "Fine. I love you."

He kissed her forehead. "Say it like ye mean it."

"As soon as you ask Bart."

He kissed the tip of her nose. "Bart, may I have yer permission to marry yer stubborn ma?"

Bart chuckled. "Yes! Is tomorrow too soon to marry Mum?"

O'Malley smiled at Bart and turned back to the woman in his arms. His lips were a breath away from hers when he demanded again, "Say it like ye mean it, lass."

Harry slowly smiled. "I love you, Michael. Now kiss me!"

O'Malley kissed the breath out of her. He wanted to linger but had a duty to fulfill. "I need to get back. There are a few details I need to see to before we wed."

From the dazed look on her face, he wondered if she was listening, or if her mind had gone where his had been tempted to go. Making love to Harry would have to wait until they were legally wed.

She blinked, and her eyes cleared. "When will you be back?"

He brushed a lock of fiery hair from her lashes. "As soon as I can. It may be a few days, as things were in an uproar when I left."

"Send word, and I'll have a batch of scones and a hearty meal waiting for you when you return."

He hugged her tight, then eased back to stare down into the eyes that begged him to stay. O'Malley needed to hear her say the words. "Promise me, lass."

"That I will wait? Of course."

His sigh was long and deep. "Nay."

She bit her bottom lip, and her eyes lit up. "I promise to bake two batches of scones for you."

He grabbed hold of her upper arms, fighting the urge to shake her until he rattled the words he needed to hear from her sweet lips. "Bloody hell, can ye not remember what ye promised?"

She flexed her biceps. The hard muscle there surprised him. Harry took advantage of his inattention, curled her hands into tight fists, and swung her arms up and around to break his hold.

"Apparently, I have promised a number of things, O'Malley. Just spit it out and be on your way."

"Is that any way to talk to the man ye agreed to wed?"

The boys and the men were snickering, clearly enjoying watching him make a fool of himself. The woman was making him daft! This should have been a private conversation.

"You're making me daft, O'Malley!" Harry said.

He laughed. "Ah, lass, I was just thinking the same about ye." When she lowered her brows and glared at him, he told her, "Ye promised to stay in bed for at least two days. I'll be sending someone around to make certain ye keep yer word."

Her expressive eyes welled with hurt. "Do you doubt that I will keep my promise?"

"Ye might not be able to help yerself. Ye're more like me than I'd care to admit. When there's work to be done, I cannot ignore it. No matter if I've just taken a lead ball to protect someone."

She blinked, and the sorrow was hidden once more. "I was not shot, and since you do not believe I would be able to keep my word, I will rescind that promise. You have my word that I will not rest."

Shocked to the bone, O'Malley stared at her. When she put her hands on her hips and growled at him, he was aghast. "Are ye looking to start our first fight?"

Anger turned to laughter in a heartbeat. "First? Have you forgotten the times you've tried to tell me what to do and I refused?"

"*Bollocks!* 'Tis our first fight since ye agreed to be me wife!"

"Mum, promise O'Malley you'll rest. He has a duty to report to the viscount," Bart urged. "He's given his word."

"And what of *my* word?" she demanded. "Does it count for nothing as I am a woman?"

Bart clamped his jaw shut, and O'Malley sensed this was not the first time she'd used that particular ploy to get her way.

"Ye'll not belittle yer son to get yer way, lass. As ye demanded I ask him for permission to wed ye, I'm thinking ye value his opinion enough to do as he asks." He turned to her son and asked, "What do ye expect yer ma to be doing for the next few days?"

Bart squared his shoulders and lifted his chin. *Good.* O'Malley had achieved what he wanted to accomplish. The lad's pride had been repaired in the eyes of the men and woman surrounding them.

"Mum, Mrs. Clarke, Mrs. Johnson, O'Malley, and I have all asked that you rest for the next two days. If you hadn't hit your head so hard, you'd listen to reason and accept that the four of us are not demanding you do something against your will. We're asking so that you allow your body time to heal. I would never ask you to do something just because I'm a man and think what I want is more important than what *you* want."

Harry remained silent.

Bart stepped around O'Malley to draw his mother into his arms. "Father was right—you're not a woman a man should cross without expecting you to put up one hell of a fight."

She laid her head on her son's shoulder and sighed. "Your father was a smart man."

Bart grinned at O'Malley. "Once the swelling has gone down, you can work from dawn until dark, Mum, if that's what you want to do."

"Fine. Then that's what I'll do. I'll *rest*—but I will not *rest* in bed."

Bart frowned at his mother. "Just how do you intend to rest, Mum?"

"I can rest as I wash the—"

"Enough, Harriet!" O'Malley boomed. "Ye'll stop being insensitive to those who care for you and are smart enough to recognize that a knock to the head—no matter if it's from a fall or a blow—should not be ignored. If I have to ask Lady Calliope to leave her infant son to come and talk sense into you, I will. But you'll bear the brunt of the guilt for causing her ladyship to leave the comfort of her home to convince you what is plain enough for the rest of us to see!"

Harry lifted her chin and met him glare for glare. "You've made your point, O'Malley. I'll concede to your wishes and those of everyone else who thinks they know what is best for me."

"Bloody buggering hell, woman! Do ye hear yourself? Ye've just insulted the lot of us again." Spinning around on his heel, he stormed to the door and yanked it open. Hurt lanced deep into his soul, carving out bits and pieces of it until he could barely draw in a breath.

O'Malley did not bother to turn around. Burying the emotions slashing through to his soul, he said, "I'll need the next few days to decide whether or not to rescind me offer of marriage. Even me own dear ma knows when to be gracious and accept the care others offer. She knows when to continue to rage at me da, or when it's time to make amends and toss a bucket of water on the bridge she'd just set aflame."

He didn't bother to say goodbye. His throat had started to tighten the moment he blurted out the words *rescind me offer of marriage*. It would be easier to cut out his heart and hand it over to her while he slowly bled out than to tell the woman who had the power to send him to Heaven or consign him to Hell that he had changed his mind and did not want to marry her.

O'Malley mounted his horse and did not look back.

# CHAPTER THIRTY

HARRY SLUMPED INTO the nearest chair and stared at her hands. How had her need to assert her independence created such a chasm between herself and the man she loved? Dear God, she *did* love him, but how could she make amends? What if he decided he didn't want to spend the rest of his life arguing with a stubborn, hardheaded woman like her?

"I'll come by tomorrow," Mary informed her, walking past. "To help with the laundry."

"It can wait another day or two," Harry murmured.

"I thought it was of the utmost importance," Ethan said.

She shrugged in answer. How could she explain the confusion swirling in her aching head? Her damnable pride had her going too far, and now she didn't know how to apologize to O'Malley.

"I'll come by and help Bart with the harvesting," Matthew offered.

She nodded, watching as the Clarkes followed in O'Malley's wake.

"If you really don't need our help," Cynthia began, "I can send over a pot of soup and some bread with Robbie."

"Midday would be best," Robert told Harry. "He'll be helping me turn over the far field in the morning."

She wanted to thank the Johnsons, but her voice wouldn't work. She nodded as they too walked past her and through the door.

The flood of tears she'd been holding back broke free. She bent in half and sobbed her heart out. She knew without anyone telling her that she'd ruined any chance of O'Malley forgiving her. She had forced him to lose his temper. By the time he reached the manor house, he would have realized he would be better off without her and mayhap had been infatuated with her…not in love with her.

Her body shook as the realization that she was unlovable hit home. She did not deserve a second chance at love. And there would never be another man in this lifetime who had a forgiving nature like her Bartholomew. He would have grabbed her and kissed her until she stopped fighting with him. Why couldn't O'Malley see that was what she expected—what she needed?

*How would he know? Why didn't you tell him?*

Footsteps echoed in the emptiness of their cottage and her heart, stopping near her chair.

"I'm sorry you feel as if we've all ganged up on you, Mum. You twisted our caring and good intentions around to suit your own purpose. If you've lost any chance of a future with O'Malley, you've no one to blame but yourself."

She didn't raise her head, was too embarrassed to meet the derision she expected to see in her son's gaze.

"After I round up our livestock, I'll be sleeping in the barn. If you need me, though I doubt you'd ever admit it, you know where to find me."

The door opened and closed with a finality that gutted her. A sob snaked through her. Apparently she had not cried herself dry.

⇛⇛❈⇚⇚

O'MALLEY HAD NOT expected anyone to be waiting for him to return. That it was the viscount and Coventry had him thinking the worst.

He dismounted quickly and handed his reins off to the stable master. "Did we declare victory too soon? Was there another wave of Chellenham's men waiting to attack?"

"Neither," the viscount replied. "I've been waiting to speak to you. I have excellent news."

The tension that had twisted O'Malley's insides until they ached eased at the viscount's tone of voice. "Ah, good news, is it, yer lordship?"

"We think so. Walk with us."

O'Malley was Irishman enough to worry at the command to *walk* with them—two Englishmen had said the same to Da and Uncle Patrick right before someone clubbed them on the back of the head and dragged them off to prison on trumped-up charges.

"Do ye mind if I use the privy first?"

Coventry nodded. "We'll wait for you."

As O'Malley closed the door, he heard the captain proclaim, "Something's bothering him."

When he returned to their side, the viscount stared at him for a few moments before asking, "Is there anything wrong that I need to know about?"

O'Malley frowned. "Nay."

Coventry motioned for them to walk past the stables toward the quarters O'Malley shared with his cousins. "Is there anything wrong that we *do not* need to know about?"

O'Malley turned to gape at them. "What makes ye ask that?"

"Do you think I don't notice when one of my men is troubled? Angry? Injured?" the viscount asked.

Coventry narrowed his eyes on O'Malley and hit the nail on the head: "Heartsick."

O'Malley's shoulders slumped. "Not one of those instances would keep me from performing me duty to ye, yer lordship."

"We realize that," Coventry said, "but the fact remains these emotions may interfere with your reasoning."

"Nothing's ever interfered with me reasoning...well, except for the time I fell out of a tree and landed on me head when I was a lad of ten summers."

Coventry chuckled. "Good to know, O'Malley." The captain glanced at Chattsworth and inclined his head.

"Coventry and I were speaking with Sean and were led to believe that you may need this." The viscount held out a missive.

"Is it a letter of recommendation, then? Are ye after letting me go?"

The viscount stared at him.

Coventry snorted with laughter. "Open it."

For the first time in a long time, O'Malley felt a flicker of fear. Snuffing it out, he read the missive, blinked, and read it a second time. "'Tis a Special License."

"Aye." Coventry grinned. "After speaking with your brother, the viscount and I decided it would behoove us to send a missive to His Grace advising that another of his men wished to marry."

O'Malley's stomach clenched as pain seared through it. "Did ye think mayhap ye should have asked me and not me brother?"

The two men exchanged a glance. Coventry said, "Tell me what happened."

"If ye don't mind, I need to mull it over before I speak of it."

"I'll keep this for you until you need it," Chattsworth said.

O'Malley wanted to shout at the men for interfering when their help wasn't asked for or needed, but chose not to, just as Harry had chosen to twist his words around until they suited her selfish need to be independent of any man—although mayhap just one man. Himself.

"The constable sent word," Coventry said. "He will be arriving with the enclosed wagons to transport the prisoners."

"At Garahan and Sean's suggestion, and my request," the viscount said, "the men have split into four groups. They will split their time between patrolling our perimeter and guarding the men."

"Where are the prisoners?" O'Malley asked.

"We're using the outbuilding adjacent to your quarters," Coventry said. "We thought it best to keep them close at hand, as the constable was not clear whether or not he'd arrive tonight or tomorrow morning."

"I'd best speak to our men," O'Malley said, and started to leave.

"O'Malley?" Coventry called.

He looked over his shoulder. "Aye?"

"Sometimes it is best to let hard words sink in before making a decision that may affect the rest of your life."

He shrugged in response.

"O'Malley?" This time it was the viscount.

"Aye, yer lordship?"

"A strong woman requires an equally strong measure of patience on the part of the man who loves her."

"I didn't say I loved her," O'Malley grumbled.

"You didn't have to."

"Take an hour to clear your mind," Coventry said. "Then report to whoever is standing guard by the outbuilding."

"Aye, captain." O'Malley started walking away again, then paused to turn around. The viscount and Coventry seemed to have been waiting for him to do so. "Thank ye," he rasped. "Thank ye both."

"Even a strong man must listen to his heart when it whispers of love," Chattsworth said. "Had I ignored it, I would have lost the love of my life and the babe we made between us."

Coventry cleared his throat and added, "I would have never realized the healing power of family that accompanied the love of a woman and her grown son, that I have protected and admired for years."

O'Malley's heart felt as if it had been pulled from his chest and then shoved back inside. "Ye've both been blessed." Thinking of the bloody visions he'd been cursed with, he added, "Not all of us in this life are deserving of it." He turned on his heel and strode off past the stables to the path to the tree line.

"Do you think we should interfere?"

Coventry stared after O'Malley. "I think we should give him tonight to mull things over and let the finality of whatever he and Mrs. Mayfield argued about settle in his gut."

The viscount slowly smiled. "He'll be beating a path to her door come sunrise."

# CHAPTER THIRTY-ONE

O'MALLEY WOKE TO the sound of shouts. He sprang from his cot and bolted for the door, racing toward the rear entrance to the manor house, Garahan hard on his heels.

Bart wheeled his horse to a stop. "O'Malley! Mum's burning with fever! Mrs. Clarke cannot get it to break."

The blood drained from his head, pooling at his feet. A strong hand clamped hard on his shoulder, steadying him. "We'll be right behind ye, lad," Garahan told Bart. "Go back home and tell Mrs. Clarke we're bringing help!"

O'Malley couldn't think straight. The woman he loved was ill! What happened? Had everyone missed that she'd suffered an injury to her back that somehow began to fester? Bloody hell, had the stubborn woman gone outside without a shawl or a coat in the dead of night and caught a chill?

"Hargrave!" his cousin called. "Tell her ladyship we have urgent need of her herbal draught for a fever."

"At once, Garahan." The butler hurried back inside.

Garahan whacked O'Malley in the back of the head.

"What in the bloody hell did ye do that for?" O'Malley demanded.

"Just wanted to help clear the sleep from yer brain."

They faced off, with O'Malley shoving his cousin back two steps.

Garahan knocked him off balance with his shoulder. "Do ye want to take a piece out of me, then?"

O'Malley roared and dove at his cousin.

At the last second, Garahan grinned and stepped to the side.

O'Malley landed on his twice-injured arm. "Ye bleeding, buggering *eedjit!*"

"I'll thank you not to use such language in from of her ladyship!" Chattsworth bellowed as he arrived.

O'Malley knew then he'd be sacked for sure. He struggled to his feet and met the viscount's gaze and then Lady Calliope's. "I beg yer pardon, yer ladyship, yer lordship. 'Tis inexcusable to lose me temper. Forgive me."

Lady Calliope shoved a basket at him. "I've written down explicit instructions. Follow them to the letter. It should break Mrs. Mayfield's fever within the hour."

"And if it doesn't?" O'Malley asked.

Lady Calliope reached for her husband's hand as if to ground her. "Pray."

⤜⤜⤜✳⤛⤛⤛

O'MALLEY AND GARAHAN urged their horses into a full-out gallop. Rounding the bend, they noticed two wagons by the corral and the light pouring from the Mayfield cottage windows.

"Go!" Garahan said. "I'll see to our mounts."

O'Malley did not need any further urging. He leapt from his horse, basket still clutched in his hand, as he ran to the door. Bursting inside, he held it up. "Lady Calliope sent an herbal to break the fever."

Bart turned from where he stood beside his mother's bed. His eyes were lifeless…hollow.

*God in Heaven, am I too late?*

Mary stepped around Bart and held out her hand. "I'll take that."

"There's instructions," Garahan announced from where he

stood in the open doorway.

"Her ladyship's," O'Malley added. "She said to follow them to the letter. Lady Calliope said it will break her fever within the hour."

"And if it doesn't?" Bart demanded.

O'Malley felt as if hands were gripping his throat, closing off what he wanted to say.

"We'll bloody well have to see that it does," Garahan barked.

Garahan's words were all that was needed to get everyone moving. Bart lifted his mother while Mary coaxed the feverish woman to drink the herbal.

When she shook her head, refusing to drink the whole of it, Garahan stalked over. He shoved O'Malley from the spot where he'd been standing just inside the door as if he'd turned to stone. "You want to marry the woman, don't ye? Pinch off her nose if ye have to, then she'll have no choice but to swallow."

O'Malley stared at Mary and Bart's worried expressions. The lad probably thought his ma would perish from a fever just as his da had.

"Bugger it!" *Not if I have anything to say about it.* He took the bottle from Mary's hand and stared hard at Bart. "Keep her lifted up but tilted back just a bit."

The boy nodded.

"No matter how much she fights, do *not* try to stop me from pouring this down her throat!"

Harry tried to shove O'Malley's hand from her nose, but she was weak from the fever. He was far stronger and determined to get the herbal into her.

It sounded as if she was choking, but Bart—bless the lad—held her while O'Malley got every bloody last drop into her.

When he released his grip on her nose, she immediately stopped fighting and opened one eye to glare at him.

"That's right, ye stubborn terror of a woman. I'm the one ye can take a swing at when yer back on yer feet in a few hours' time."

Her lips were moving, but he could not make out what she was saying.

He leaned closer. "What did ye say, lass?"

"Bugger off," she rasped.

O'Malley grinned. "We make a good team, Bart. Between the two of us, we'll keep yer ma in line and see that she obeys our every command."

Bart's eyes widened at O'Malley's words. "My father should have thought to do that more often. He only had harsh words for her the one time that I heard."

"I'm thinking we'll be needing to keep her busy with mindless tasks suited to a woman until she sees the error of her ways."

"Go to blazes!" she said.

O'Malley and Bart smiled at one another. "That was a bit louder, don't ye think, lad?"

"Aye." Bart was smiling as he leaned closer to his mother's ear. "Mrs. Clarke mentioned that she has a lovely length of cloth that she has no use for—isn't that so, Mrs. Clarke?"

"I do," Mary answered as she handed a damp cloth for O'Malley to wipe the bit of concoction off Harry's cheek. "I often like to spend my afternoons sitting by the window watching my men hard at work outside, while I ply my needle and thread."

"You cannot make me sit and sew!"

"What did you say, Mum?" Bart asked.

Harry's eyes shot open and then narrowed at O'Malley. "You cannot make me sit inside and sew a blasted dress to suit yer own need to prove I'm inferior to you because you're a man."

"That's enough, lass," Garahan bellowed from where he stood off to the side. "O'Malley and I rode our horses to a lather to bring that bloody herbal cure to ye."

She turned her head to meet the angry man's gaze.

"Yer son did the same, asking help from the man you'd cut to the bone with yer harsh words and evil assumptions. Me cousin may be hard of head, but his heart 'tis as soft as a newborn babe's. Ye owe the man, Lady Calliope, Bart, and meself for yer life, such as it's worth."

Guilt drew down the corners of Harry's mouth. For long moments, she did not speak.

Mary urged the men toward the table. "I've made a pot of tea and sliced the butter cake I brought with me."

Bart rose and Garahan followed him over to the table.

O'Malley glanced longingly at the butter cake but could wait to have a slice. The need to sit with Harry until the fever broke was more important than his empty stomach. From what he observed, the herbal was working, but he wouldn't rest until they knew for certain it had.

"I'm so sorry, Michael," Harry murmured.

"Michael, is it?"

"Aye. I have pride enough for three people."

O'Malley chuckled. "I won't be arguing with ye on that count, lass."

"Forgive me for the harsh things I said to you. I've felt as if I've been a failure ever since Bartholomew passed. Holding on to my pride was the only thing that kept me upright when I wanted to lie down and weep."

"What about yer son?"

"I did it all for him. His father was so proud of him. It was our plan to have Bart marry and seek the viscount's approval to add more acres to what we till and plant. To add on another room or two to our cottage. More revenue for the estate and enough room for two families."

O'Malley nodded to Mary as she brought a small bowl of cool water and set it on the table beside the bed. He dipped the cloth into it, wrung out some of the water, then bathed Harry's face, gently, slowly, afraid if he pressed too hard, she'd break.

"I'm far from fragile," she said.

"To me ye're as delicate as the petals of a rose."

Her mouth opened, but no words emerged.

O'Malley leaned close and pressed his lips to her forehead. "Ye're cooler."

"I should be the one caring for you."

"I'm not the one who's been burning with fever."

"But I—"

O'Malley sighed. "And here ye've been so agreeable."

She closed her eyes. "I truly am sorry. I do not mean to be disagreeable, but…"

"But?"

"You'll tire of me wanting to work beside you when you'd rather I sit inside mending shirts, darning socks, and scrubbing the floor." Her voice broke when she confided, "I'm afraid you'll leave me."

"Never will I leave ye, Harry," he said. "It nearly killed me to ride away from ye when all I wanted to do was stay."

"Then why did you?"

"Because you needed to understand there are boundaries."

"What boundaries?"

"Ye really do not have an inkling, do ye?"

Color was slowly seeping back into her cheeks. "I wouldn't ask if I didn't want you to explain."

"Ma and me da have had an understanding between them since I could remember."

"And what is that?"

O'Malley swept the cloth across her cheeks. After he bathed her forehead, he leaned close to press his lips once more to check for fever.

Harry sighed. "My mother always kissed my forehead like that when I was ill."

"Ma still would, if I were home and happened to look a bit peaked to her."

Harry's smile blossomed. "Tell me about your parents' understanding."

"There is always work to be done around the farm and within the household. Da encouraged Ma to work in the herb and flower gardens, as it gave her pleasure, and she encouraged him to help her with the making of the soap or the rendering of tallow for candles."

"Your father would do woman's work?"

O'Malley chuckled deep in his throat. "Ah, lass, don't ye realize that it's *all* work? It doesn't have to be assigned to suit anyone but the ones who are tasked with it. Ma and Da decided long ago that if one noticed the other flagging, they would pitch in with whatever task needed finishing. Me brothers and I were raised to lend a hand, no matter the task."

Harry scooted back against the pillows until she was sitting up. "And I lectured you—"

"Nay, lass. Ye screamed."

She stared at him, and a miracle happened…her pride seemed to dissolve like honey in hot water. A look of understanding and remorse took its place. "Forgive me, Michael. I know I don't deserve it, but I'm asking you to forgive me. I will work hard to change the way I think and promise to make you and Bart proud of me."

"We're already proud of you, Mum," Bart remarked as he rose from where he had been sitting at the table. "You need to be proud of yourself."

"Ye and yer husband have raised a fine son, Harry," O'Malley said. "Ye should be proud of him."

She held out her hand to Bart, and he grasped it. "We are. I know he's smiling down on us right now, Mum. On the three of us."

"I dreamed he was standing over me, frowning at me, castigating me for my sharp tongue and stubborn pride," Harry said.

"Well then, it seems as if ye've listened to his advice," O'Malley replied.

"I have. Forgive me, Bart?"

"Of course, Mum."

"Mary?"

Her friend walked over and handed her a cup of weak tea. "Drink up."

"I'm so sorry for my harsh words, Mary. Please forgive me?"

"Aye."

"Would you please ask Ethan to come inside so I can apologize to him, too?"

"I'll fetch him in," Garahan announced as he strode to the door.

A few minutes later, Ethan entered the cottage, while Garahan stayed outside with Robbie.

"Harry! You're sitting up!"

"The herbal draught worked. My fever broke."

Ethan smiled. "I'm so glad. Bart was worried—we all were."

She patted her son's hand. "I'm sorry for it."

"You wanted to speak to me?"

"I'm so sorry for my harsh words, Ethan. Please forgive me?"

He glanced at O'Malley before turning back to Harry. "You are forgiven. We've all seen how hard you have worked to keep your farm after losing Bartholomew. It is not a task for one man—or one woman. It takes a team."

"And the help of your family," Mary added.

"That too," Ethan said. "We understood your worries, though you never confided them. We shoulder the same ones, only ours were spread between two adults…not all on myself or Mary."

"I should have spoken about it," Harry said.

O'Malley agreed. "Aye, ye should have, but we understand about pride, too. If ye're willing to start afresh with a man such as meself, me offer of marriage still stands." Harry tossed aside the covers and was about to stand when O'Malley frowned at her. "Ye'll stay put in that bed, or I'll be asking me cousin to give ye another piece of his mind."

When she stilled, he nodded. "Now don't be getting another chill, lass. The lot of us will leave ye and Mary to the changing of the bedding and yer sleeping gown, while we check on the horses."

"You won't leave without saying goodbye?"

"I won't if ye promise not to let loose with such venom

again."

"I promise, I won't." She looked at Garahan, who stared at her. "I'm sorry, Garahan—forgive me?"

He grunted, and O'Malley snickered. "That's Garahan speak. He forgives ye." His gaze met hers. "I promise to always say goodbye to ye, lass."

"And kiss me goodbye too?"

He chuckled. "If I kiss ye now, will ye be meek as a lamb for Mary?"

Harry's eyebrows rose. "You want me to be meek, too?"

Bart groaned. "Mum—don't argue!"

O'Malley was laughing as he kissed her forehead.

Harry pouted. "I thought you were going to kiss me."

"I did. If ye're a good lass and do as Mary asks, I'll come back and kiss ye again before I leave."

"It had better be worth it."

A SHORT WHILE later, O'Malley stalked into the house and strode over to where Harry sat in bed. His gaze never left hers as he knelt by the bed, pulled her into his arms, and kissed her with an ardor that she hadn't expected.

Her heart pounded and her limbs went slack as he deepened the kiss.

He ended the kiss and eased her back against the pillows. "I trust that'll hold ye until I return tomorrow."

Hand to her breast, unable to look away from his brilliant green eyes and handsome face, she sighed deeply.

"I'll take that as a yes, lass. See that ye rest for the next few days. Ye'll be needing yer strength for our wedding night."

The last thing O'Malley saw before he closed the door was the look of wonder on Harry's lovely face.

He planned to enjoy every moment of their wedding night—

from the moment he carried her over the threshold, through the night, and until the dawn.

"Are ye ready to leave?" Garahan asked as he stood by the horses.

"Aye."

"Have ye remembered Lady Calliope's basket?"

Bart stepped outside as O'Malley was headed to the door. "Mum penned a note for Lady Calliope. It's in the basket."

"I'll see that she gets it, lad," O'Malley replied.

"Will we see you tomorrow?"

"There's more than I can accomplish in one day waiting for me. I'll try, but if I can't make it, I'll send someone to check on yerself and yer ma."

"Thank you." O'Malley and Garahan were about to leave when Bart called out, "O'Malley!"

"Aye, lad?"

"I'm glad you didn't let anger rule your thoughts. Mum does sometimes."

"'Twas a near thing, but yerself and yer ma are worth the trouble. Ye're a good man…a good son to yer ma."

Bart's eyes filled. "She loves you."

"I love her more."

They were about to urge their horses into a fast trot when Bart called O'Malley's name and ran over.

"Is something wrong?"

Bart hesitated, then raked a hand through his hair. "I have missed having a father to look up to. When you marry my mum, I'll have you."

As they rode away, Garahan blew out a breath. "Ye're gaining a beautiful wife and a fine son, O'Malley."

"Faith, I know it."

"Make sure ye continue to be deserving of them, or ye'll answer to me!"

O'Malley grinned all the way back to the manor house.

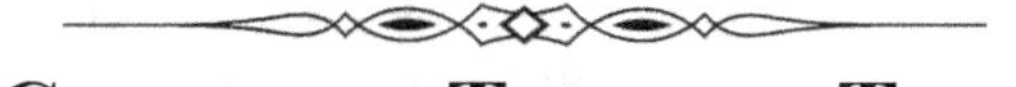

# CHAPTER THIRTY-TWO

A FEW DAYS later, Chattsworth Manor was abuzz with activity as the viscount's carriage pulled up to the front doors. Bart leapt down from the carriage and held out his hand to assist his mother from the conveyance.

Harry took his hand and stared at her handsome son—the spitting image of his father. "I love you, Bart."

"I love you, Mum." He tugged on her arm. "Let's go get married!"

She was laughing when the front door opened and Hargrave greeted them warmly. "Mrs. Mayfield, Master Bart. They're waiting for you."

Harry hesitated, and Bart asked, "You haven't changed your mind, have you, Mum?"

She smiled to ease his worry. "No. I'm just not accustomed to such splendor."

"Their ladyships are in the upstairs sitting room," Hargrave informed them. "Mary Kate will show you the way."

Harry thanked the butler and walked toward Lady Calliope's maid.

HARGRAVE TURNED TO address Bart. "You're expected in the library. His lordship wants to speak to you."

"*Me?* Did I do something wrong?"

Hargrave assured him, "Not a thing. Follow me."

At the viscount's bidding, Bart entered the room.

"Ah, Bart! We've been waiting for you." The viscount waved him over to where he stood with O'Malley.

He hesitated, taking in his surroundings before greeting them, "Your lordship, O'Malley."

"Now then," the viscount began. "I'd like to ask a favor."

"Anything, your lordship."

"How would you like to work with the duke's guard for the next few days?"

Bart's eyes widened. "Ride on patrol with them? Target practice, too?"

The viscount smiled. "Aye. Lady Calliope suggested that your mother and O'Malley should have a few days to themselves. What do you say?"

"Aye! Do you want me to bring my blunderbuss?"

"No need. We have plenty of weapons for you to practice with."

"Thank you, your lordship." Turning to O'Malley, Bart confided, "Mum's a bit nervous."

O'Malley tugged at his cravat. "She's not the only one."

"Really? I didn't think anything worried you."

"Well, lad, when it comes to me position among the guard, I'm in me element. But I've never been married before."

"You'll be fine. Mum loves you." Bart leaned close enough to say, "I...uh...love you too."

O'Malley pulled his soon-to-be son into a rib-cracking hug and stepped back. "Faith, I've always wanted a son. I love ye too, lad, though to tell ye the truth, I was afraid ye might not want me to."

"Weren't you listening when I told you I miss not having my father and that I won't have to anymore because I'll have you?"

"I heard ye but thought ye might change yer mind once yer ma and I exchange vows and we're living under the same roof."

Bart shook his head. "Not going to happen. You're stuck with the both of us."

"If you two are ready," the viscount said, "I'll send the others in."

O'Malley smiled at Bart. "Ye'll get to meet me cousin, Dermott, and me older brother, Sean."

⊁⟫⟫⟩✖⟨⟨⟨⟨⟨⊰

"THERE YOU ARE, Harriet!" Lady Calliope exclaimed, rushing over to pull the bride into the sitting room. "Mary Kate, come in."

"It's my shift in the nursery," her maid reminded her.

"Oh. Well then, we shall see you at the wedding."

"I wouldn't miss it. Thank you for including me."

"You're very welcome. See you soon." The door closed, and Lady Calliope turned around to Harry and beamed. "Ladies, it is time to help our bride get ready!"

Mary Clarke and Cynthia Johnson rushed toward Harry, hugging her between them. "We are so happy for you," Mary declared.

"You deserve to be happy," Cynthia added.

"We don't have much time," Lady Aurelia told them as she walked to Harry. "We have a lot of work to do."

Lady Calliope waved her hand toward a gown in the palest of pinks. Mesmerized by the color and the drape of the fabric, Harry slowly walked over to it. Fingering the material, she smiled. "Where did you get it? It's lovely."

"O'Malley told us you were partial to pink," Lady Aurelia commented.

"I have never worn this gown," Calliope told her. "Now that I'm nursing our babe, it will be some time before I can wear it. Aurelia's a talented seamstress. She made the alterations."

Harry held it up and sighed. "I've never had anything so lovely. Are you sure you want to let me borrow it?"

"It's our gift to you," Calliope replied. "From Aurelia and me."

"Thank you, from the bottom of my heart. My husband—" Harry paused, worry churning in her belly. "Is it wrong of me to mention him?"

"Whyever would it be?" Lady Calliope asked. "He is Bart's father, and you were married for years. You loved him."

"Just because you have been blessed with a second chance at love does not mean that you have to erase your first love," Lady Aurelia said.

Relief swept through Harry, brushing away any doubt she had about the rightness of this day. "I'm ready to get married!"

The ladies joined forces and soon had Harry dressed in the whisper-soft gown, with her hair swept up into a knot on the top of her head, silken tendrils pulled free to frame her face.

Lady Calliope and Lady Aurelia stood back to admire the bride. "O'Malley's going to swallow his tongue," Calliope predicted.

"This I have to see," Aurelia said.

At the knock on the sitting room door, Calliope smiled and said, "Enter."

"Ah, Hargrave, you've brought Bart to us," Aurelia said. "Excellent—his mother is ready."

Bart stepped into the doorway and stared. "Mum, you look beautiful!"

"Thank you, I feel beautiful."

"I can't remember the last time you wore a gown," he said.

"I do. It was when you had started to outgrow every pair of trousers and shirt you owned."

"I'd forgotten that you used your gowns to make clothes for me."

"We did what we needed to do to keep you in clothes until you grew tall enough to wear some of your father's."

"Mayhap you could ask O'Malley to buy you a gown or two," Bart suggested.

"Not just yet. We have so much to do around the farm what with everything that's been happening."

"Time to go," Calliope said.

Bart offered his arm. "Ready, Mum?"

She beamed at him. "Ready, Bart."

⤞⤝

O'MALLEY STOOD WITH his brother by his side and his cousins flanking them. "What's keeping them?"

Sean chuckled. "Anxious to get married?"

O'Malley grumbled, "Aye. Weren't you?"

Sean's gaze sought that of his wife. "Couldn't wait to marry Mignonette."

"Then ye know why I'm wondering what's taking them so long to walk down the bloody staircase."

A chorus of chuckles erupted around them. "The lass'll be here shortly," Garahan told him.

The door to the library opened and a vision of loveliness draped in pale pink, with sunset hair and mist-laden eyes, floated toward him.

He blinked, but she did not disappear. "Harry?"

The vision slowly smiled. "Aye."

"Ye look like an angel."

The sound of her happy laughter filled the room. "Looks can be deceiving."

He grinned at Bart. "Faith, I'm a lucky man."

"We both are," Bart said.

A hush fell over the room as the vicar cleared his throat and began the service.

O'Malley only heard half of what the man said—he couldn't take his eyes off his bride. She'd turned his head and set his blood

265

to racing dressed in her husband's cast-offs. Clothed in the entrancing gown, fitted to perfection, she was exquisite.

He frowned when he noticed his cousins noticing. They smirked in return. He'd be having a word with them after the ceremony was over.

Sean nudged him, and O'Malley stared at his brother.

The vicar harumphed. "I repeat, Michael O'Malley, do you take this woman to be your wedded wife?"

"Aye."

Sean nudged him again and mouthed, *I do.*

O'Malley repeated, "I do." He was too busy staring at his bride to be embarrassed by his inattention. Harry was going to be his. He was already counting the hours until they could be alone.

"Harriet Mayfield, do you take this man to be your wedded husband?"

Her gaze met his, and she slowly smiled. "I do."

O'Malley blocked out the rest of what was said, until he heard the word *kiss.* He yanked on Harry's arm and pulled her against him. "I've got ye now, lass. I'll never let ye go."

The room erupted in cheers as he kissed his bride. The taste of her went straight to the part of him that would be celebrating later—when they were alone—until a thump on the back of his head got his attention.

"You have the rest of your life to kiss your wife," Sean reminded him.

"And I intend to use every opportunity." When he would have continued kissing Harry, Hargrave announced that the wedding breakfast was being served. "How long do we have to stay?" he whispered into his wife's ear.

Harry leaned into him and replied, "Long enough to have a bite to eat and raise a glass, then you will be all mine for three whole days."

"And three nights," O'Malley reminded her. "You take a bite of food. I'll raise me glass."

A quarter of an hour later, they were laughing as he swept

her into his arms and strode from the dining room.

BART SHOOK HIS head at their hasty departure. He had a feeling he knew what their hurry was—after all, he *had* been raised on a farm. "I guess they weren't hungry."

Laughter erupted around him, but he took it good-naturedly. Raising his glass, he toasted, "To my new family!"

"Welcome to the madness, nephew," Sean said.

# EPILOGUE

"I THOUGHT WE'D never escape them," O'Malley said, carrying his bride over the threshold.

"They only wanted to give us a proper send-off," Harry reminded him.

"The only send-off I wanted was a hearty handshake and a fast horse." Harry's snort of laughter had him smiling down at her. "Ye're beautiful, wife of mine. In case you don't remember me telling ye before."

She traced the tip of her finger along the line of his strong jaw. "A woman doesn't forget the first time the man she loves tells her she's beautiful."

He kicked the door shut with the heel of his boot and carried Harry to the new bed his brother had promised would be delivered while O'Malley and his bride were exchanging vows.

Grinning, he raised his eyes to the ceiling. "Thank ye, Sean."

Harry noticed the bed. "I never thought about sleeping arrangements."

O'Malley chuckled. "Ye were too busy thinking about getting yer hands on me."

She pressed a kiss to his jaw, and then another and another. "You are absolutely right."

His eyes darkened with desire. "How careful do I need to be with yer gown?"

"Very!" she said. "I'll never own another so beautiful."

"Well now, I think I like seeing me wife wearing something other than a man's trousers and shirt…covered in dirt."

Harry had already turned her back to O'Malley, who was unfastening the buttons on the back of her gown. "Are you ashamed of me?" she asked.

"Are ye daft? I'm proud of ye."

"But you said—"

"'Tis called teasing, lass. Have ye never heard the like?"

"Oh. I thought…"

"Come here, lass. I've a powerful need to kiss ye."

Their lips met, and words were soon forgotten as he helped remove her gown.

She unfastened the buttons of his frockcoat and waistcoat, urgency tearing through her as she watched him remove each article of clothing. Excitement streaked through her as she reached for the placket of his trousers.

He stayed her hand. "Not yet. I want to see all of ye, lass."

Harry lifted the chemise over her head and stood before him, anticipation driving her to the brink of madness. "Michael…"

He traced the tip of his finger along the line of her collarbone, then traced the same path with the tip of his tongue. "Ye taste of roses."

She moaned as his tongue dipped into the hollow of her throat and traced a path between her breasts, then shuddered when his clever mouth suckled one breast and then the other.

He slid a hand along her spine, cupping her backside, drawing her closer as he teased and suckled her. "Ye're a bounty for a starving man." He tore off his cravat and drew his cambric shirt over his head.

Harry brushed his hands aside as she quickly undid his buttons and shoved his trousers off his hips.

"Are ye after me lasting five minutes, then, lass? I'd planned to take me time bedding ye."

"Later," she rasped. "I want to wrap myself around you."

Surprise quickly faded as she wrapped one long, supple leg around his waist. Their eyes met, and the desire simmering in hers had his need surging once more. He slipped a hand beneath her other leg as she locked her ankles. Her sultry smile had him bracing his legs apart. Heart pumping, need churning, he groaned. He would not spill his seed before she gained her pleasure!

Frantic to regain control, he forced his mind to concentrate on numbers—it had worked in the past. It would work now! He slowly started to regain control, counting the number of right crosses he'd leveled opponents with during his reign as Wexford County's bare-knuckle champion.

When he had a firm grip on his control, she snatched it away, demanding, "I need you inside me. *Now!*"

O'Malley answered need with need, plunging into her welcoming warmth, damp with her passion, throbbing with her need. Her legs locked around his waist, his hands gripped her firm backside, and he drove into her, filling her to the hilt.

Her gasp fueled his hunger as he drove into her again and again. The satisfying sensation of damp flesh pounding against damp flesh had him desperate to prolong their lovemaking, but his need would not be denied. He plunged deep, threw back his head, and roared with triumph as his release clawed through him.

Harry screamed his name as she followed him over the edge of madness into the abyss of pleasure.

When he felt himself tipping to one side, he braced a hand to the wall to gather the reserves of his strength. "I need a few minutes to catch me breath."

She uncrossed her ankles and slowly slid down his battle-hardened, sweat-slickened body. With a wicked grin, she laughed. "Time's up!"

THE NEED TO gobble her in huge bites had eased by the third time they made love. "Remind me to thank me brother for the bed in case I don't have any of me brains left by morning."

"I'm older than you. Shouldn't I be the one exhausted?"

He was about to answer when her fast hands wrapped around him and gently squeezed until his eyes crossed and his breath whooshed out. "I promise to take me time—the next time we make love."

The speed of their loving nearly blinded him. The ache of his need nearly stopped his heart.

She gasped as another wave of pleasure grabbed her by the throat. His hands splayed across her backside as he locked her in place, plunging deep, then deeper still, as he drove her once more to oblivion and took her under.

O'MALLEY WOKE AS a now-familiar damp warmth clamped around him. He groaned low in his throat, gazing at his wife with her back bowed and her glorious sunset hair streaming over her strong shoulders. He'd already tasted paradise in her arms...and he wanted more!

"Ye've bewitched me, lass."

She slowly smiled, and he watched her soft gray eyes turn to smoke as she leaned forward...closer, until her bountiful breasts were inches from his lips. He accepted the invitation, drawing her breast into his mouth, teasing her with his tongue, drawing every ounce of pleasure from one breast before he suckled the other. Their hips began a rhythm as old as time while she rode him for all he was worth. She gasped, he growled, as they soared to the heavens as the sun came up.

HOURS LATER, HE woke with his hand wrapped possessively around her waist, and their legs tangled together. Pressing a kiss to the nape of her neck, he inhaled the subtle scent of roses mingled with musky undertones of their lovemaking. He would crave that scent for the rest of his days.

Harry turned in his embrace to face him, tracing the tip of her finger along the rim of his mouth. She leaned close, claimed his lips in a kiss that promised another bout of mind-boggling lovemaking.

Her kiss intoxicated him, and even though he felt the stirring of need for her, he ended the kiss and sighed. "I've never in me life refused so tempting an offer."

"A man as handsome as my husband would have had many, many offers."

His grin was lightning fast. "Aye. That I have...but too long ago to remember," he added when he noted the glint of temper in the depths of her mist-laden eyes. "I think the last time we made love may have rubbed me a bit raw, lass. 'Tis tender skin there. I'll be no good to ye until it heals."

Concern replaced temper as she drew the covers back. Sweet replaced wicked as she offered, "Let me kiss it and make it better."

He grabbed her hand before she could wrap it around him. "I think that's enough for now, lass. It'll take a bit for the tenderness to heal."

"Does that happen often?"

He snorted with laughter and pulled her back into his embrace. "Nay, but I've never made love so many times in one night. Faith, but ye're a delightfully demanding, lusty woman."

Her beautiful smile and lighthearted laughter eased the worst of his embarrassment.

"I have never spent a night like last night either," she confided. "Since you admitted your...er...condition, I'll admit mine."

"And what would that be, lass?"

Her gaze met his, and she murmured, "I'm not sure I can

stand up without my legs wobbling."

When she looked away from him, he said, "Tell me the rest, lass. Mayhap I can kiss it and make it better."

She snickered. "It's your fault that I will not be sitting comfortably for a day or two."

His laughter filled the room. "We're a pair, aren't we, lass?"

"We certainly are." She snuggled closer to him. "Michael?"

"Aye, lass?"

"I love you."

"I love ye more."

"Kiss me?"

"With pleasure, lass."

Their lips met in a kiss that promised of a lifetime of love.

A kiss that promised of forever.

# About the Author

*Historical & Contemporary Romance "Warm...Charming...Fun..."*

C.H. was born in Aiken, South Carolina, but her parents moved back to northern New Jersey where she grew up.

She believes in fate, destiny, and love at first sight. C.H. fell in love at first sight when she was seventeen. She was married for 41 wonderful years until her husband lost his battle with cancer. Soul mates, their hearts will be joined forever.

They have three grown children—one son-in-law, two grandsons, two rescue dogs, and two rescue grand-cats.

Her characters rarely follow the synopsis she outlines for them...but C.H. has learned to listen to her characters! Her heroes always have a few of her husband's best qualities: his honesty, his integrity, his compassion for those in need, and his killer broad shoulders. C.H. writes about the things she loves most: Family, her Irish and English Ancestry, Baking and Gardening.

*Slàinte!*
*CH*

C.H.'s Social Media Links:
Website: www.chadmirand.com
Amazon: amazon.com/stores/C.-H.-Admirand/author/B001JPBUMC
BookBub: bookbub.com/authors/c-h-admirand
Facebook Author Page: facebook.com/CHAdmirandAuthor
Facebook Private Reader's Page ~ C.H. Reader's Nook:
facebook.com/groups/714796299746980
GoodReads: goodreads.com/author/show/212657.C_H_Admirand
Instagram: c.h.admirand
Twitter: @AdmirandH
Youtube: youtube.com/channel/UCRSXBeqEY52VV3mHdtg5fXw

www.ingramcontent.com/pod-product-compliance
Lightning Source LLC
Chambersburg PA
CBHW071222210726
48293CB00002B/533